PACT MATES

♥

C. M. CONNEY

Realms ⦁f Man

Ace
Lyon
BOOKS
LLC
March 2025

*Ace
Lyon*

Published by
Ace Lyon Books
Acelyonbooks.com
First Edition
Cover Design by S. M. Savoy
Pact Mates C. M. Conney

ISBN: 978-1-947122-55-0

CONTENTS

Chapter 1

May 28

Pain traversed Kelly's body in increasingly painful waves. Muscle spasms traveled from her hips to her shoulders every time she moved. The shot Matti had given her made her feel strangely disconnected from the pain as if it were happening to someone else.

Mark and Matti moved and spoke in between blinks, and she knew she was losing time. Their words were hard to focus on as were her own thoughts. Is all she wanted was sleep. Even worry over her children felt difficult as if she'd dreamed them.

I'm a werewolf and we don't get sick. Maybe this is a nightmare, she thought and let herself drift into sleep.

A sharp jab of pain brought her back to the here and now.

"We need you to look alert," Matti said as she gave her another injection.

"I'm trying," Kelly said irritably, batting at Matti, giggling over how weak she was, then groaning when the light brightened. The light glittered oddly. Long streamers of color hid the detail of the room and she puzzled over what she was seeing for a minute before giving up and just admiring the lights.

Mark shook her hard. Or maybe it just felt hard. Every small movement hurt.

The room swam in dizzying circles before settling into understandable images. But she'd lost time again. She bit back her groan as two paramedics lifted her stretcher from the back of an ambulance—and the night crashed back on her. She remembered her sister and the cage and the long hours of pain and fear. Terror made her breath come hard.

A baby's soft cry startled her, and she remembered she'd already delivered and Mark had come for her. They were safe as long as she didn't give them all away.

"The kids?" she asked.

"Barb is looking after them," Mark said. He glanced over his shoulder and turned back glowering.

"I'm sorry," she said.

"It's not your fault and they're fine. Let the doctor examine them while Matti gets you situated." He released her hand, stepping away, saying, "What the hell?"

He'd barely gotten the words out before people began yelling questions. Bright flashes made her eyes tear. She turned her face away but the light followed and noise grew.

"Mark," she said weakly, not knowing what she expected him to do.

"Who's in charge here?" Matti snapped. Then softer. "Get her inside. I'll handle this. Room three fourteen."

Kelly wanted to see who had her children but the effort to lift her head caused her muscles to seize in painful cramps. She lay back and panted, trying not to cry out with the pain. She didn't know what expression she was supposed to be conveying but what they were getting were tears. The crowd overwhelmed her with their bright lights and shouted questions, and she couldn't pull her scattered thoughts together over the growing pain in her muscles.

Reporters continued to yell questions over men telling them loudly that they had to leave. To Kelly's relief, the sound grew muted when they entered the hospital although the brighter inside lights made her eyes tear harder.

"Doctor Sorenson arranged a room," Mark said.

Kelly tried to turn to see who he spoke with but the slight movement flooded her eyes with tears. She squeezed them closed, forcing her expression to smooth. She almost laughed despite the pain. *What did normal look like in this situation?*

3

The thought distracted her.

"I just need you to fill out this paperwork," a woman said, jolting Kelly back.

"Mark," Kelly whispered.

Mark snapped, "Don't be ridiculous! We aren't stopping here. Look at them. This is a circus. Take her to her room and I'll fill out any damned thing you like!"

"Yes, of course. Security will have them cleared away in no time. Right this way. Jean, can you give me a hand here? Room three fourteen. Let's get Mrs. Miller settled."

"How are you doing?" a new woman asked as the stretcher began to move again.

"How do you think she's doing?" Mark sighed hard. "Sorry, we're both stressed. I'd like to go see my children as soon as I get my wife settled."

"They'll be here in the nursery. Your wife's room is right down the hallway. Normally, we like to bring the newborns into the room, but she looks exhausted." She paused before an open door. "Yes, right in here."

"I'll help her into bed. She has a sprained ankle," Mark said.

Pain made Kelly moan when Mark lifted her.

"Soreness is perfectly normal," the nurse said cheerfully. "Let's see here… has the doctor ordered any pain medicine?"

Kelly pried her eyes open as Mark set her down on the bed. A small blond woman stood at the foot of the bed peering at a clipboard.

"I'd like the children in here," Kelly said, trying to look alert although the room swam alarmingly.

"I need to take your blood pressure and–"

"I'll see to Mrs. Miller," Matti said as she entered the room, interrupting the nurse. "I've ordered bloodwork. Doctor Reyes will be assisting. Mrs. Miller has refused pain medication but perhaps some Tylenol? Hand me those pillows there, and let's see if we can make her more comfortable. Mr. Miller, if you'd accompany Doctor Reyes and get your wife all signed in?"

"I'm fine," Kelly lied, releasing his hand.

"I should take her home," Mark said.

"Tomorrow, if the blood work comes back okay. Your wife has had a very trying ordeal. Let's make sure she's recovering, shall we?"

Matti leaned over her with her stethoscope out. Mark hesitated then followed Barbara and the nurse from the room. As soon as the door closed behind them, Matti said, "Where does it hurt?

Kelly said, "My hips mostly but all my muscles hurt. Did I permanently injure myself by holding back the wolf?"

"Honestly, I don't know. I doubt it though. I think it's a reaction to the shot I gave you to keep you awake. You need sleep. Are you having any trouble holding the wolf back now?"

"No. I don't even feel her. Is that bad?" she asked when Matti inhaled sharply.

Matti frowned, pursing her lips. "I'm not sure. Normally, a female wolf sleeps for about three days after giving birth. I've never spoken to one immediately afterwards before. I wish I could let you sleep but we need you to walk out of here tomorrow." Matti chewed her bottom lip, absently turning the stethoscope in her hands. "Damn it, I should've sent you home!" She sighed hard, shaking her head. "Too late now though. Try to rest. I'll give you another shot in the morning and we'll get you out of here as soon as we can."

"This doesn't feel real," Kelly murmured. She closed her eyes, trying to relax. Sleep sounded like heaven, but she was growing tenser by the minute.

"Well?" Mark asked as he entered the room.

"Your wife will be fine. I'll bring the children to you."

Mark took her hand and Kelly turned toward him, wishing he was laying beside her. His scent relaxed her and she sighed with relief. They should be tucked in her den on a pile of soft leaves. She smiled as she envisioned the den she'd prepared for her children. She couldn't wait for them to be born.

Chapter 2

"Is this normal?" Mark asked, uneasily eyeing his sleeping wife.

Matti said, "The sleeping is. I'm a bit worried about her pain."

Mark leaned over to kiss his wife, wrinkling his nose at her scent. She smelled of blood and fear, antiseptic and illness.

"She said her hip hurts and it shouldn't," Matti continued. "She's shifted three times now. The damage she caused by holding back the shift should've mended by now. But I've never seen or even heard of a partial shift like that. I have no idea what to expect."

"But she'll be okay?"

"She needs rest. I'll bring the children to her. They need rest too."

"They're okay though, right?"

"I've never seen a child attempt to shift before either." I'm sorry, Mark. I wish I could reassure you, but

7

the truth is I just don't know. But I'm worried he'll do it again."

The door to the room opened and Barbara entered.

Matti said, "*Ah*, Barb, great. Fill out the paperwork, would you?"

Barbara said, "I spoke with the nurses but if anyone does pick them up the heartbeat will be noticeable."

"Right," Matti said as she strode to the door.

"There's a problem with their heartbeat?" Mark asked.

Matti shook her head, calling, "Later!" over her shoulder.

"No. Newborn wolves have very fast heartbeats. It's perfectly normal," Barbara said as she reached for the clipboard at the foot of Kelly's bed. "Has she been sleeping long?"

Mark glanced back at his wife. Matti had given her enough adrenaline for five people and it worried him that she'd fallen asleep so quickly. He sat on the edge of her bed. "No. She just fell asleep."

"I'll keep the other nurses out as much as I can but we need some to see her all normal like this."

"Is this normal?"

Barbara grinned at him as she signed her name with a flourish at the bottom of the clipboard. "Yep. The nurses change shifts and won't know she hasn't woken. Just pretend she just fell asleep when the new nurse comes on duty." She hung the clipboard back on the foot of the bed and removed a stethoscope from her pocket.

"I'll take her stats. If you notice her breathing slow that's normal for newly delivered wolves but tell me or Matti because we don't want the nurses to see it."

She quieted as she listened to Kelly's heartbeat and took her pulse. "Nice and normal. There will be three shift changes—"

Barbara straightened, turning to the door as it opened. A strong odor of garlic accompanied the woman who entered.

"Leave the tray," Barbara said. "She just dozed off..." Barbara's eyes narrowed and she let her stethoscope fall from her hand. "What do you think you're doing?"

Mark stood, Barbara's angry tone surprising him. He turned from his wife right as Barbara snatched a cell phone from the woman's hand. "Let me see some ID!" she snapped.

"I'll just leave," the woman said as she placed the tray on the counter right beside the door.

"ID— now!" Barbara reached to block the door.

The woman tried to grab her phone but Barbara pushed her away. "Security!" she called.

Mark grabbed the woman's arm.

"Hey, let me go!" the woman yelled.

She turned to slap at Mark. Barbara stepped into the hallway, the closing door muffling her as she called again for security.

"What the hell are you doing?" Mark asked as he grabbed both the woman's arms.

9

She stopped struggling to grin at him. "I just wanted to see the werewolf up close. Did you know she was one? Have you ever seen her shift?"

"Are you kidding me?"

"You know you can make a lot of money. Get me my phone back and I'll cut you in on my connections."

The opening door cut her off. A man in a blue security guard uniform strode in followed by Barbara.

"A reporter," Mark said disgustedly. He thrust the woman away. "Tell all your friends that if they try this again, I'll be pressing charges. My wife needs peace and quiet. You can see she isn't a werewolf or vampire or whatever crazy thing you're thinking. What she is, is traumatized by her crazy sister."

"I can get you an interview—"

"Get out!" Mark hollered, then peered over his shoulder, worried he'd woken his wife, but she slept on undisturbed.

"Let's go," the security guard said gruffly. "This floor is off limits. It's illegal to impersonate hospital personnel."

The closing door cut him off. It opened again a second later and Matti entered followed by another woman. Both women pushed clear plastic bassinets.

"We heard the commotion," Matti said. "I'll arrange for a security guard. Thank you, Nurse Hansen, we've got this."

Barbara busied herself straightening the bed linens as Matti leaned over the basinet she'd pushed into the room. She used a stethoscope, nodding as if she liked what she heard.

Hansen picked up the discarded tray of food and wrinkled her nose. She leaned over to sniff and then held the tray at arm's length. Mark had thought the strong smell of garlic just his heightened senses. He and his wolf were so tense that every sound seemed explosive and smell overpowering, but it was clear from her expression that it stank of garlic to her too.

"I'd better bring this to security. Maybe she wasn't a reporter at all but trying to poison her. Jesus, the nuts…" She shook her head, making a tsking noise.

Mark joined Matti to examine his son. The boy slept on his back swaddled in a blue blanket. A blue hat covered his brown curls. Matti or someone had cleaned him, and he looked pinker than he had. He also looked angry. His little face was screwed up in a grimace and the most casual of glances showed he breathed in quick shallow breaths.

"Probably just trying to prove it, not poison her," Barbara said as she strode to the door. "I better see about the children's milk though and speak to security."

"Isn't garlic for vampires?" Hansen asked.

The closing door cut off Barbara's reply.

Matti reached into her pocket and took out her cell. "Send him in, Richard." She snapped her phone closed as she stepped away from the crib.

"Place him with Kelly and see if he settles. Barbara washed and examined him. We upset him. Your

11

daughter is sound asleep, but your son keeps waking. We're running some tests." She glanced at her watch and reached into the other crib. "Richard arranged for a reporter to sneak into the room and get some pictures."

Mark straightened in surprise. "What?"

"Relax, the man doesn't know who arranged it, but we need to set the stage. Help me with this. Let's see…" Matti pursed her lips, cocking her head before nodding decisively. "Sit beside Kelly and act like you're sleeping. We'll uncover one leg." As she spoke, Matti pulled back the sheet and draped the light blanket strategically across Kelly, covering her breasts but leaving most of her left leg exposed.

Mark placed his son in the crook of his wife's arm.

Kelly stirred, turning more toward the baby.

"Perfect," Matti said softly. "I'll be back in two minutes. Let him take pictures. If he tries to touch them, pretend to wake."

"My daughter?"

"Leave her in the crib." Matti waved him to a seat, glancing at her watch again. "I'll be paged in a minute." Her voice softened as she cooed to the baby, "Who's a little angel. You're a good girl aren't you, sweety."

Mark rose to check on his daughter. "What are you doing?"

Matti waved him back down. "She's sound asleep and breathing normally. I'm just uncovering her so he'll be able to see she's perfectly normal."

The beeper on Matti's waist trilled and Kelly stirred. Mark took Kelly's hand and leaned over her, hoping his scent would soothe her. She muttered and rolled farther toward him.

"Got to run. Remember, you're pretending to sleep. We need these pictures, Mark."

Matti reached for her cell phone as she exited the room. Mark hurriedly straightened the blanket, being careful to leave his wife's leg and one arm exposed but covering the rest of her. His son mewed and fussed.

"*Shh*," he whispered, laying his head on Kelly's pillow, lightly resting his hand on his son's chest and closing his eyes. He wished he really could relax and sleep. He tried to relax his shoulders but was sure he appeared tense. The thought of a stranger near his helpless family infuriated his wolf. He took deep breaths, hoping the smell of them would calm his wolf.

Air currents and muted clattering from the hall warned him the door had opened, and he had to fight himself to hold in his growl and stay still. He cracked his eyelids the barest slit as light footsteps approached.

A man paused beside his daughter's crib. The soft clicks of the camera made Mark twitch and he tried to play it off as sleepy movement.

His wolf struggled to get free, cramping his muscles and making his skin crawl. Blood pounded in his ears, drowning the small sounds the man was making. He could smell the man's nervous excitement and track his progress across the room. He'd made no attempt to touch any of them, but Mark didn't think he'd be able to pretend sleep much longer.

"Can I help you?" Matti asked.

"*Um*— wrong room," the man said.

Mark sat, making a production of rubbing his eyes and yawning. The man was slipping a small camera into his jacket pocket as he turned to face Matti.

"Sorry, I thought you were someone else," he said as he headed to the door.

"Who are you looking for?" Matti asked.

She held the door, stepping back so that the man could exit.

"*Um*, my wife. She's here visiting a friend. I thought she said room three fourteen, but I must've been mistaken. I'll call her and find the room number. Sorry to disturb you."

Matti let the man leave, grinning at Mark when she closed the door. "Thinks he got away with it," she whispered as she approached. "How's he doing?"

She peered over Mark's shoulder and her smile softened. "He looks happier already. Leave him with her. See if you can place these on his chest or at least tuck them beneath the blanket." She handed Mark small electrodes attached to thin white wires. "Hook the wires to this box. I'm telling people I'm monitoring for a heart murmur."

"Does he have a murmur?"

"No. But it makes a good excuse to keep others from disturbing him. The pack is here, guarding. Try to get some rest, Mark. No one is getting in that we don't want in."

Mark snorted and grimaced. He rose to stretch, and Kelly murmured in her sleep.

"Lay beside her. She knows you're here."

"This is all wrong, Matti," Mark said as he settled beside his wife.

"I know," Matti said sadly. She leaned over his daughter and a minute later handed her to him. He tucked the baby beside her brother and placed Kelly's hand over them. She sighed deeply and her breathing slowed. He hadn't even realized it had been fast.

"Great, she's relaxing too. We got this, Mark. Barb will be bringing breakfast in three hours. No other nurses will be checking but if you need anything at all, call. Hopefully, Kelly will stay sleeping. Leah and Richard need to be seen visiting but they'll make it quick. One night here, Mark, and you can take them home."

Chapter 3

A tap on the hospital door was immediately followed by Mark's friend Officer Derek Reynolds poking his head into the room. "Mark, I have two people out here claiming to be Kelly's parents."

Mark placed his son into the plastic basinet beside his wife's bed and covered him with a light blanket before heading to the door. He hated to release him. The baby slept so soundly that only feeling his heartbeat reassured him.

Flashes and shouted questions greeted Mark when he stuck his head from the doorway. Hospital security immediately began ordering the people away. He ignored the commotion, offering his hand to his father-in-law who looked to have aged ten years since he'd seen him last.

Alice had obviously been crying. Her eyes were red and her face pale. She turned to glare at the people being escorted away.

"Alice, John, glad you could come. Kelly has been asking for you. Thanks, Derek." Mark held the door open as Derek stepped forward with his hands raised, waving back the reporters. "This is a private ward. You'll be charged with trespassing—"

The closing door cut Derek off.

"This is unbelievable," Alice whispered as she gave him a quick hug. She hurried from him to peer into the basinet.

"The children? My daughter?"

"Doing good." Mark waved John forward. "The doctor gave Kelly a mild sedative," he lied.

"But she'll be okay?"

"Physically yes. Mentally—she loved Stacy. Her sister hurting her like that... I can't say how that will affect her."

John rubbed his temples. Alice flushed, whether in anger or embarrassment Mark didn't know as she patted her granddaughter's back.

"You can hold her. She's a bit cranky." Mark ran a fingertip over his daughter's soft cheek. "He's a bit weaker than her, but the doctor says he should pick up. He has a heart murmur. Those electrodes are monitoring it."

Alice peered doubtfully at the wires connected to the baby. Mark ran a finger over his son's cheek then pulled up the blanket to hide the fact that his son's heart was beating wolf fast.

"They're beautiful," Alice cooed as she picked up the baby girl. "Have you named them?" Her smile was tender, full of love. Mark was relieved that seeing her hold his child didn't alarm his wolf at all.

"Not yet. We've picked names, but I want to wait until Kelly wakes to make them official."

"I'm so sorry I didn't hide the address better..."

"It's not your fault," Mark interrupted hastily. "I'll be honest. I hope they throw Stacy in prison for a long time."

John snorted, slumping into a chair beside his wife. "We all hope that."

"Kelly might not. We haven't spoken about it..."

"She must see that it isn't safe for Stacy to run free." John stood to lift the shade to peer from the window. "Reporters are lurking outside."

"Richard or his father will give a statement. They'll handle it," Mark said.

John turned back, his gaze sweeping his sleeping daughter and the plastic crib. "I don't think you realize the publicity this has generated."

"We were shocked," Alice said as she stood to pat her husband's arm. She rocked the baby she carried, kissing her head. "How anyone could believe Stacy's craziness... I hope they throw her in prison forever. God, poor Kelly. She must've been terrified. The things her sister wanted to do..."

She clamped her lips and spun away, crooning softly to the child she held.

Mark opened his mouth, then closed it. He didn't know what to say. Stacy was vicious but not crazy, and if they eventually told Kelly's parents the truth, every lie he told them now would forever stand between them.

Mark leaned over the plastic crib to check his son, trying to be casual about feeling the shape of his legs. So far the child had remained human normal, but he worried his son would revert to wolf form. The baby slept as deeply as Kelly. Matti had tried to reassure him, but he knew she was guessing too. He couldn't wait to get his family out of here and into the hills.

When Mark straightened. John peered worriedly over his shoulder.

"A heavy sleeper? He seems really still. Are you sure he's okay?"

"Not really. All the tests so far have been inconclusive. The doctor is hoping he picks up and they're monitoring him closely. Richard has provided a private nurse, Barbara Reyes, so that we can keep him with us. Doctor Sorenson assures me I'm worrying for nothing, and I trust her, but…"

John laid a hand on his arm. "When did you eat last? You look exhausted."

"I'm fine."

It hadn't occurred to him to fix himself up. He smoothed his hair back and felt his bristly chin. He should shave and clean up, not look so uncivilized. The

19

thought of leaving his wife alone in this room made him growl softly.

"We'll stay with them," John offered.

"I'm fine. Leah will bring me clothes."

"Your cousin offered us rooms at his home. Will your parents be coming?" Alice asked.

"I asked them not too," Mark lied. Before he had to elaborate on the lie, the door opened again and Matti and Richard entered.

"Mr. and Mrs. Anderson," Richard said, extending his hand.

John shook his hand. "Please, call us John and Alice. We're family now. Thank you for taking such good care of our daughter."

Alice said, "I shudder to think what Stacy would've done." Alice rose from her seat to peer over Matti's shoulder as she examined her grandson.

"He's doing very well," Matti said reassuringly. She shook her head, holding her hand out when Richard stepped forward. "Let him sleep." She flicked a meaningful glance at Alice, and Richard nodded slowly.

Mark pursed his lips.

"Change might rile him and he needs rest," Matti continued, giving Richard another pointed glance.

Mark stepped between Richard and his son.

Richard gave him a sad smile and stepped away.

"Leah?" Mark asked.

"On her way. She stopped at your house for clothes and to get Kelly's bag."

20

Matti said, "Please keep visitors to a minimum. Let the babies and Kelly sleep. I'll release Kelly when she wakes, but I don't think you should go home."

"He'll come to my house," Richard said. "I want everyone safe under my roof until this settles down. My father is arranging security for you," he continued, speaking directly to John.

John said, "That won't be necessary."

"It's entirely necessary for Kelly's peace of mind. Until this blows over there'll be a guard at your farm, and I'd like one to accompany you whenever you leave the farm. No one need know they *are* guards; you can say they're new hands, but Kelly was hysterical worried over you."

The lines on John's forehead deepened.

Richard said, "As you just said, we're family now. My father is sorry he hadn't considered your safety until now. His wealth does make our entire family at risk. With this added craziness..."

John exhaled heavily, returning to the seat beside his wife. She handed him the baby, and both leaned over her.

Matti winked, saying, "Mr. Miller, I've asked the nurses to page me when your wife wakes, which should be this evening. Don't worry if she sleeps through the night though."

"Will Kelly need any special equipment?" Richard asked.

Matti smiled at Mark and nodded at Kelly's parents. "With your permission, Mr. Miller, I'll speak with Mr. Henderson about follow up care for your wife?"

"Sure, and thanks. You've been great."

Kelly's parents added their thanks as Richard and Matti left the room.

To Mark's surprise, the presence of Kelly's parents soothed him. Their obvious love and joy with the children calmed his wolf and he was able to settle in a chair beside his wife. The thick doors and walls of the hospital kept the talking in the hallway to an indistinguishable murmur although he heard Derek speak and sat straighter right as Leah entered.

JJ ran to him and hugged him hard.

"Mamma says we need to be quiet," he whispered. He eyed Kelly with a dubious expression. "Is she sick?"

He sounded so amazed that Mark laughed.

"Just tired."

"Hello," Alice said shyly as John stood and offered his hand.

Leah handed Mark the bag she carried and shook John's hand. "It's nice to see you again. I'm sorry about the circumstances."

"Your family has been very kind," John said.

"More than kind," Alice said as she rose and adjusted the baby on her shoulder. "The newspaper reported how you oversaw the computer search that located Kelly. I can't thank you enough."

"It was nothing. We have a division that works on tracking poachers by the pictures they post. Granted, most don't bother trying to hide their tracks as if they're too stupid to worry about posting pictures of illegal activity, but we've had experience. And I thank God we did. We almost weren't in time..."

She grimaced apologetically at Mark and gave him a quick hug. He tightened his hold and breathed deeply of her scent, not releasing her until JJ said, "Mom," in a worried voice.

"Everyone is fine," Leah said as she pulled away from Mark to wipe her eyes. She squatted to be face height with her son. "Want to see the babies?"

He pursed his lips, looking so doubtful that Mark laughed again. "You're not the baby in the family anymore, sport."

JJ brightened, nodding eagerly. Mark picked him up to let him lean over his son.

"Don't touch him. We don't want to wake him," he whispered as JJ reached out.

"Would you like to hold her?" Alice offered as she lowered Mark's daughter so JJ could see her.

JJ frowned doubtfully. "She's really red and wrinkly."

Leah laughed, smoothing his hair back. "Perfectly normal. In a few days they'll look just like your baby pictures."

Mark was angry all over again at the lack of woods and moonlight for his children.

Leah put her arm around him, saying firmly, "Go take a quick shower. I'll stay here until you get back."

"I'll watch over my cousins too, Uncle Mark."

Alice grinned at the boy. "These are your only cousins?"

"Yeah. I have lots of aunts and uncles though."

Mark grabbed the bag and stepped into the small adjoining bathroom, letting the door swing shut on JJ's excited babble— JJ wasn't old enough to know that speaking like he was could lead to trouble.

Reporters would be checking the facts. If one heard that JJ had twenty 'uncles' they might think to investigate them and most of the pack had no ID. They didn't work or own homes but people had seen them— maybe even with JJ.

The pack was always careful to keep their relationships as distant as they could for public perception in case one of them was caught doing something illegal but police had to follow laws that reporters didn't and police wouldn't be the danger that other packs would be. Werewolves had one universal pact—keep their existence secret.

His family were not only pack mates but pact mates. They all knew that breaking that pact was death sentence whether you'd done so purposefully or not.

Conspiracy theorists would be looking for mistakes. Mark doubted they'd believe that JJ had so many 'imaginary' friends. He hoped Richard had been really careful about their backstories. Mark had never worried about it before because he'd never imagined they could be so publicly outed as werewolves.

He was worried about it now though…

Chapter 4

He showered in record time and emerged shaved in clean clothing to find JJ holding his daughter, sitting between Leah and Alice.

"She hasn't made a peep," Leah said as she rose to hug him again. "Give her back to Alice, son. We'll set up a nursery for them, right, sport?"

"Yep." JJ kissed the baby's cheek and handed her to Alice. "I love her already. Take good care of my cousin."

"I will," Alice said, blinking back tears.

JJ hesitated beside the plastic crib, peering anxiously at Mark and his mother. "We shouldn't leave him if he's hurt."

"He's just sleeping," Mark said.

JJ leaned closer, sniffing hard.

Leah pulled him away.

"He isn't hurt, sport. His father is here, and Daddy is coming."

"We should wait."

The panicked sound of his voice made Mark tense.

"Mom, we should wait, or get Matti," JJ repeated in a higher voice as Leah tried to lead him from the room.

"I'll take good care of him," Mark said as he squatted to hug JJ. It was clear the baby's scent was affecting him. This was his first exposure to it and his instincts would be to protect the child.

Leah leaned down and whispered something that Mark couldn't hear and JJ took a reluctant step away. Tears filled his eyes as he glanced back, and Mark said, "We'll be home before you know it, and you can sit with him as long as you like."

JJ nodded, wiping his face on his sleeve. It made Mark feel like crying too.

"JJ, we have to go. Say goodbye," Leah said.

The command in her voice shivered across Mark's skin and calmed her son.

"Bye," JJ mumbled without looking back at the Andersons. He reached for the door handle.

Mark tensed when JJ opened the door but the hall outside remained quiet.

"When can I hold him?" JJ was asking as the door closed behind them. Leah's reply was cut off by the closing door.

"He's cute," Alice said.

"Yeah, JJ's a good kid. He's been looking forward to cousins to play with..."

"What names made the final cut?" Alice asked.

Mark made small talk until Richard returned accompanied by Barbara who carried diapers and bottles. An insulated black pack swung from Richard's shoulder from which he removed a stack of sandwiches while the women introduced themselves and changed the baby.

"Should we wake him to feed him?" Alice asked.

"No. Let him sleep." Barbara offered Alice the bottle. "He'll wake when he gets hungry."

"Nurse Reyes will be staying at the house for a week or so to oversee them," Richard said.

Mark nodded. He didn't care who stayed as he had no intention of staying himself. He planned to take his family into the woods the minute they left here. What he would tell her parents, he didn't know, but he was going.

"How long will you be staying with us?" Richard asked John. "You're welcome as long as you like but I know you have responsibilities at home."

"We hadn't talked about it," Alice said anxiously.

"And let's not worry about it now," John said and kissed his wife's cheek. "Stein can see to the cows until I get back and I'm sure our neighbors will help. Let's talk it over with Kelly." He rubbed his cheeks, exchanging unhappy glances with his wife. "I'd been hoping you'd come for a long visit with Kelly and the children over the summer, but now... I'll work something out," he said to Alice.

Alice forced a smile and stared at the bottle with such absorption that Mark knew she was avoiding his gaze. Guilt roiled Mark's stomach. Alice thought it was her fault that Stacy believed like she did.

Mark ate his sandwich even though he wasn't hungry just to have something to do while Richard made small talk with Kelly's parents.

His daughter refused the offered bottle, making small noises of discontent. Kelly slept restlessly, twisting beneath the thin hospital blanket. Mark wished he could lie beside her. He had to settle for holding her hand.

Her low growl startled him, and he jumped to his feet.

Richard was already standing.

"Let's give them a private minute," Richard said as Kelly growled again, thrashing, yanking gracelessly at the light blanket covering her.

"Kell, sweety, your parents are here," Mark said as he pulled the blanket over her to tuck the edge around her hand that now sported black claws and a dusting of fur.

"We could use a few minutes," Mark said, giving Richard a desperate glance.

Kelly sat and screamed his name.

"You're safe. I'm here." Mark tried to wrap her again in the blanket as Alice and John hovered uncertainly.

"Mark!" Kelly snarled, sniffing hard. She turned her golden eyes to the door, making an odd coughing snort.

The eyes sent a shiver of apprehension over Mark. He'd never seen anything like the shape of her pupils and hoped it was an affect from the drugs—one that was common enough that humans would believe it, although the color was different enough to be noticeable all on its own.

"They need a minute," Richard said as he pulled John from the room. Alice followed, reaching for John's arm but glancing back with an expression that said she wasn't sure if she should go or pull her husband back into the room.

"Is everything okay?" Derek asked.

Mark glanced at the door and could only see his shoulder. He hoped Derek couldn't see any better because his wife was shifting.

"Kelly, honey," Alice said, and Kelly's shift halted with only her legs becoming wolf like. She yelled, "The babies!"

"It's fine. We're okay. Relax, sweetheart!"

She strained in his arms, her nails cutting into his shoulders.

"She's a little confused," Richard said loudly. "The sedative—"

To Mark's relief the closing door cut Richard off and not a moment too soon. Kelly growled again, pushing him away to jump from the bed. In seconds, a wolf hunkered before him, showing her teeth and growling low in her throat. She leapt over his head and crashed into the door.

Mark grabbed her, using the hospital gown still tangled about her to wrestle her to the ground while she snarled and snapped at him.

"Kelly!" He clamped her muzzle with his hand and shook her head hard while she whined and struggled to get free.

"Kelly," he said again as he fell forward to pin her with his weight. He released her muzzle to stroke her head and she snapped at him, biting into his shoulder and tearing away a gob of flesh. The scent of his blood seemed to calm her. She stopped snarling but kept scrambling to get away.

Mark tightened his hold as her claws scratched along the tile floor.

"Sweetheart, the kids are fine. You're safe. I'm okay. I need you to calm down. We can go home if you calm down." He continued to babble, using the calmest voice he could manage until she stopped struggling.

Her eyes had reverted to their more normal wolf yellow when she turned to glare at him, lifting her lip but making no attempt to move when he sat. Her lip lifted further when he reached for her, so he withdrew his hand and released her. She shook herself hard whining, looking from the door, to his shoulder, to the crib.

"Go see them. This is nothing." He'd been about to say Richard was outside, thinking it would comfort her but she began growling again as she sniffed the insulated bag Richard had left behind.

Mark took off his shirt, wincing at the blood stains. *Damn*, he thought in aggravation as he wadded the cloth to jam it against the wound she'd made before going to lock the door.

Kelly stood on her hind legs staring into the crib. Mark almost laughed at the comical sight. The hospital gown dangled to her back paws with her tail sticking out between the ties. Her ears were back and her teeth showing, a low growl rising in pitch as she sniffed the baby.

He knelt beside her to stroke her head.

She flicked him a glance and her ears twitched upright a moment before laying back on her head but she continued to sniff.

"Your mother has our daughter. They're right outside the door. Can you change back?"

She made that odd coughing snort again that rose the hairs on his arms, then sneezed and shook her head.

Mark didn't know if she were saying no she couldn't shift or just shaking her head to clear it.

"You must be hungry."

He stood to unwrap a sandwich and offered it to her. She snarled but took it and gulped it down, hardly chewing it. He fed her all the remaining sandwiches, then got her water while she sniffed and growled but she was doing it quietly and seemed more in control of herself.

While she drank, he cleaned the blood from the floor then tossed his bloody shirt into the bathroom sink.

He lifted their son from the crib and unwrapped him so she could see him.

She licked the baby then Mark's cheek before turning away and pawing at the robe.

Mark yanked the ties and the robe fluttered to the floor. A shiver shook her followed by a motion that looked like a wave beneath her fur as her back hunched. The fur receded, replaced by skin and ten seconds later Kelly sat before him. She began to cry, reaching for the baby.

Mark let her take him.

"I'm so sorry," she wailed as she reached for him.

He hugged her to his chest.

"It's okay. Everyone is fine."

"I need our daughter."

"I'll get her. Can you get into bed?"

"I need her," she repeated in a voice laced with hysteria.

"I need you to put on a fresh gown." Mark shook her lightly and nipped her neck.

She shivered and stilled, taking deep breaths through her nose.

"It stinks in here." She rose, still holding their son, glancing about and frowning.

"There's robes in the cabinet."

"I want to go."

"I know. Me too. But we have to stay and act normal just a while longer."

Anger made Mark's skin feel tight. Her tears were infuriating. He began to remove his clothes. "I need to shift for a minute. I'm afraid it will make you shift too. Want to wait in the bathroom or should I go in there?"

"No."

He half laughed as he let his pants fall. His laughter died when she huddled against him. He could feel her shaking and she smelled odd. Blood, antiseptic, the sour smell of fear, and a weird medicinal smell mixed with an earthy scent that he thought might be her milk coming in.

"Let's take a shower."

He reached for his pants to grab his cell and called Richard.

"Everything okay?" Richard asked.

"Give us a few minutes before you come in. Kelly wants to shower. I'm going to help her. Call her doctor and see about getting her released as soon as we can. Our son will be in the bathroom with us."

"Matti is already on the way," Richard said and hung up.

Mark hesitated and then unlocked the door. A nurse was unlikely to try to enter the bathroom, but she might call security for a locked door. Kelly watched him with a bewildered expression, her gaze darting around the room.

He grabbed the bag Leah had brought and pushed the plastic crib to the bathroom. The bathroom had been made to accommodate wheelchairs; the crib fit through the doorway with no problem, leaving plenty of room for the three of them. Mark dropped his dirty clothes to the floor while she leaned over their son and breathed deeply.

The shower was large with safety bars and a plastic chair that Mark shoved into the corner.

"Wash up and you'll feel better."

She shook her head but took his outstretched hand.

He'd hoped the weird odor surrounding Kelly would wash away, but even after he washed her hair twice he could still smell the sickly smell. She stood shivering beneath the spray and he'd made the water as hot as he could stand.

"I can't stay here much longer," she said as she grabbed the soap.

"Just a little while longer."

Her breath hitched in a sob as she turned away half crouching to wash herself. He felt like a bully for forcing her to stay. He should've insisted they go to the woods and to hell with the rumors.

Chapter 5

Mark rinsed his wife and then himself before stepping out and offering her a towel.

"I should call my mom. She'll be worried," she said, her voice muffled by the towel she was using to dry her hair.

Mark paused with the only other towel in his hand.

"They're here; remember?"

"Oh." She stopped toweling to glance around the room as if she expected to see them in the bathroom.

"Kell?" he reached to feel her forehead.

"I'm okay," she said. She cocked her head, sniffing deeply. "I hate it here," she mumbled as she wrapped the towel around herself.

The towel gaped, leaving a long line of exposed skin along her left side.

He offered her the dress she'd packed. She ignored it to peer into the crib, jerking back and again staring around the room. "Where is she?"

Before Mark could answer, Kelly was fumbling with the door.

"Mark, where is she? Did Stacy take her?"

She sobbed, yanking at the door. Mark reached for her, seriously alarmed by her memory lapses. "Your mom has her."

"Mark?" she said in a bewildered tone as he hugged her, swaying and staggering as if she wasn't certain if she should push away or let him hold her.

"*Shh*, it's okay. Wait right here and I'll get her. I'll bring her to you."

She was nodding now and clutching him, but he wasn't certain she'd heard him. He threw her dress over his shoulder to hide the bite and wrapped the towel about his waist before opening the door.

"You'll get her," she mumbled. "Stacy wouldn't hurt her." She rose her hands to her temples, her eyes widening. "She would! God, she would!"

"Our daughter is here and safe! Stay here!" He tried to extract himself from her now desperate clutch.

"Mark?"

"Stay with our son!"

As if she just remembered him, she jerked away, reaching to her stomach. A puzzled expression crossed her face before a look of panic set in. She spun and sniffed the baby.

"What's wrong with him?"

"Stay here!" Mark said and eased out the door.

Alice and John stared in shock when he exited the bathroom in the towel. Mark bit back his curse, angry they were back in the room. He should've sent them away.

"Kelly is really sick. Get the doctor. She's confused, a bad reaction to the sedative maybe," Mark blurted as he reached for his daughter. Behind him, Kelly wailed his name.

"Where are we? Mark are you here? Mark?" Dear God did Stacy—"

She broke off and snarled. Before Mark could do a thing, she jumped forward, her hooked fingers reaching for Richard's face.

"Kelly!" Mark reached for her, hampered by the baby he held.

"Kelly?" Alice said as John stood. "Honey?"

"Daddy?" Kelly partially turned as the door to the room opened. "No!" she shrieked and tried again to hit Richard.

He caught her hand, yanking her forward.

Kelly's skin rippled, and Mark grabbed her arm, not knowing what he planned to do. It was clear she was shifting.

Richard knew it to. He pulled her into a hard embrace, lifting her off her feet.

"Kelly, calm down. It's me, Richard."

She snarled and inhuman sound, struggling in his grasp.

"Get her on the bed," Matti said at the same time.

"What's happening?" Alice asked.

Mark turned to hold Alice back.

"If everyone except Mark could step outside," Matti said loudly in a futile attempt to empty the room before Kelly shifted.

Fur sprouted and receded on her back.

She wouldn't be able to hold back much longer.

Richard ignored everyone and pushed past Mark and into the bathroom, taking Kelly with him.

"Mark," Kelly gasped, then snarled again.

Mark hesitated, torn between stopping his in-laws from going to her and going to her himself. His wife shrieked, making all the hair on Mark's body stand up.

"Richard, let her go."

Matti said, "Mr. and Mrs. Anderson, would you please wait outside?"

A nurse Mark didn't know stepped into the room. Derek peered over her shoulder. To Mark's surprise, Arny stood in the hallway, wearing dress pants and a doctor's coat. He'd cut and dyed his hair and wore it brushed back or maybe wore a wig. Star stood beside him dressed as a nurse, including a mask dangling around her neck. Strands of blond hair peeked from the paper hat on her head and she conferred with Arny, both pouring over a clipboard he held.

Mark turned away; glad they were present but wondering what they thought they could do. He banged on the bathroom door. The thick wood muffled the sounds from the bathroom, but Kelly's scream was audible.

"Kell, sweetheart, you're safe. It isn't Stacy!"

Mark pounded again.

"What's going on?" Derek asked.

Matti said, "Get me two cc's of Atropine and I want a full blood work up. This isn't a simple reaction to a sedative. I think we're dealing with a toxin. She had no needle marks and told us they didn't inject her with anything. Did she eat or drink anything while she was caged?"

Mark's heart rate accelerated. "Richard, so help me God!"

Richard said something the door muffled, and Kelly shrieked again.

Matti yanked Mark's shoulder half turning him. "Did she eat or drink anything while with her sister?"

Mark nodded as he gazed about the room at the staring crowd. Her parents stood in shock. Derek had dropped his hand to his holstered gun. The nurse gaped. Barbara ran up and pushed past Derek as Kelly screamed again.

Mark whipped around and pounded on the door again. "Let me in!"

The noise from inside the room had changed to muffled growling.

40

Mark glanced around again, wondering if they could hear the growls with their weaker human hearing or if they thought them sobs.

"Officer Reynolds, was there any hallucinogens on the men arrested?" Matti asked loudly.

"She couldn't remember where she was," Mark said. "She didn't remember giving birth. What's wrong with her?"

"I'm trying to find that out. Can you—"

Warm wind buffeted Mark and he swayed, not hearing Matti over Richard's voice in his head. Without his will he dropped to his knees and scratched at the door.

"Mark," John said as he took the baby and tried to pull him up.

Matti yelled, "Okay, I need everyone out right now! Nurse..."

An unfamiliar nurse pushed past Matti and took Alice's arm as Alice stared about with wide eyes and a gaping mouth.

Barbara grabbed Alice's other arm, "Come with me, please. Let the doctor examine your daughter. I'm sure everything will be fine." Barbara gestured to the door. "Mr. Anderson, if you would?"

"Yes, of course."

The bathroom door opened, and Mark fell forward, catching himself on his hands.

"Mark!" Kelly wailed and fell into his arms.

His son began to shriek and Alice and John both turned back.

Matti gestured to Barbara. "Settle Mrs. Miller. I'll see to the baby."

"Yes, doctor," Barbara said and tried to pick Kelly up.

"I've got her," Mark said and stood, taking Kelly with him.

She cried and shook in his arms. Richard had made her pack, it was clear by her smell. Mark hoped Richard could help calm her through this added stress. Mark wasn't certain what her tears were for. Becoming pack was an emotion laden time as you bonded with your packmates. She'd be more attuned to their feelings and feel compelled to help them and some wolves had a hard time adjusting to that. But Richard could command her to be calm now and force her wolf back, so Mark supposed it was a fair trade off.

The other nurse ripped open a packet of gauze and stepped forward. "Just a quick pinch."

She continued to speak but Mark was certain Kelly didn't hear a thing. Barbara reached past his shoulder as he set Kelly on the bed and injected something into her arm.

The other nurse gave her an annoyed glance, making a tsking sound as she fumbled for a vial to withdraw blood.

Kelly continued to cry into Mark's shoulder. Someone draped a sheet over him, but he couldn't spare any attention for anything beside his wife's sobs and his son's cries.

"Go to him," Richard said.

Mark shrugged, trying to force the command away.

"Go!" Richard said again and pulled him up. "We'll be right back, Kelly. You'll feel better in just a minute. Let Mark see to your son."

She nodded and sniffled, dropping her hands from Mark to wipe her face.

Mark let himself be hurried to the bathroom both angry with Richard for commanding them and relieved to see to his son.

"Jesus," he breathed as he peered past Matti's shoulder at his son's deformed body.

"Richard," Matti said urgently.

Mark glanced over his shoulder at Richard who half-closed the door with his foot, his hands busy removing his shirt.

Mark held up his hand then dropped it. It was unheard of to make such a young child pack. Mark hated to contemplate what it would do to his son's developing psyche.

"He needs to," Matti hissed.

Mark debated slamming the door closed but couldn't think of a reason for doing so that her parents and the other nurse would believe. He took a small step back angling himself to block as much of the half-opened door as he could.

The skin on Richard's arm shivered and hair sprouted. His arms bent in as he fell to the floor and he stood in the shower enclosure ten seconds later as a wolf. Matti held the screaming boy's arm out, and Richard grazed the offered arm with his front left incisor.

The baby shrieked.

"Is everything okay in there?" Alice called.

Mark turned on wobbly legs. The smell of his son's blood made his stomach flip. He glanced at Kelly who stared at the door with wide eyes and then his in-laws who stood just inside the doorway of Kelly's room.

"Yes, I think—" he broke off and turned as his son gasped and shrieked again.

Richard had already resumed his form and held the crying baby.

"You better bite him, Mark, he has no teeth to do it himself," Matti whispered.

Mark glanced back into the hospital room.

"Leave the door open," she whispered, pointing to the shower.

Mark exhaled heavily and headed to the shower enclosure. Matti stepped into the open doorway, half closing it as she spoke with the nurse, sending her for a portable monitor.

"Let us make you more comfortable, Mrs. Miller," Barbara said. She continued to talk loudly as she straightened the pillows and resettled Kelly in the bed.

Mark let his wolf loose. His son continued to cry as he contorted, his body changing shape and fur sprouting to cover his legs and back. It took Mark thirty seconds to shift, the entire time hoping he'd beat his son to wolf form. He bit the offered hand harder than necessary.

Richard rolled his eyes, shaking his head. The baby stopped screaming abruptly when Richard pushed his bloody finger into his mouth.

Mark watched anxiously, praying it would be enough to reverse the change.

"Is he okay?" Alice called again, by the sound coming closer.

"I don't like his color." Matti stepped from the bathroom, closing the door more. "I'm going to take him when they're through changing him and run a few tests. We shouldn't be long."

"My son?" Kelly asked sounding tired and confused.

Another nurse who Mark didn't recognize said. "Temperature ninety-nine point three. She has a slight fever, Doctor, but no pain in the abdomen."

"He'll be just fine," Matti said speaking to Kelly, ignoring the nurse.

"I need to go home," Kelly said.

"Soon. Let the nurses see to you."

Matti continued to speak over Alice's low murmurs of reassurance and the small fussing of his daughter.

"Get dressed, Mark," Richard said softly, not whispering but trying to be casual.

45

Mark shook his head hard. There was no way he'd be able to force his wolf back yet. He needed to see his mate and child.

"Mark—" Richard placed the baby at Mark's feet and stepped into the doorway.

The baby's slow transformation continued. Mark watched anxiously as paws replaced feet and a snout pushed from his son's face. The boy whimpered and shook, unable to get his feet beneath him. He appeared unfinished, more a furry human than a wolf. Mark nuzzled him gently.

"Get dressed," Richard said again in a commanding voice.

Mark whined and pushed himself, the power of Richard's voice helping him force his wolf back. His inner wolf was just as alarmed as he. Pins and needles raced across Mark's arms and legs. He forced himself to move when he wanted to lay and pant. His son sniffled and snorted when he picked him up.

Mark cringed at the misshapen feel of him.

Footsteps approaching startled him and he realized Richard had left the doorway although he hadn't seen him go.

"Just me." Matti halted in the doorway. She glanced over her shoulder saying, "Help Mrs. Miller feed the baby and get a stat on that bloodwork. How's he doing?" she asked as she turned back. Her lips tightened as she examined the baby, but she continued to speak in a normal voice. "Settling down now that he's dry, I see. Let me bring you a bottle for him."

"Shall I take him?" Alice asked.

Richard pushed past Matti and entered the bathroom, blocking the door. "I'll hold him while you dress."

Mark glanced down, realizing he was naked and had to bite back his annoyed growl. His son needed Kelly and she needed him.

"I need to speak with Mr. Miller," Matti said, waving Richard back. "Barb, see to Mrs. Miller and then speak with my team."

"Yes, ma'am," Barbara answered as Alice asked again what was going on.

Richard turned away, an anxious odor blooming around him. Mark's pulse picked up and his hands began to sweat.

Matti closed the door, reaching into her pocket to withdraw a syringe. Before he could ask what it was, she gave him a shot.

"Give me the baby." Matti held out her arms.

Mark handed him over, absently rubbing his shoulder.

Matti leaned closer and whispered. "Kelly needs to be in the woods with her children. She wasn't affected by anything other than her wolf's confusion. And her wolf is seriously alarmed. I've ordered more sedation for her as I don't think she'll be able to hold herself back, but we need her out of here."

And the shot you just gave me?"

A tranquilizer. We only have a few minutes."

Matti slapped his face when he growled.

"Pay attention. Your wife and child are fine but I'm going to go out there and lie. Now go!"

Mark yanked up his jeans and staggered into the other room.

Chapter 6

Mark sat on the edge of Kelly's bed hoping he didn't look as out of it as he felt. The room swam alarmingly. *No wonder Kelly was so confused if Matti was giving her this crap*, he thought angrily.

"What's going on? What was all that about?" John asked.

Alice stared open mouthed, clutching Mark's daughter to her chest.

Matti said, "I need to run more tests. I don't want to alarm you, but his blood pressure is low and his pulse is erratic."

Before Mark could reply Matti hurried from the room with the baby.

It's a lie, he told himself, closing his eyes and rubbing his face hard.

"What the hell was all that?" John repeated angrily.

Mark opened his eyes to see John glaring at Richard.

Richard tossed Mark a sweatshirt.

Mark put it on as Richard, said, "I thought if we could have a private moment that Kelly could say what she wanted."

"Did you threaten her?" John's glare ratcheted up and he stepped closer.

"Of course not," Richard said.

Mark said, "Why would he?"

"I don't know what the fuck is going on, but something is! My daughter was hysterical and angry with him!"

"John," Alice said nervously.

He spun to glare at his wife. "You don't think it's suspicious as hell he had to drag her off kicking and screaming?"

Alice bit her lip.

Richard said, "Kelly needed to take it out on someone. I know she didn't mean it and would be embarrassed later. I thought it better to let her yell at me privately. In hindsight that probably wasn't the best idea..."

"Kelly—" John broke off and hurried to the bed.

Mark followed his glance to see her eyes were closed although her breathing was fast.

Mark said, "She's sleeping."

John glared at him as he felt for her pulse. "Kelly! Wake up. You're scaring me!" He shook her shoulders.

Alice said, "I'll get the doctor!"

Mark batted John's hands away. "Leave her alone!"

"Christ, Mark, she could be dying!"

Richard said, "The doctor gave him a sedative too. Mark, I'm sure she's fine. Kelly, wake up! Open your eyes!"

Kelly moaned and opened her eyes.

"Daddy?"

"I'm here, honey. Did he threaten you?"

"Who?"

She rubbed her eyes, trying clumsily to sit. Mark pulled her up to hug her.

"Let her go," John said.

Richard said, "I assure you—"

John cut Richard off with a sharp gesture. "And I want to hear it from my daughter without either of you speaking for her! Give us a few minutes to speak privately!"

Mark said, "I swear Richard would never threaten her."

"Look, son" – John took a deep breath, spreading his hands— "She's my daughter and has acted oddly since you met. I lost one daughter by not paying enough attention. I won't lose another. If you or anyone else is keeping her from us, I'll do what I need to do to keep her safe!"

Alice said, "Kelly loves him, honey."

"Does she? You don't find it alarming that he takes her away for months at a time and doesn't let her speak to us?"

51

"Mark?" Kelly clutched him tightly.

"Just rest, sweetheart. Your dad is worried is all."

John said, "Let me speak to her alone and this can all be cleared up."

Richard said, "I'm so sorry. Of course you can speak to her."

Alice said, "I'm sure this is all a misunderstanding."

Richard pulled Mark to his feet.

He reluctantly released Kelly.

"Don't go," she said.

He said, "I'll be right outside."

"Don't go!" she said again, reaching to pull him back. "I need you. The children…" her eyes widened, and she sniffed the air.

The door opened and Matti entered. "We have a situation. I've found a small blood clot in your son's left ventricle. We're assembling a team now. The procedure shouldn't take more than two hours but I'm afraid it really can't wait."

"The procedure?" Mark stared in perplexity.

Matti said, "We'll need to operate to remove the clot."

"He's sick?" Kelly began to cry. "Can you help him?"

"We'll do everything possible."

Alice gasped and sagged, sitting weakly in a chair, clutching the baby to her chest.

Matti said, "I need you to sign these releases so that we can proceed. Doctor Reyes will be in shortly to go over the procedure with you, but time is of the essence. We need to get him prepped."

The loudspeaker in the hall emitted a tone then, *Doctor Sorenson to the NICU. Doctor Sorenson to the NICU. Code Blue.*

Matti ran for the door.

Richard followed her.

John hesitated and then followed them.

Alice said, "Dear God," and began to cry.

Mark sat beside Kelly again to hug her. "He's fine," he said.

"Is he sick?"

"I swear to you, our son will be fine!"

"What's going on?"

"*Shh*, just sleep. The sedative is making me sleepy too."

"I feel like I'm dreaming," Kelly muttered.

"Don't worry about anything. Just go to sleep."

Alice sniffed loudly. "Mark, she should know."

"Know what? She heard Matti." Mark settled Kelly to the pillow and tucked the light blanket around her. He kissed her cheek and smoothed her hair until her eyes closed.

Alice bit her lip but said nothing. Mark waited until Kelly's breathing evened out before turning to face Alice.

"Kelly is beyond exhausted. Between whatever they hell they gave her and the sedative, she must be more confused than not and there's no point in making this worse. She needs time to get the drugs out of her system. You can see she isn't acting rationally." He grimaced and stood to take the baby from Alice. "Believe me, I'm worried enough for both of us." He placed the baby beside Kelly. "Let her hold her. Can you watch them? I want to check on my son."

"Of course."

Alice stood and hurried to the bedside where she hesitated and then hugged Mark.

"John's upset. He's worried we're missing the signs." Alice grimaced. "No, he knows we're ignoring them, but I'm certain she loves you. Something is going on though and don't try to tell us it isn't. Is it Richard? You can come stay with us."

"Can this wait?"

She flushed and sat on the bed.

Mark exited the room right as John and Richard returned.

Richard said, "I've given permission, but they need you to go sign the papers."

Shock rooted Mark to the spot. He'd thought the operation a ruse.

"Is he—"

"Holding his own," John said gruffly.

Code Pink! Code Pink! The lights in the hallway flickered as a distant siren sounded. *Code Pink! Code Pink!* The echo of it came to him through the floor. Whatever was happening was happening to the entire hospital.

"What the hell!" John said and returned to the hall.

Mark started to follow and Richard grabbed his arm.

Gunshots sounded, muffled by distance but distinct to Mark's ears. A woman screamed and glass broke.

The nurses at the duty station all jumped to their feet.

The woman on the intercom said, "Code Silver. Please remain in your rooms with the doors closed. An armed intruder has entered the hospital! An amber alert has been issued. The hospital will be locked until an all clear is sounded."

Code Silver! Remain in your rooms with the door locked! The message repeated as Richard pulled Mark into the room.

"What's going on?" Alice asked.

Mark turned to see if the noise had woken Kelly. Alice held the baby again and Kelly thrashed restlessly but her eyes remained closed.

Richard pulled a phone from his pocket and made a call.

John stood in the open doorway.

"Close the doors, please!" a nurse called as she ran for a room across them.

Another two shots sounded accompanied by screaming and a group of people ran through the swinging doors at the end of the hallway. A nurse there waved them into a room.

Richard said, "Dad, I think someone is trying to kidnap the baby. We need more guards and we need them right now!"

John said, "Son of a bitch!" and he ran through the door.

"Sir!" a nurse called.

"Oh my god!" Alice wailed.

Mark hesitated torn between running after John or going to Kelly. He knew Richard wasn't speaking to his father, but his brain felt muzzy and he couldn't decide if this was Richard's plan or if Richard was putting on a show of expected actions for a kidnapping.

Richard said, "Get someone to the police station and see if we can get one of them to talk." He turned away and lowered his voice, "The baby won't live long without that operation."

"Oh God," Alice said again and she began to sob.

Mark said, "We don't even know if it was him."

He yanked open the door and a security guard waved him back. Four nurses had congregated at the far end of the hallway. Two who were crouching behind the desk.

John was yanking at the closed door at the end of the corridor while an officer tried to pull him away.

The guard said, "Return to your rooms, please. We'll be sweeping floor by floor. You're perfectly safe."

"My son. He's going for surgery."

One of the crouching nurses ran to the guard and grabbed his arm. She whispered something and the guard nodded and motioned Mark forward. "I'm sorry, Mr. Miller, but it was your son they took."

Alice let out a keening cry.

Mark said, "Who took him?"

John released the door handle, turning to glare at them.

"I'm sorry. I don't know the details, but everything is being done to retrieve him."

The room wavered. The guard's voice grew dim in his ears.

Richard said, "Mark, remain calm. Sit right here and take a deep breath."

Richard pulled him to the floor and squatted beside him. "Everything will be okay. Trust me. Take a deep breath."

Barbara ran through the doors, peering behind her. Her hair was mussed and blood stained her white jacket.

She called, "Mr. Henderson—"

Richard interrupted. "I want my family out of here. Help Kelly dress. We're leaving."

Mark growled low in his throat as he caught the scent of the blood. Richard cocked his head and his eyes narrowed and Mark knew he realized it was Matti's blood too. It shocked Mark that his wolf was remaining so passive. Whatever they'd given him seemed to be working.

Alice said, "My daughter needs medical care."

Barbara said, "Her tox screen came back positive for THC. We can treat her—"

Richard said, "You'll treat her at home. I want her out of here before another crazy comes."

"Of course, Mr. Henderson. I'll arrange transport. I'm so sorry…"

Mark said, "My son's operation?"

"Hadn't started yet. Doctor Sorenson was injured in the attempt as were two nurses."

Richard said, "How bad?"

Mark sniffed deeply but they both smelled nervous. The entire floor reeked of nervous perspiration.

"I really don't know, sir," Barbara said.

Mark told himself Richard wouldn't be standing here so calmly if there was danger. He lowered his head to his hands and concentrated on slowing his breathing.

Three police officers ran through the door and the guard joined them.

One of the officers approached and Richard stood and offered his hand.

"Mr. Henderson, Mr. Miller," the officer said.

"My son?" Mark stood, bracing himself against the spinning room.

"No word yet, I'm afraid."

Alice said, "Are they still in the hospital?"

"We're sweeping now, ma'am, but we know three escaped."

"With the baby?"

"I'm afraid so, ma'am."

"How did this happen? He needs an operation!"

"We're doing everything we can."

Richard said, "How much time does he have?"

Alice pressed her hands to her face, sobbing.

Mark swayed and Richard grabbed his arm hard.

The officer said, "A doctor could answer that better than me."

The police officers began going room-to-room trailed by two of the nurses.the other four had disappeared, into the rooms, Mark supposed.

The loudspeaker again warned them that the hospital was locked down and armed intruders were present.

"Why would they take him? He's just a baby…" Alice patted her chest, and Mark was suddenly worried she'd have a heart attack.

Richard released him to take her elbow. "Nurse! Can we get a doctor here?"

He led Alice back into the room.

"What am I supposed to do?" Mark said, flushing when he realized he'd said it aloud.

"Wait," the officer said kindly. "Go be with your wife."

"But why?" Alice asked again. "Who did this? Stacy is locked up, isn't she?"

The officer said, "I'm afraid she had more confederates, but we'll catch them all."

Richard said, "How did they get passed the guards?"

The radio on the officer's belt squawked and he stepped away without answering Richard.

"Do you know what the codes mean?" Alice asked.

Mark nodded, shock and fear stealing his breath.

Richard said, "Suspect in custody. One fatality."

Alice drew in a sharp breath.

Mark's muscles tightened painfully, and his heart began to pound. He sniffed the air again, trying to discern if Richard was sincerely worried but the scent of Matti's blood on Barbara's clothes distracted him.

"The baby?" Alice asked.

Richard said, "No. They would report a victim differently. Let me see what I can find out. Mark, stay here and stay calm!"

The power of Richard's voice pushed Mark back. He staggered as he caught his balance.

One of the nurses headed to them.

Alice laid a hand on Mark's shoulder. "Come sit down. You're as pale as a ghost."

"Stay with Kelly," Mark said and followed Richard.

"We've got this all under control," Richard said softly but not whispering.

Mark sniffed deeply and couldn't identify a change in Richard's scent.

Doors up and down the hallway were opening, and two nurses passed them, heading to the soft sounds of call buzzers.

One of the nurses headed to Alice. Mark glanced back as she took Alice's arm, feeling for the pulse in her wrist as she led her back into the room.

The officer with the radio called after them, "I'm sorry, but you need to wait here until we get the all clear!"

Mark ignored him, pushing through the double doors leading to the nursery. He caught the scent of blood before he saw it and his pulse began to pound. The smell of his pack was clear in the corridor over the other smells.

A group of whispering and crying nurses were huddled before the open door to the nursery. Two men wearing doctor's coats spoke with a police officer and John. Another four officers were setting out crime scene tape. One of the glass windows that allowed visitors to see the babies lay in shards on the floor.

"My son?" he asked loudly.

"Mr. Miller!" One of the nurses left the others.

Mark recognized her as the one who'd taken Kelly's blood earlier.

Two of the officers headed to him as Richard, the guard, and one of the other officers from the other room entered.

Mark reached the intact window and stopped to stare at the blood splattered floor. A headache joined his pounding pulse. A feeling of pins and needles suffused his arms and legs. He staggered, catching himself with a hand on the glass. Three paramedics and two doctors were crouched around a nurse, and with a shock that made him moan, he recognized Star was the nurse.

A man with his back to Mark was stitching her arm. Blood trickled from a cut on her forehead and she held a bloody cloth to the side of her head.

Star gave him a quick smile, then turned away, wincing as her arm was stitched and speaking to a police officer who held a notebook and was taking notes.

Richard said, "Let them do their job, Mark. Come sit down."

The command in Richard's voice shivered across Mark's skin but Richard sounded as if he spoke from the end of a tunnel.

"Come with me!" Richard repeated forcefully. "I'm sorry. I think he's in shock."

Mark turned to see who Richard spoke to.

The officer said, "Mr. Miller, if you'd please accompany your friend."

"Mark," Derek said, and Mark turned to see his old friend was one of the officers who'd been laying out the tape. He shook his head and breathed deeply, trying to clear the fuzziness in his head.

The door to the nursery opened, stirring the air, and the pins and needles feeling intensified when he caught a vague whiff of Arny and Alan's blood.

Chapter 7

"Mark, come with us," Derek said, taking his arm and trying to pull him away.

Mark pressed closer to the glass to scan the cribs. Only two contained babies and both seemed to be sleeping peacefully despite the hubbub around them. A few of the cribs were overturned and sprinkled with blood. Medical implements and broken glass littered the floor. It was clear a fight had taken place in this room.

The door at the other end of the corridor opened and a group of men in suits entered.

"Get him out of here!" the first police officer said to Derek, giving Richard a hard glance. He headed to the new group saying, "Hold it right there! This is an active crime scene!"

Derek said, "Come on. You shouldn't be here."

"The babies?"

63

Pins and needles assaulted his limbs again. The pack would never endanger a child and blood was splattered across the cribs. His son was really taken. He began to shake.

Richard said, "They're all fine. Most are in with their parents. You should be with your wife and daughter."

"Kelly..." Mark shook his head hard, pinching the bridge of his nose. "How many are hurt?"

"No one you need to worry about," Richard said firmly.

He pulled Mark away from the window.

Mark peered over his shoulder, but Star didn't glance back at him. She was speaking to Arny, one of the men wearing a white coat that Mark had thought a doctor.

"Is this..." He clamped his lips, shaking his head again. Whether this was staged by Richard or had been a real attempt made no difference. He needed to get control of himself.

"I need to get my wife out of here!"

He pulled his arm from Richard's grasp and tried to run but his legs wouldn't obey him, and he staggered awkwardly.

Richard grabbed him again.

John said, "They caught two of them, but the rest got away."

Mark hadn't seen or scented him coming. John took Mark's other arm. Tears filled his eyes and his face was pale.

Richard said, "Let's not worry him about that right now. Everything is going to be okay. We've got it all under control. You just worry about Kelly."

The men continued to speak but their voices couldn't dent the haze around him. Only Richard's voice was clear, and he eagerly grasped the reassurance in it.

Richard released him when they reached the door to Kelly's room.

Alice said, "John," in a quavering voice.

The nurse who'd been taking her vitals laid aside a blood pressure cuff and patted Alice's hand.

John shook his head, releasing Mark's arm to hug Alice. Mark sat beside Kelly, resting his hand on his daughter's back. Her pulse beat fast but steadily and he leaned closer to smell her. She smelled just as she had, and he breathed deeply, letting her scent calm him.

Kelly turned more toward him, moaning softly.

Richard said, "I want you guys out of here. There's too many people coming in and out to secure you here. Nurse, get her doctor and get her discharged."

"I'm afraid I can't—"

"We're going with or without the damned discharge! If this hospital ever wants to see another dime of my father's money, a wheelchair better be here in three minutes!"

Barbara exited the bathroom and handed Mark Kelly's overnight bag. "I thought it best to wait for you to help her dress. It would be kinder to let her reach home before telling her…" She bit her lip and hurried to Alice. "There, there, now. You have a beautiful healthy granddaughter."

"He didn't even have a name," Alice said, and her tears came faster.

"His name is Marcus," Mark said.

Richard said, "Kelly wanted to call him Wilson for his grandfather and I think that would be better."

He said it so forcefully that Mark nodded. The power in Richard's voice made him slightly nauseas and the pins and needles returned.

Derek said, "We have leads. Good strong leads. We could find him."

Richard stepped into the hallway. "I know you mean well, but I think it's false hope. Wilson needs that operation. I think we should prepare him for the worst."

Barbara fussed about them, giving Kelly an injection, the furtiveness of her actions convincing Mark that she didn't want anyone to see her do it. He craned over his shoulder to see if her parents or the nurse had noticed, but her parents were hugging each other, and the nurse had left. He was growing woozier by the second, and he cursed softly as he struggled with Kelly's clothing.

Richard continued to speak but his voice was just a soothing murmur of sound. He wished John and Alice would stop crying. Kelly grumbled at him, slapping weakly at his hands. Men and women spoke loudly in the hallway over the sound of the loudspeaker but it was all an indistinguishable blur to Mark.

"We're going home," he said. "I'm taking you out of this place. I never should have brought you here. God, what was I thinking? You need peace and quiet, not this circus."

"Mark?" Kelly coughed and cleared her throat.

Barbara handed her a glass of water and two small white pills. "I'll see about that chair," she said to Mark.

Mark held the glass so Kelly could drink and took the pills from her.

"Mom?" Kelly said, sounding scared and confused.

Richard said, "Your mother is perfectly all right."

"I'm here, honey. Your father and I are right here." She leaned passed Mark to take Kelly's hand. Mark took the baby from her and held her to his face.

Richard said, "Derek, could you escort the Andersons to my car? I've arranged for private guards at the house, but a police escort would be nice to get us there."

"I'll call it in," Derek said. "Mark, I'm so sorry, man..."

By the time Mark realized he should reply, Derek, John, and Alice had left the room.

Richard crouched in front of him and took his hands. "Marcus is fine and with Leah. Everyone is fine. Just keep it together for ten more minutes. Kelly, keep your eyes open. That's right; look at your hands. Just keep looking at your hands. Mark, hold her hand. Barb, what the hell did you give them? They're like zombies!"

"WBGDP13," Barb said. "We haven't experimented with it much. But—Oh good, Nurse Hightower, help me get Mrs. Miller settled. Mr. Henderson, if you'd take the baby?"

Richard took the baby from Mark. "Let's go home!"

The power of Richard's voice pulled Mark to his feet and he followed to the elevator before he remembered Kelly.

"We're going to the car!" Richard said when Mark turned back.

Barbara pushed Kelly closer and Richard leaned down to pick up her hand. He pressed Kelly's hand to on his. Kelly's harsh pants alarmed Mark and he found himself matching her breath for breath.

The hospital corridors were crowded. Lights, noise, and motion dizzied him. He closed his eyes and followed his nose, concentrating on the smell of his daughter. Smells were growing erratic, fading and flaring for no discernable reason.

A barrage of sound startled him, and he opened his eyes to see a line of news vans lining the street. Policemen were laying out a barricade and waving reporters back.

The air refreshed Mark and he slowed to breathe deeply. Richard stopped beside him.

Kelly said, "Mom?"

"In the car," Barbara said.

Mark took his daughter from Richard and followed him outside.

Richard's limousine waited by the door.

Richard said, "Mark, give me a hand with your wife. Barb, take the baby."

Richard took the baby and handed her to Barbara.

Barbara said, "Officer Reynolds, tell those assholes this is a hospital zone and the noise ordinance is in effect. They're disturbing our patients with that ruckus!"

Derek said, "Yes, ma'am. Mark, my partner and I will follow you home. If there's anything I can do…"

Richard said, "I'll tell him. Thank you."

John said, "Do you need a hand."

"Get in," Richard said.

Mark got into the car, sighing with relief when Richard placed Kelly in his lap.

"Sit beside him, Barb." Richard sat on his other side, crowding against him.

Mark closed his eyes, laying his head on Kelly's.

"Sleep, sweetheart. We'll be home soon."

He must have dozed off because when he opened his eyes the door was opening and they were at Richard's house.

Three men that he didn't know waited. All three wore armored vests and carried rifles and radios. He knew the sight should alarm him but he couldn't manage more than mild interest.

"It's been quiet, Mr. Henderson," one said.

Richard said, "Mark, go with Barbara. Barb, if you'd settle them in the room we prepared?"

"Of course. Come with me, Mr. Miller."

John said, "Has there been any word?"

Mark leaned from the door, absently settling Kelly more on his shoulder.

"Nothing new, I'm afraid, sir," one of the guards said.

Mark climbed awkwardly from the car carrying Kelly. The air was laden with scents and felt warm and soft on his skin. He took a few deep breaths, holding them and releasing them slowly, sorting the smells.

His gaze drifted to a tight grouping of pines that he knew Andre was in and slid to the roses where he knew Andre's mother was. No outward sign betrayed their presence, but he could smell the pack surrounding the house.

Six strangers had stood here recently, three of them the men with the guns. Motor oil and exhaust was heavy in the air. A distant sound of talking came from the road where motors ran. He peered over his shoulder and could just make out a news logo on the side of a van through the trees.

They all paused and stared at the sky when a helicopter passed overhead.

Richard said, "Barb, get them inside."

Mark cradled Kelly and followed Barbara.

Behind him, Richard said, "John, Alice, the police will be by soon for our statements. I was hoping you'd have some idea where Stacy might go, who she might be working with?"

The closing door cut off sound and Leah greeted him with a hard hug.

"We've caught two reporters over the fence so far. You need to stay inside until we're certain it's safe outside.

"My son?"

"With JJ and Audrey. Settle Kelly first. I made a spot in the conservatory."

Mark nodded.

Leah said, "Are you okay? You look a bit…"

Barbara said, "It's the sedative that Matti and I developed. We need more trials. Mark, I'd like to take a few blood samples from you both."

"Do whatever you need to but don't give me that again."

"It helped though, didn't it? You didn't feel your wolf, right?" Barbara felt for the pulse in Kelly's wrist. "She needs her children and to rest undisturbed. See if you can get her to drink."

Barbara followed, still giving directions that he didn't really hear until they reached the glass French doors of the conservatory. Iron scrollwork and wood held leaded stained-glass panels that Audrey had made over a hundred years ago. Banana trees formed a dense wall in front of the floor-to-ceiling windows and shaded the stone floor to the left of a kidney shaped pool. Sunlight streamed in from the right, sparkling on the slow-moving water.

Leah headed for the mechanism to close the blinds on the windows and Mark said, "Leave it open. She needs the light."

The windows looked out onto a private patio bordered on three sides by wings of the house. The fourth was open to the side lawn but bushes and trees made it private. Kelly wasn't going to be stirring from the cave even if someone did wander by. Mark doubted an intruder would even make it onto the lawn without his pack knowing about it and the angle was bad for a helicopter to get shots inside the house.

Potted trees and dense ferns were spread around the room interspersing and shading the lounge chairs and couches. Mark headed to the back wall and indoor garden that surrounded a redwood that grew through the ceiling. The room had been constructed around the tree, the earth left how it was and planted with shrubs. Mark knew there was a small cave built into the earth because he'd used it in the past. This room was their version of a hospital. Leah had made it to be a safe place to rest and relax and recuperate from injuries. A place they could be a wolf or human as the need took them but still be close if they needed her or Richard.

Audrey had lived in this room for three years and she waited now, sitting cross-legged beside the cave.

"He's sleeping," she said, offering Mark the baby she held.

JJ jumped to his feet. He still had a few feet of clearance, but Mark needed to duck to enter.

JJ said, "I put my blanket in the cave just like you said, Mom."

Mark laid Kelly on the blanket.

"Let's go make lunch." Leah held out her hand to JJ.

JJ hugged Mark's knees. "He's sick, I think. We should get Daddy."

Mark squatted to hug him. "Thanks for looking after him, sport. He needs his mommy now."

JJ peered doubtfully at the baby.

Mark examined him with equal doubt. Blankets covered him but he could tell by the shape and angle Marcus hadn't resumed his human legs. Sparse patches of fur covered his back and arms. His face and head seemed to be caught halfway between man and wolf with the wolf winning.

Leah said, "We have guests and Uncle Mark is tired. Come help me make lunch. We'll go talk to Daddy."

Barbara laid their daughter beside Kelly. She said, "You need sleep too. Richard has a handle on all this."

"Does he?" Mark quirked a brow and Barbara made a face.

"As much as anyone can. And it's a good plan. Do your part by recovering." Barbara swung a small pack from her back and knelt to rummage in it. "I'll be out of your hair in just a minute."

"Is he okay?"

"Not really but I'm hoping is all he needs is his mother. He can't seem to decide what shape he should be in. Moving him caused that." She pointed vaguely at the child's face. "It's settled down some with Audrey and JJ. Let's get him as comfortable as we can beside Kelly. He's probably hungry too."

Kelly didn't wake when he removed her clothes or when Barbara took her samples. She sighed deeply when Mark placed Marcus on her chest. Audrey handed him a pillow.

"Prop this under her arm. I doubt she'll move. And look, he's doing better already."

Mark laid a hand on his son's back. The baby's breathing had eased, and it eased more as he watched. Within moments both his son and wife breathed slowly. He undressed his daughter and laid beside them, settling her to his chest.

Audrey fussed around him, propping his arm with a pillow and kissing both babies.

"Stay," he said sleepily, sighing gratefully when she lay beside him. Audrey would make sure neither of them rolled onto the babies.

Mark let the smell of fresh earth and trees relax his tense muscles. The room smelled strongly of pack and JJ. The trickle of water lulled him to sleep.

Kelly still slept deeply when he woke.

Audrey said, "Neither woke. She hasn't moved a muscle."

"How long?"

"Twenty-two hours."

"Did you get any sleep?"

"I'm fine. Barb says Kelly will probably sleep longer than the normal three days and that you shouldn't worry."

Mark grimaced and Audrey smiled wryly.

He knelt to examine his family.

His daughter slept in the crook of Kelly's arm and his son still slept across her chest but without the blanket now. His legs were paws complete with tiny claws and covered with fur. The fur ended midway up his chest, becoming thin patches. It looked to Mark as if he had a bit more fur on his head but maybe he was misremembering.

He leaned closer to sniff them. The weird sickly odor still clung to Kelly although it was weaker now. Her breasts looked swollen and sore. Clear liquid oozed from the nipple when he ran his finger across it.

"See if she'll suck," Audrey said.

Mark lifted his daughter, cradling her gently, holding her to Kelly's breast. He rubbed her mouth lightly against Kelly as he'd been told to do by Matti and Leah.

Anger heated his face. His wife had none of the comforts he'd prepared for them.

"Sometimes they don't wake enough to eat," Audrey said. "Give her a minute."

Marcus made a coughing snort and Mark set his daughter down to pick him up. He placed Marcus's lips against Kelly's nipple. Marcus mewed but wouldn't drink. His cries picked up in volume and Audrey leaned closer. "Maybe lay Kelly on her side more and lay him on his back. His mouth is the wrong shape. Let gravity do some of the work."

Kelly mumbled when he turned her, but she didn't open her eyes. Her breathing escalated to the same panting that had alarmed him when they'd left the hospital.

Mark held his son to her breast until the baby cried himself to sleep.

Audrey said, "Try again in an hour or so. We can try a bottle too."

Kelly curled around her children and her breathing slowed.

Audrey stood and eased through the shrubs at the cave mouth. Mark followed.

She said, "Kelly could use some privacy."

"She trusts you."

"I know and it's good for the pack to be near her. But she's a human woman too, Mark, and she'll be embarrassed when she wakes if she thinks we were hovering over her while she was naked like this."

Mark scowled at his sleeping wife.

"Does she need…"

"The blood is normal and nothing to worry about. It'll stop in a week or so. She isn't injured or at least I don't think she is. Shifting will fix her right up but this is a private personal moment and she won't want us around for it. She hasn't bonded with us yet and even if she had she's more human than not. Trust me on this. She won't want us around. Cover her if Richard comes to check on you."

"Has he been by?"

"No one has come in." Audrey bit her lip, glancing over her shoulder. "Her parents are going to be a problem."

"She'll never forgive us if we harm them."

"We have no intention of harming them!" Audrey winced, glancing over her shoulder again. Mark turned to look and caught the shadow of one of his pack outside on the patio.

Audrey said, "You should go speak with them but clean up first and get something to eat." I'll stay with Kelly. Leah left you clothes in the hall bath."

Mark hugged her for a minute, enjoying her calm company and the sun on his back. She kissed his cheek when he finally pulled away.

"I'll take good care of them," she assured him.

Mark left to clean up. His in-laws were sure to be angry and worried and he had no idea what to say to reassure them.

Chapter 8

Mark knocked once and entered Richard's office. Star and Arny were already there, sitting on a couch to the side of Richard's desk. Two chairs flanked the desk on the opposite side and Mark headed to the closest. The double wide, floor-to-ceiling windows were open, letting in the soft spring breezes and Mark sniffed deeply. To his relief Star smelled healthy without any signs of distress.

Richard wore casual clothing, jeans and a t-shirt. He sat at his desk, watching his monitor intently. He smelled relaxed though. A whiff of uneasy perspiration lingered around Arny. His gaze was on the widescreen television hanging above the fireplace between the windows. The sound was muted on a local news channel that was doing a recap of the deaths during the abductions. Two doors lay on opposite sides of the room. One led to Leah's office and the other to a bathroom.

Mark's stomach roiled unpleasantly. Kelly would be horrified innocent civilians had been murdered in the cover up and Mark still had no idea how he was going to pacify her parents.

Star stood to hug him. "How's Kelly?" she asked as she resumed her seat.

"I have no idea." He lifted trembling hands to rub his cheeks. "Marcus hasn't gotten any better. Kelly is going to freak when she wakes up and realizes we killed—"

The door to Richard's office swung open and John strode in.

Mark stiffened as he smelled the gun.

Richard leaned back in his seat, waving to the empty chair beside Arny. Arny scanned John slowly and Mark knew he'd scented the gun as well.

Richard said, "John, I was just going to go look for you. Please, have a seat.

"I'm fine right here. I've been doing some looking of my own." He glared at Mark.

Star stood and passed Mark, going to the sideboard and pouring a glass of whiskey.

"Care for a drink?" she asked.

John ignored her, half turning his back to face Richard directly.

"I walked the grounds earlier to check out the security, but you know that already, right? You're having me followed the instant I step out the door."

He shot Mark another scathing glance.

Arny half stood, and Richard waved him back to his seat.

John was highly agitated and more afraid than angry. It showed in his scent and the way his hand hovered by his waist.

Mark said, "I'm sure you're as worried as we are, and you can see Kelly when she wakes. My sister—"

"Save it! I'm not interested in your lies. Does Richard know about you two? Is she even your sister?"

Mark's heart thudded. *It had been John outside the conservatory windows.*

John said, "I just want my daughter safe."

Richard gave Mark a speaking glance and said, "Audrey isn't Mark's biological sister but both she and Mark were raised by my father. I consider them my cousins."

"Did you know they're having an affair?"

Star snorted a soft breath of laughter.

John glared over his shoulder at her. "I don't give a shit about that! That's between him and my daughter, but I sure as shit care about this asshole keeping her from her family! Every time I ask to see her, I get put off and I'm not taking no for an answer again!"

Mark said, "She really can't see him now, Richard."

Richard said, "We can handle this. We knew it might happen. John, take a seat, please, and I'll explain."

John glared at Mark. "You're talking to me, not him!"

Arny gestured for them to be quiet, saying, "Turn up the television. It's a special report."

Richard reached for the remote as Mark peered over his shoulder at the television. From the corner of his eye he spied John reaching for the gun and he turned back as glass shattered and the smell of whisky suddenly filled the room. John pulled the gun from his waistband as Star grabbed his arm. Mark had run forward, but he halted and put his hands up.

"There's no need for this," he said as John and Star struggled over the gun. "Don't hurt him, Star!"

The gun went off, blowing a hole in the couch, right as Star yanked it from John's hand.

"Sit!" Arny said and pulled John to the couch. He thrust him into the seat.

Star stuck the gun into her waistband. "I told you we need an alarm on the gun case."

"Not now," Richard said,

He turned up the volume and they all stared at the screen as the words *Special Report Miller Kidnapping* faded from the screen.

Mark said, "I swear to God, John, that I'm doing everything I can to help Kelly! If you could just be patient a few more days, Kelly will speak to you herself."

"And give you time to brainwash her or terrorize her into doing what he says?" John jerked a thumb at Richard. "I see how you all jump when he speaks. Mark, you need help. Can't you see how he's controlling you? You let him name your son…"

Mark said, "I'll do whatever you want after Kelly speaks with you."

Leah stuck her head through the doorway.

Richard said. "It's all under control. Make sure the guards outside didn't hear anything and keep everyone calm."

Leah nodded and withdrew, wincing at Mark as she closed the door.

"I demand you let me speak with my daughter!"

Richard said, "*Shh*, I want to hear this."

Star sat on the arm of the couch beside John.

"I hope I didn't hurt you," she said.

John ignored her other than a quick scan to see where she'd put the gun.

Mark pinched the bridge of his nose. John wasn't going to take later for an answer. He couldn't think of a logical reason he'd have been naked and hugging Audrey. Of course John thought he was having an affair... He couldn't bear the thought of dressing Kelly and putting her in a hospital bed with all the tubes and wires someone in her condition should have and it was clear John wasn't taking no for an answer. If he was willing to shoot to get to his daughter, he'd go the police the minute they let him go. This was spiraling out of control.

With dread he turned to the television to see what else his pack had been up to.

Chapter 9

The woman on the television said, "This is Andrea Corman with a special report. We've just received word another arrest has been made in the Miller kidnapping case. This is the fourth conspirator apprehended this week."

A picture of the house where Kelly had been held flashed behind Andrea. "We're going live to the courthouse in Minnesota with Bill Bradly. Bill, what can you tell us?"

A man in a blue suit stood on the steps of a courthouse. He had a notebook balanced on his arm and looked down at it as he spoke into the mic he held in his other hand. "I've just been informed three men were apprehended and are being held for questioning on the abduction of Wilson Miller. Police Chief Gerald Connell will be issuing a statement momentarily." Bill tucked the notebook under his arm and faced the camera. "We've received footage pertaining to the arrest, but I warn the audience it makes for grim viewing."

The picture on screen changed to a photo of a wall. At first glance it appeared to be covered by diagrams of the human body, but the camera zoomed in to show someone had drawn in fangs and claws and the limbs were angled wrong. The camera panned the drawings of joints and muscles, lingering on autopsy photos tacked in layers to the stained wall as Bill said, "The men living in this house have been collecting pictures to substantiate their delusion, and I hope the police are investigating to be sure none of these people were victims to gather the information displayed here. Almost every one of the people portrayed in these pictures was believed to be the victim of a serious animal attack of some kind. We can see where joints and muscles have been measured and if you look at the back of the pictures you can see their theories."

The picture changed again to show a weed covered backyard and two dilapidated doghouses. Half-rotted tarps had been hung over a chain-link fence surrounding the yard. The camera panned slowly, stopping when it reached a shallow hole beside one of the doghouses.

"The bones you see there are what the police believe to be the remains of two timber wolves stolen from the Edmonton Zoo last year. The freezer inside the house held several dismembered canine carcasses and numerous vials of blood that are undergoing testing.

These men believe they can become werewolves by drinking the blood of wolves."

The picture changed again.

"Jesus…" Mark said breathlessly, "Did we?"

"Nope. This was all of them." Richard sounded both pleased and horrified.

A human skull laid in the center of a pentagram beside a wolf skull. Bones from both feet and paws had been placed with precision in a circle around the five-pointed star. Flies were clustered thickly on a piece of meat of some kind. It was clear by the scuff marks and faded paint lines that this wasn't the first pentagram to be drawn there.

The picture switched back to Bill who said, "The police are still combing that house for evidence but there's no doubt that the men who lived there were working with the kidnappers. The police found pictures, maps, plans, and receipts for the equipment used to broadcast the abduction of Mrs. Kelly Miller."

The camera panned over a cluttered desk with drawers opened and obviously newly emptied.

"The men who lived here kept lists of other living victims of animal attacks and we've been informed that the police confiscated plans for further kidnappings that included the means to hold their victims and in some cases devices or further equipment and thermos on how they could get those victims to reveal they're true shapes. I can't go into the detail but suffice it say I believe it's clear they had no intention of ever releasing these people."

The picture changed again to a video of Bill on the street talking to an older man before a rundown house. Police cars with flashing lights could be seen in the background.

Bill said, "This footage was recorded earlier today. On the video Bill said, "Mr. Haller, you called and informed the police—"

"I been calling for years, and they always ignore me. The damned place reeks and the dogs bark something awful. They always got new dogs and some I think were coyotes. They kept them caged up in the back there. The whole neighborhood knew they were crazy—up to no good."

"You say you reported them before. Had you heard or seen anything that might make you think they were a danger?"

"Look at that place! It's clear as shit they're a danger! Just last week I called in a complaint about screaming."

"Did the police respond?"

"Sure; they showed up and knocked and left two minutes later. They didn't even go inside."

"Did you ever find out what the screaming was about?"

"One of their skanks came to the door. Said she saw a rat. I think it was that girl, the ringleader girl, but I can't swear to it. There's two or three who come around regular like. They all wear dog collars and I even seen them on leashes a time or two. Their sick crazy—"

The audio was beeped out and the scene changed to Bill on the courthouse steps. Banner on the bottom of the screen said 'Live.'

Men had gathered on the stairs behind him and they were busily setting up a podium and microphone. Andrea said, "I'd be interested to hear more about those police reports. I'm sure our viewers would like to know why nothing was done."

Bill said, "I spoke briefly with Chief Connell." Bill broke off to peer over his shoulder at the door at the top of the stairs opening. "Oh, here he is now. Let's hear what he has to say." Bill joined the other men and women hurrying up the stairs with their mics thrust out.

The chief grabbed both edges of the podium and leaned forward. "Let me start by reassuring the populous that so far no human remains have been found at the scene, except for the skull and foot bones that I've been assured are over seventy years old and we believe to have been stolen from a local cemetery. Tests are being conducted as we speak to identify the remains and families will be notified. I know we all hate the idea that we lived so close to serial killers, but it looks as if this group hadn't quite reached that level yet.

"Mr. DaSilva, the owner of the home, has admitted that he does practice animal sacrifice and that he was involved with the abduction of Mrs. Kelly Miller. He's denying involvement with the abduction of Wilson

Miller and our investigation is ongoing. Mr. Fortier and Mr. Wiles, the two men picked up in the raid, collaborate his story and numerous witnesses can attest to the whereabouts of these three men during the abductions. They've given us new leads to pursue and my officers are still questioning them."

One of the reporters shouted, "Why did it take so long for the police to respond to all of the complaints?"

Chief Connell said, "It's true that numerous calls had come in prior to this incident and every single one of them was answered within the letter of the law. Dogs were removed from the house two times and fines levied. Mr. DaSilva was warned that the next instance would result in a criminal case.

"The house was entered on two separate occasions but not searched. The law prohibits the search of a residence, except in the case where an officer believes a person is at risk. Animal cruelty, while heinous, is not a criminal offense in this county unless the abuse can be proved to be ongoing. If you don't like the three-strike rule, I suggest you take it up with your congressmen. Meanwhile, my officers will continue to enforce the law as written."

"There were over twenty dog skeletons!" someone yelled.

"And all were buried. The skeletons came to light during our investigation and the men will be charged appropriately once cause of death has been established."

"And the missing child?"

Mark leaned forward in his seat, flicking a glance at John who glowered at him.

"There was no sign of the child nor any indication of their direct involvement." The chief held up his hand as the reporters began yelling questions. "This is a trying time for the parents, and we should all remain sensitive to their distress. I won't speak publicly about it, except to say that the men kept a book, a grimoire if you will. It's a hodgepodge of superstition and they seemed to have adopted a type of vampirism into their beliefs. Their book speaks of a sacred circle, the spot of sacrifice, and describes it as a meadow with blood red poppies, a stream following a ley line, and I'm quoting here, the tree that guards the portal. This tree might or might not be an apple tree.

"We're asking anyone who might have heard them speak of this place or has any further knowledge, to contact this station immediately."

A barrage of questions followed. The chief answered them for twenty minutes or so but had nothing new to say that Mark didn't already know.

The chief returned to the building and an image of Andrea replaced Bill. She sat at her desk with pictures of all of the people who'd been arrested so far behind her.

Mark was shocked by the amount of them. Over twenty people had been involved in Kelly's abduction and they'd barely started investigating.

Andrea gave a brief synopsis of how each was involved and the picture had just changed to show images of people wanted for questioning when a buzzer sounded and a light came on at Richard's desk.

Richard took out his phone as it rang.

He listened for a moment and said, "Send them right in." He replaced the phone in his pocket.

He said, "The police are here and would like to speak with you."

"And Kelly?" John rose an eyebrow, his expression challenging.

"Kelly is sleeping," Mark said.

"Then wake her up. I'm getting tired of this shit!" John stood and headed for the door.

Arny grabbed his arm.

Mark said, "Don't hurt him," as Richard said, "Keep him quiet but let him listen." He jerked his head to the far door as the doorbell rang.

Mark winced as Arny slapped a hand over John's mouth.

John began to struggle, yelling something but the hand over his mouth made his words indistinguishable.

"I'm sorry and I'll explain," Mark said.

Star stepped into the doorway. She held the gun in one hand and grabbed at John's flailing feet.

Mark said, "Give us ten minutes and I swear to God I'll tell you everything."

Mark didn't know if John had heard or believed him. The door between the rooms closed. Richard sat on the couch over the bullet hole as Leah entered followed by Derek and another officer Mark didn't know, two men in suits, and JJ.

JJ ran to him and Mark swung him into his arms. Richard muted the television.

"Mr. Henderson. Mr. Miller, will your wife be joining us?"

"My wife has been sedated. Did you find him?"

"Please, I think you should sit."

"Did you find him?" Mark asked again as he sat. Leah sat beside him and took his hand, placing her other hand on JJ's back.

"It might be best if the child leaves."

"Derek, did they find my son?"

Leah said, "JJ, honey, go to the kitchen and ask Willa to give you lunch. She made your favorite but save some for us."

JJ hesitated, and Richard said, "Give your uncle a kiss and go to the kitchen, son."

JJ kissed Mark's cheek and ran from the room.

One of the suited men offered his hand and said, "I'm Special Agent Joel Carvalho and this is my partner Agent Alphonse Prescott. You can call me Joel. I see you've been following the news."

Mark said, "Did they murder him?"

Carvalho winced. "We don't know. Human remains have been found and were sent to the lab for testing. "

"What—"

"There wasn't much left. They'd burned the body."

Leah squeezed his hand.

Joel continued. "The remains are consistent... I'm so sorry but there's a real possibility that the body was that of your son."

"But you don't know for sure?"

Mark didn't have to fake his horrified expression. It sickened him to contemplate his pack had killed a child.

Derek said, "We have blood evidence and are testing that but, Mark, her sister was talking to a cellmate about ransom. There's hope."

Richard pursed his lips. Mark agreed. Stacy of all people had to know the kidnapping was a hoax perpetuated by them. "Stacy thinks she can ransom him back? No one called us..."

Carvalho shook his head at Derek. "This is one of the worst cases I've ever been on. I hate to speak of the details to you, but I think you need to hear them to understand how we've reached the conclusions we have."

Richard gestured them to seats, pulling Leah down to sit on the arm of the couch beside him.

Prescott said, "Stacy Anderson confided in her cellmate. The woman is cooperating with us and so far all of her information has checked out. We found another small cell of these lunatics in California. That cell was more concerned with the zombie apocalypse, but they drank the blood of animals and humans as a regular thing. In their pathos doing so will empower them, making them able to withstand the coming zombie plague. These are deeply disturbed people."

Derek said, "They had lists of people they suspected of being vampires and werewolves and all kinds of crazy things. Kelly wasn't their only target. She was just the first."

Carvalho nodded. "We're still trying to figure out what escalated them. But we think it was just old-fashioned greed. Stacy Anderson bragged to her cellmate that she'd be able to sell Kelly's child. She called it a win-win. She doesn't appear to care who pays for the child, the werewolf wannabes or you. The court appointed psychiatrist say she's suffering from delusions exasperated by mild brain damage caused by the drugs she takes. Her beliefs shift and she's sometimes convinced your wife is a werewolf and at others she's just angry that she married well and sometimes she thinks Kelly is safe at home and she speaks of her with a sort of fond lightheartedness."

Prescott said, "Stacy Anderson is a deeply troubled young lady."

Mark said, "I don't care about any of that."

Carvalho leaned forward, resting his elbows on his knees and clasping his hands. "She's also very well known in this fringe group and has been trying to sell her plan for months. Her plan called for the abduction of her sister. She intended to keep the child and either ransom it back to you or sell it to them. I'm not a hundred percent convinced she believed her own hype.

I think she saw an easy way to make a quick buck. Her sister met their criteria of surviving an animal attack. But the plan got away from her. I think when she was arrested that they decided to go for the child themselves for their own reasons."

"Which are?"

"They believe that drinking the blood of –

"Enough," Leah said. "You think they sacrificed him."

"I'm sorry but the evidence supports it."

"What evidence? Is all I've heard is supposition and hearsay."

"The intel from Stacy's cellmate led us to a trailer park in Flathead where we found the burnt remains of an infant and enough blood to be considered a mortal wound. Most of the blood was tainted by either the fire or cleaning products but we've taken swabs, which are being compared to the samples taken at the hospital.

"When will we know?"

"Any time now. We wanted to wait but were afraid you'd hear it on the news."

They all turned to the muted television. The chief of police had left but the two reporters still spoke while pictures of the house and the people there played in the background.

Mark said, "Did you catch them?"

"They took their own lives when we arrived on the scene. We still have agents there, but we think we've got them all. Anderson's cellmate gave us a pretty comprehensive list of names."

Mark frowned as he considered why Stacy would volunteer the information. She wasn't stupid and it wasn't at all in character for her to admit she'd done a thing wrong.

Leah said, "What about his daughter? Is she in danger?"

"As I said, we're still tracking down leads and we should know more in a day or two."

Richard said, "And what about them?" He gestured to the television where women in black robes held out golden cups, offering blood to people passing by their shop.

"Unfortunately, it isn't against the law to be crazy. I'm sure there will be some who persist in their beliefs and some who don't believe will jump on the bandwagon because fools are easy targets. Mrs. Miller had the misfortune of having a greedy sister, but I think you can expect your fair share of the crazies to show up here. The work you do, your logo, all will be grist for the rumor mill."

"You think our son will become a target?"

Horror sent a cold chill down Mark's spine. He closed his eyes and covered his face with his hands.

"Maybe. It's hard to say with these kinds of things. Any sane person will see the truth, but we aren't talking about sane people."

"So what should we do?" Leah asked.

"Go on as you have been. Let this blow over."

"Easy for you to say. It isn't your child!" She dropped Mark's hand and jumped to her feet. "Maybe we should sell it all and move."

Prescott shook his head as he stood. "You can do what you like but running will make the conspiracy nuts certain that you're hiding something."

Leah wrung her hands and Mark lifted his head to sniff. She didn't smell at all distressed although she sounded scared.

She said, "This is crazy. They had her most of the night. They must see she's just a normal woman!"

Carvalho shrugged. "They want to believe. They're looking for magic. You could sit in front of a camera all night long every night and they'd still come up with theories as to why you could. These people are fanatics. But you have security and these people are also disorganized and on our watch list now. We'll hear about it if they begin to hatch another plan. I really don't think you need to worry."

Derek said, "Mark, if there's anything we can do…"

Richard said, "Let us know as soon as you hear anything."

"Of course. We'll be running extra patrols here and the offices when they open back up."

Richard said, "My father has taken to his bed. The stress…I haven't given the offices a thought. I suppose I better though."

Leah said, "Maybe it's time to quit your job. We always knew this day would come."

Prescott said, "I was under the impression you already ran the sanctuary."

Leah said, "He does basically. He works too hard. His real job is game warden."

"I love that job," Richard murmured.

Mark winced, leaning forward, resting his elbows on his knees to cradle his throbbing head.

Richard said, "None of this is your fault, Mark. If I need to take over more of the day-to-day operation at Howls, then I will. That was always the plan. We knew my father would retire someday."

Leah said, "I better go check on JJ. If you'll excuse me."

Richard sighed heavily, leaning back in his seat.

Mark didn't know what to do or say or how he was supposed to react. Worry for JJ kept intruding on his thoughts. Richard had made himself a target to save his family. The entire pack was now at risk. His breath caught hard.

Richard laid a hand on his back.

"I'll take care of them," Richard said.

Derek said, "We're a phone call away."

The soft buzz of a phone on vibrate interrupted him. Mark picked his head up as Prescott answered the call. He turned away and spoke softly, but they could all hear him. Derek's eyes filled with tears and he turned away and cleared his throat.

"Thank you for calling," Prescott said and placed the phone back into his pocket.

He turned back, spreading his hands. "That was the lab and the blood was a match. I'm so sorry."

Mark stood and he'd reached the door before he remembered Star and Arny had brought John into the next room. He rested his forehead on the door, wiggling the handle to warn them.

"I need to speak with my wife but she's resting."

"Go be with her. I'll see them out," Richard said.

Mark stepped through the door, closing it behind himself and sagging against it.

John glared at him from teary eyes. He'd been tied and gagged, and he sat in the desk chair. This was Leah's home office and stuffed animals and toys were scattered around the room. Star peeked from the window. Arny stood beside John with a hand on his shoulder, but his eyes were on the computer screen. The volume was on low, but Mark could hear Richard making his farewells.

Mark said, "You can see Kelly, but let me explain."

He nodded to Arny, and Arny ripped the gag from John's mouth.

Arny said, "Don't make me shut you up."

Mark shook his head, pinching the bridge of his nose. His temples throbbed in time to his heartbeat.

Star left the window to take Mark's arm. "You look beat."

"What the hell are we going to do?"

"Nothing. We did it already." She winked at him and kissed his cheek, releasing his arm and sitting on the edge of the desk.

Mark said, "Where'd we get the dead bodies?"

John's eyes widened and he licked his lips, his gaze darting about the room.

Arny said. "We caught the fuckers who took Kelly and ran into the woods when the police arrived. We needed to know who they'd told."

"And Stacy? How'd you get her to cooperate?"

Star frowned, thumping her feet to the floor. "You're not going to like this, but we promised her we'd make her pack if she cooperated."

The blood rushed from his head so fast it left him dizzy. "Like hell you did!"

Star winced.

Arny said, "We promised to bite her the minute she gets out. Hell, you couldn't stop me from biting her!"

Mark's head throbbed harder.

John said, "Are you all crazy?"

Mark sat cross-legged on the floor. "This is a secret that you can't tell. Stacy wasn't wrong. Kelly is a werewolf."

Chapter 10

John stared for a moment and then said in a voice of forced calm, "Can I see her, please?"

Mark said, "I know it's unbelievable."

Star huffed a small laugh. "We work really hard to make it unbelievable."

Mark waved for her to quiet. "Kelly was bitten by a feral wolf. It wasn't one of us. I was sent to find that wolf and stop him. He'd killed a bunch of girls trying to make a mate.

Mark huffed in annoyance, angry at himself for rambling. "None of that matters. What matters is I found that feral and killed him, but it was too late for Kelly. I knew she was bitten and was amazed she'd lived. There was a slight chance she wasn't infected, and I was ordered to watch her.

"You're absolutely right that I took her that night and it's a good thing I did or she'd have killed you and her mother. But I taught her how to be a wolf and she's

101

a really strong shifter. I wanted her to run away, to come here where she'd be safe and wouldn't need to hide what she was, but she didn't want to leave you, so I let her stay home. So I stayed too, to watch over her, making sure she had a handle on her wolf."

John said, "You brainwashed her. You're all fucking nuts, and my God, what the hell did you do to Stacy?"

Mark continued as if John hadn't spoken. "Kelly tried so hard to be a good daughter, and it was killing her. She needed fresh air and the hills. She needed to be free. She's an amazing woman. I love her. I didn't plan it, but I knew as soon as I smelled her that first time that she was meant to be my mate. She loves me too and we were happy, but she was still worried about you.

"You have to understand, it's hard to control your wolf. The wolf wants to run in the forest and it's easy to lose track of time. She worried a lot about that. But she knew it would be a death sentence to tell you."

"So you plan to kill us then?"

He said it defiantly, but his voice shook and his gaze darted about the room again.

"No. I promised her I wouldn't, but we can't let you go. If you're a danger to our community, it's our responsibility to handle that danger. If you won't keep this secret, then we can't let you leave. It's as simple as that."

"Fine. I won't say a word. Let me speak with Kelly, and then Alice and I'll go home and pretend this never happened."

Star said, "Mark—"

Mark stood, holding out his hand. "Give me the knife."

He accepted the knife from Star and began cutting John loose.

"I'll let him see her. He'll see our children need her. He loves his daughter. He'll keep our secret for her sake. That craziness on the news, that's nothing compared to what would happen if the world really knew about us."

Mark tossed the knife back to Star who caught it one handed and slid it back into her waistband.

She said, "Fine, it's his funeral."

John followed without protest. The house was quiet and the French doors to the conservatory were in sight before John said, "All of this, losing a child like this, it's clear you need some help. Let me help you, son. Kelly doesn't deserve this. Let Alice and I help both of you. We'll be safe on the farm. I have some money put aside, enough we could go away, all five of us, and put all of this behind us."

Mark pushed the door open. "Kelly is sleeping, so let's keep it down, okay?"

"Whatever this is, however they convinced you to go along with it, I think you really do love Kelly."

John stilled when Mark stopped and held his hand out. He'd forgotten Audrey was here but her low growl reminded him.

He said, "Audrey, it's fine. John has come to see Kelly.

The low growl from the bushes grew deeper, lifting the hairs on Mark's neck. He took another step forward, spreading both his hands. "Audrey, he's a friend. There's nothing to be afraid of."

John gasped and stumbled backward as the foliage rustled and Audrey slunk forward—an enormous coal black wolf. Her hackles were raised and her teeth showing in a silent snarl.

"Jesus Christ!" John said.

"Don't run," Mark said as he took another step forward.

"Audrey, I know you can hear me. Stop right there!" He put as much command as he could into his voice and knew it wasn't going to be enough. Audrey gathered herself and sprang, a snarl ripping from her throat.

Mark grabbed her around the neck and they both fell to the ground. She snarled and snapped at him, ripping away a hank of his shirt and leaving a jagged wound in his arm.

"It's John. Kelly's father!" He thought she was going to retreat and breathed a sigh of relief as her shoulders relaxed but then her ears pricked and a second later Mark heard the soft mewling coming from the brush too.

She snarled and scrabbled frantically, using her teeth and claws.

"I need some help in here!" Mark yelled. "Get Richard!"

"Is that the baby?" John asked.

104

"Get Richard. I can't hold her long. Audrey, stop it right now! You're hurting me!"

John hesitated then whirled and ran for the door.

Audrey snarled and bit Mark's arm again.

"Damn it!" he yelled as he tried to pry her off.

She released his arm and jumped away, charging for the door before he could grab her. John closed it, cringing back when she crashed into it. Glass shattered but the frame held, and she threw herself against it again, biting down on the iron frame and ripping a pane out. She stuck her head through the hole she'd made to snap at John.

Mark embraced his wolf, letting the change sweep over him.

John glanced back then stopped and turned, ignoring the snarling wolf to stare as Mark transformed. He took a slow step backward, lifting a shaking hand to his eyes.

Mark's clothing hampered him, and Audrey had charged the window twice more, making the hole bigger each time before he reached her. He bit Audrey's left leg, yanking her backward as she pushed through the window frame. She snarled and snapped, and they rolled in the glass.

"Mark!" Star called.

She ran past John to grab Audrey around the neck. Audrey caught her with a paw to the face. Star's blood splattered Mark from a scratch that just missed Star's eye.

"Be still!" Richard shouted.

Audrey whined, shaking her head; her body falling limp.

Mark lay panting beside her.

Audrey whined again and began inching forward.

Richard laughed as he knelt. "Come here, sweetheart. John, stay behind me."

Mark licked Star's face and she threw an arm around his shoulder.

Audrey crept to Richard, growling low in her throat.

Richard said, "Go see your daughter. Audrey will be with me."

Star stood, waving John forward. "Mark won't bite." She laughed lightly, taking a step back. "None of us will. Richard can handle Audrey." She bent to try to help Mark out of his clothes.

The smile fled from her face. "The baby's crying."

His son had begun to scream. The pain-filled sound made his hackles rise again and he suddenly didn't blame Audrey for attacking. He wished there was something he could kill too to ease his son.

Mark kicked through the remains of his pants and ran to his wife. Star followed and they both stopped when they reached the cave.

Mark growled and Star stepped back. She turned to grab John's arm.

"It'll be over in a minute," she said.

Mark glanced over his shoulder. John leaned on Star, his shocked gaze glued to Kelly as she shifted.

Mark concentrated, willing himself to take his human form. His joints popped and muscles clenched and he fell to the ground. By the time he could stand Kelly was already a wolf and his son's arms had become paws. The change progressed slowly until a wolf pup lay mewling on the floor. Kelly's nose and ears twitched and her breathing was fast but she didn't open her eyes or stir.

Mark picked him up and laid him against Kelly's stomach. The pup began to nurse, and Mark picked up his daughter who nuzzled his hand with sleepy grunts.

"Jesus Christ," John whispered.

Mark cuddled his daughter, speaking without turning around. "Everything I told you was true. Kelly will speak to you when she wakes but that won't be for a few days. This isn't normal." He waved at the wolves. "She needs peace and quiet."

"That...puppy thing is Wilson?"

Mark winced. "Yes. That's our son but his name is Marcus. That isn't normal either."

Star said, "I don't think we should tell Alice until they're recovered, and we shouldn't tell her at all if she can't keep a secret."

Mark said, "John can do what he thinks best but I'm taking Kelly into the woods."

Star said, "You need to come back for the funeral."

"If she's up to it."

John said, "What funeral. Oh—the baby. What—how did you get a baby?"

Star said, "Matti. She really is an obstetrician, but she isn't a murderer. I didn't ask but I'm sure we can find out. We had the blood but only a few vials and we weren't sure it would be enough to convince the police that Wilson was dead, and we need the world to think he's dead because of this." She gestured to the nursing pup. "So Matti got us the corpse. There's no way she killed a child though."

Mark said, "Go talk somewhere else and clean up the blood."

Both Kelly and the baby sniffed continually. The scents and sounds were obviously upsetting them.

John said, "You need medical attention."

Star laughed in dismissal as she led John away, her voice growing fainter with distance. "I can shift and heal it. It's nothing, just a scratch."

The smell of his blood was likely upsetting them the most so Mark jumped into the pool to rinse off before lying beside them.

He was just dozing off when his daughter began to whine.

"*Shh*, sweetheart, Daddy's here."

He checked her diaper, which was clean, and placed her beside her brother, hoping she would nurse as eagerly as he had but his daughter wanted none of Kelly's furry teats. Her whining picked up in volume.

He tucked her to his chest and went to see about finding her a bottle before she woke Kelly.

Star sat by the broken door with a cooler and a diaper bag. Someone had cleaned up the glass and the hall smelled of cleaning products.

"She hungry?" Star asked as she opened the cooler. "Is Kelly still a wolf?"

Mark glanced over his shoulder but couldn't see his family. "They both are."

Star put a scoop of dry baby formula into the bottle and handed it to Mark.

She said, "Shake it hard to make sure the formula is mixed. Put in one scoop and use body temperature or sun-warmed water. Matti says we don't need to worry about sterilizing the bottles and there's bottled water in the diaper bag."

"I want to take them out of here."

"We can help but should you move her?"

Mark shrugged.

"Are you hungry? I've got both cooked and fresh meat here."

"No."

His daughter didn't like the bottle any better. He rubbed the nipple against her lips and she finally latched on. She sucked with her fists clenched and only drank for a minute before refusing more.

Mark tried to burp her while she screamed in his ear and Star rubbed her back, whispering endearments.

Leah and Matti approached, and Leah held her hands out.

"Let me try."

Matti said, "How much did she drink?"

Star took the bottle from Mark to hold it out. "Less than an ounce."

Leah took the bottle and offered it to the baby again. The baby stopped crying, sucking for a minute before falling asleep.

Mark ran a finger over her flushed cheek. He didn't like her shuddering breaths or red face.

"She's upset and we're probably not helping," Leah said ruefully.

A door opened in the distance. People spoke but were too far to make out.

Leah frowned, motioning Mark back into the conservatory.

"I'll get the door replaced," she said.

Mark said, "I want to take them into the woods."

Leah said, "You need to go to the police station to make a statement. I've told them Kelly is under sedation and unable to come in. That will work for a few days but we need her well."

"She needs time." Matti laid a hand on his shoulder. "I'm unsure what to advise. It's a very bad sign that she's become her wolf. Going into the woods could make you all go feral. We need to encourage her to become a human again. It might be best to let your daughter's distress wake her, but Kelly does need sleep."

Leah said, "We thought a compromise might be best. Feed your daughter yourself for two days and do your best to keep her content. Let Kelly sleep but then let your daughter wake her."

Mark said, "I hate to disturb her or let my daughter cry..."

Leah said, "You can let her sleep longer but physical discomfort can pull a new mother out of hibernation. Her breasts will be very sore if she doesn't feed them."

"He's drinking."

Matti rubbed her brow and Mark knew she was as worried as he.

He said, "I know it's not good."

Leah said, "Richard might be able to talk him down."

Mark's stomach dropped. His son would have no words, no way to communicate.

Matti took the baby from Leah and handed her to Mark. "Let's not worry about that right now. Make them as comfortable as you can."

A horn blew in the distance and they all turned to the windows.

Leah sighed hard and kissed the baby's head. "I better go take care of whatever that is. I'll do my best to keep things quiet."

"What about John and Alice?"

Star said, "He spoke with Richard. We're watching him but I think he'll keep quiet. We haven't told Alice."

"She's going to want to see them."

"We'll handle it."

A helicopter passed over the house.

Leah said, "Go be with her."

Star said, "I'll put the quad in the truck and get you some supplies and find you a spot, but you'll need help moving all of them. Don't try to sneak off. Let us help you."

Another helicopter passed and men yelled in the distance.

Leah ran from the room, calling over her shoulder, "Go to the police station in the morning!"

Matti said, "I'll be right outside the door." She winked and kissed his cheek. "I'm home recuperating from my gunshot wound."

Mark winced. "God, I'm an ass. I never even asked... How are you?"

"Perfectly fine. It didn't even hurt." She winked again as she turned away. "I gave myself some lidocaine and didn't even feel it. Alan has good aim."

Star laughed softly and gave Mark a quick hug. "Go get some rest. We've got this under control."

Mark returned to the cave and laid beside Kelly. She still breathed quickly. His son slept deeply with the limp bonelessness of puppies. His fur was soft, his ears small flaps and his eyes closed. He was beautiful.

Tears filled Mark's eyes as he stroked his feral son's head.

Chapter 11

Mark dozed beside his wife. Both children slept deeply, and her breathing gradually slowed. He rose when sunlight crept into their cave and tiptoed from the room.

Matti said, "If I hear her cry, I'll get Leah and she can try to feed her. Leah left you a suit in the bathroom. You should eat something even if you aren't hungry."

"I hate leaving them."

Matti said, "It should be fine. If you'd done this normally, you'd be leaving her for short periods to hunt and scout. If you think you can handle it, it might be a good idea to let your wolf out and sleep beside her that way." Matti smiled ruefully. "You two are doing things backward. She's supposed to be human and you a wolf."

"I'm taking them to the woods as soon as I get back."

"Going in a vehicle might be too stressful for her."

113

"Well I can't stay here!"

He winced apologetically, rubbing his face hard. Stubble rasped and he growled low in his throat.

"Go get cleaned up," Matti said, waving him away.

Mark cast one anxious look back and ran for the bathroom.

Richard was waiting when he exited the bathroom.

"John is going with us."

"Us?"

"Ted Truman from Howls will meet us there."

"I need a lawyer?"

"It's always smart to have a lawyer when dealing with the police. You know that."

"Fine. Whatever. Let's just get this over with."

Richard handed him a roast beef sandwich. "Eat first!" He glanced at his watch, took out his phone, and sent a message.

Mark ate the sandwich as they walked to the front door. John and Arny were waiting when they arrived.

"How's my daughter?" John asked stiffly.

"The same."

Arny said, "The car is here."

Alice entered the hall wearing a robe and clutching a handful of tissues.

John said, "Go back to bed, sweetheart."

"I should go speak to her too."

John shook his head, leaving the doorway to hug his wife. "And say what? Stay here and help Leah with the

114

arrangements. Kelly's doctor will be here and one of us needs to be here to speak with her."

Richard said, "My wife can handle the details. You should rest. Kelly can't lose her mother too, and you don't look at all well."

"I'm just sick about this. Just sick! To think there are so many crazy people in the world!"

John frowned and Richard said. "Those people *are* crazy. They're acting out of superstition, fear, and greed. But we're not like them. Kelly needs peace and quiet and parents who love her. It doesn't matter what Stacy believed. Treating her sister like that is unforgivable."

John's shoulders slumped. "I suppose that's true."

Alice said, "She was always difficult, and I blame myself for indulging her. We should've put a stop to all that occult nonsense, but I thought she'd grow out of it, and to tell the truth, I was tired of arguing with her all the time. It was easier to let her behave badly, so I did."

John said, "We didn't realize the depth of her desire to be different." He shook his head and kissed his wife's cheek. "Go lay down. We'll talk when I get back."

Alice hugged Mark. "I'm so sorry," she said and began to cry.

Leah stepped from the doorway and put an arm around her shoulder.

"Let's go get some tea," she said kindly.

John watched them from sight with his hands on his hips and a deep frown marring his brow.

"She's perfectly safe," Richard said.

"I know. Your wife is a kind woman and there'd be no point to killing my wife, not with the police right outside. And Kelly does need her." His lips tightened and he glared at Mark. "Not that I don't think you couldn't engineer an accident and get away with it. You're a master of manipulation."

Mark said, "That's true but I do love your daughter."

"You murdered my daughter!"

Richard said, "*I'm* the one who sent Mark after the wolf that bit her. Mark did everything he could, but it was too late. He's been as kind to your daughter as the situation allowed."

John's expression lightened and he threw his hands into the air. "I know. It's just so damned unfair! My daughter is gone, and her mother doesn't even know it yet!"

Mark said, "This is exactly why we don't tell. Kelly will be crushed, really destroyed that you think she's dead to you."

He stalked away before John could answer and got into the car. Alan was driving and greeted him with a subdued hello. Mark closed his eye, resting his head on the seat back. His wife would be so upset about all of this. He could bear to contemplate the ramifications of any of this himself. He didn't open his eyes until they reached the police station.

John grabbed his arm and said, "My Kelly *was* killed in that wolf attack. My dreams for her future, the life she should've had—that asshole killed all of that. But I do love the woman she's become. You're right, she does need us. This must be so difficult for her. I'm angry she hid this from us although I'm starting to understand why she did. She should've trusted us though. I might've been able to help her and save Stacy."

"And that's exactly why we wouldn't let Kelly tell you! You do want to help her. You'd have gone to doctors. You'd have done anything to help her but the help she needs isn't something you can give her. Now that you've seen, we're trusting that you'll let us help her."

John released his arm. "You're using hostages to ensure my silence. That's not trust."

Mark pushed past him, saying over his shoulder, "Let's just get this over with."

Richard said, "Alice is free to go whenever she likes."

"But my daughter isn't. You own her soul."

Chapter 12

Mark ran up the stairs and into the police station. Ted waited, sitting on a bench in the hallway across from a glass-fronted reception desk. He stood when Mark entered and offered his hand.

"I'm so sorry."

Richard and John entered, and Ted left Mark to shake their hands and offer condolences.

He said, "This is just a formality. Answer the questions as truthfully as you can. I've arranged for you to speak with Stacy, but I think we should finish the interview first."

Men had gathered behind the glass partition while Ted spoke, and Mark felt their regard like a weight on his shoulders. These men pitied him and the falseness of it suddenly struck him. If they knew the truth, they'd likely be hunting him. The thought made him shiver. His family would die. They were defenseless, unable to even move. If they were found out the least he could expect was a lifetime of experimentation and study.

Cement walls and iron bars would crush him. He'd go feral and die caged like an animal, taking his entire family with him.

Richard laid a hand on his shoulder, leaning closer to whisper, "It's okay, Mark. This will all be over soon and you can go home and rest."

Mark shrugged off his hand to straighten his suit, wiping his sweaty palms on his pants.

Ted cleared his throat and led them to a metal door. "I can't imagine how horrible this is. We'll get this done as quickly as possible."

Special Agents Joel Carvalho and Alphonse Prescott waited along with three police officers and a man in a suit who Mark didn't know.

Ted made introductions, introducing the stranger as the district attorney and Mark sat and answered their questions, most of which concerned the search Leah had done by helicopter.

Carvalho said, "Had you been contacted previously by Stacy Anderson or anyone at all and offered money or been threatened?"

"I gave Stacy ten grand when Kelly and I left town. She'd tried to extort Kelly. She'd seen us together and thought she could blackmail her sister. So I bought her plane tickets to California and gave her some money to live on."

"When you say she'd seen you together..."

Mark said, "Kelly's parents didn't want me around her. They thought I was too old for her, and I was when we met. But Kelly and I had kept in touch. We were friends and she really needed a friend. Stacy made her life miserable. My wife is the sweetest woman..."

His breath caught on a sob and he rose his hands to rub his face, embarrassed to have lost control.

Carvalho said, "So Stacy thought she could blackmail you into giving her money and it worked."

Mark dropped his hands and cleared his throat. "I guess, but she had nothing to blackmail us about. I didn't pay her to keep her quiet. I wasn't going to give her a dime, but Kelly wanted to help her."

John said, "My wife and I disapproved of Mark and were strict with Kelly, maybe stricter than we should've been, but Stacy was a mistake that we didn't want to repeat.

"Stacy had been extorting money from Kelly right along. Her sister had learned how to guilt Kelly into giving her all of her spending money. She'd been taking her lunch money and had gotten her to give her anything else she had of value. We put a stop to it when we found out and sent Kelly to therapy. That's when Stacy tried to get her sister to pay her off by embarrassing her."

Prescott turned to Mark. "And where were you during all this?"

"South America. I knew about it though. Kelly told me all about it. I think Stacy hates her sister. She did everything she could to make her life miserable."

John said, "I never understood why she hated her so much. I still don't. Kelly was always good to her." He peered off into the distance, avoiding all of their eyes, saying, "Alice and I reached out so many times. We tried everything... I never really considered before how much you must hate someone to do what she did..."

"What did she do?"

John clamped his lips together, staring down at his hands, clearly sorry he'd said anything.

Mark laughed harshly. "She used to go to Kelly's games and give the kids blowjobs for ten bucks. Kelly was mortified. It's why we moved away. Kelly wanted to go to school where no one knew her. She was and is a good student but the pressure at school was affecting her schoolwork."

"But she'd dropped out of college."

Richard said, "She was working as an intern at Howls."

Mark said, "She'd changed her mind about her major and I talked her into going away on a long honeymoon. We hadn't intended to get pregnant..."

Thinking of his children riled his wolf. Sweat broke out on his brow and he gritted his teeth against the wolf's urge to leave.

Richard clasped his hand. His touch comforted Mark's wolf. But he withdrew his hand after a moment as he didn't think human men would hold hands, even under these conditions, unless they were lovers.

John said, "How is any of this relevant?'

Carvalho said, "It shows Stacy had a pattern of abuse, which isn't helpful on the case at hand but will help our profilers, and maybe we can apply what we learn here to help someone else."

Richard said, "I assume you're warning anyone you think might be a target?"

"The people on the lists we took have been warned but how many unknown cells of would-be werewolves are out there? If we can figure out what motivated one attack, perhaps we can stop others."

Prescott sighed heavily. "Unfortunately, greed seems to be the motivating factor with a heavy dose of sibling rivalry. It's not that uncommon for criminal behavior to escalate in proportion to another sibling's scholastic, athletic, or career achievements."

John said, "How concerned do we need to be about another attack?"

"We have agents in place and are monitoring the online activity. The people directly involved have been apprehended and you'll be notified when they're released from jail but there's a large fringe group that we can't touch legally. Most of them seem like harmless flakes and we'll be keeping an eye on them, but I can't guarantee one won't decide to try again."

John said, "That's hardly reassuring."

"There are over a million Wiccans in this country and while most of them would consider the magic they practice white magic they have their fair share of dark magic practitioners. And that's not taking into account the actual Satanists. And then there's the people who believe they're vampires and the people who donate blood to them. My point is there are millions of potential suspects and we can't possibly watch them all. What we can do is offer witness protection to your family."

Mark said, "Kelly is in no shape to stand a trial."

"Surprisingly, a trial might help her. A trial can be healthy closure to victims of violent crime."

Carvalho said. "Stacy has already pled guilty to all charges and will be remanded to a secure facility for the criminally insane as soon as a bed opens up. Her lawyer is still working out the details with the court, but she'll be sentenced to a minimum of seven years.

Prescott said, "Stacy is shrewd. I'm not at all convinced she's insane. Accepting a guilty plea will make her eligible for parole at the doctor's discretion. She could be back on the streets in as little as three years.

"Some of the men who abducted your wife have also pled guilty while others are going to court. Trials are weeks away. We're still making our cases. We can worry about that later, but meanwhile we could put you up in a safe house."

Richard said, "I believe my security is adequate."

"I think so too but I know Mr. Miller doesn't have access to the same funds—"

"I'll take care of them. He needn't worry. If he and his wife decide they need to disappear, I can set them up somewhere if you'll supply new identification for them."

"And we'd be happy too."

Carvalho said, "I think you should hire extra security for the funeral."

"The funeral will be held privately at my home with just the family as soon as the remains are returned to us."

Ted said, "I can see to the cremation and the permit to bury the ashes in the family plot."

"He won't be buried there. We'll release his ashes. We'll also release footage of it to keep people out of our graveyard."

Ted winced, clearing his throat and shuffling his papers, clearly uncomfortable with the reminder.

John said, "That poor baby. Where is *his* justice?"

Richard said, "That child is beyond helping but we have another child at home who needs our protection."

"He needs to be free," Mark said, rubbing at his suddenly tearing eyes.

Richard hugged him and Mark let himself lean against him a moment.

John cleared his throat.

Ted said, "I think we're done here?"

"Yes." Joel stood and gathered his briefcase.

Prescott said, "We'll give you a few minutes and then bring Stacy in."

The rest of the men filed from the room and Mark slumped.

"I'm very sorry for your loss." Carvalho said as he closed the door behind himself.

Richard stood and took a seat across from the door with his back to the wall.

John sat beside him and said, "Is this room monitored?"

Richard said, "It doesn't seem to be, but since this is an integration room…"

John said, "That child—"

Richard held a hand to his mouth as if covering a yawn and whispered, "Was born dead two years ago. Matti had permission from the parents to use the corpse for medical research. Doctor Reyes switched the lab results that needed switching but there wasn't much left from the fire."

Mark whispered, "We shouldn't talk about this here."

Richard shrugged. "It's a lesser risk than letting John begin screaming that we're murderers."

John snorted, and Mark rested his head on his folded arms.

Richard said, "You can go home, Mark. I'll stay with him."

"He's my problem."

John snorted again.

Richard leaned closer to hug him and whisper, "You need to rest or you'll go feral too."

Mark shuddered and stood.

John said, "That can happen?"

Richard opened his mouth but closed it as the door handle turned. Mark resumed his seat. An officer escorted Stacy into the room and shackled her to the chair in front of the door while she grinned smugly.

Mark wanted to beat the smug smile from her face.

She said, "Hi, Dad. I see you're all chummy with them now. Whatever happened to hating Mark?"

"I never hated him. I barely knew him. I thought he was too old for your sister, but I didn't come here to talk about her. I came to talk about you."

The officer said, "I'll be right outside. Knock when you're finished."

Stacy said, "The fuckers hate us and hope you're here to beat me."

The officer paused with his hand on the door.

John said, "Don't be ridiculous."

The officer said, "She isn't wrong," and closed the door.

Mark was tempted too. He didn't think the police would rush in to stop him. She knew it too by the way her eyes narrowed.

John said, "When did you really believe about werewolves?"

"The minute I saw one."

Mark said, "You're delusional. You know that, right? Nothing you thought you saw could possibly excuse what you did to your sister."

John nodded and Stacy's eyes widened.

"You told him?" She threw her head back and laughed. When she finally stopped laughing, she gasped for breath and wiped her eyes. "Oh, that's priceless."

John said, "Why didn't you tell us? Why didn't you let us help?"

"You still don't get it, do you? I didn't want your help or your life. I hate the farm and the stupid cows and the smell of cow shit." Her voice rose until she was yelling. "You never heard me! You forced me to go to the dumb fairs and to join fucking 4H and I hated every minute of it! I wasn't meant to be a farmer and you never even tried to understand that!"

"That's bullshit! Your mother and I asked you all the time how we could help you!"

"I didn't need your help," she said derisively. "Your help was endless rules!"

Mark said, "She wanted to be a skanky whore. I can still smell all the men you fucked this week on your skin. Don't you ever shower?"

Stacy crossed her arms, smirking at him. "Jealous?"

"No. Sickened. You're disgusting!"

"I'm your sister-in-law and I'll be more soon."

"You're a fool. You'll never be the woman Kelly is. You reek of jealousy!"

"Kelly's a lying little whore. I never pretended to be something I'm not. I don't sneak around. I go for what I want. I'll be way better than she could only dream of being. She stole my life!"

"I'd never have wanted you. Don't kid yourself about that."

"I'm not talking about you, asshole! I'm talking about Brandon. I stuck around hoping he'd come back."

She clamped her lips, but her smile gained depth as if she knew a secret.

Mark stood to lean over the table and whisper, "Don't wait by the phone for him to call. I killed that fucker years ago."

He smirked when she glared.

"I fucking hate you!"

"The feeling is fucking mutual, skank!"

Richard laid a hand on his arm, and Mark sat. Richard resumed his leaning position with his elbows on the table with his hands folded blocking his mouth.

John said, "And Kelly?"

Stacy leaned forward and spoke as if imparting a secret. "I thought it hadn't took, but she *had* survived the bite. So I knew I'd survive too and I'd let him try as often as he needed to until I became a wolf."

"Jesus Christ!" Mark said, pushing away from the table, stumbling to his feet. "You did it on purpose!"

Stacy smirked and then pouted, staring at her clenched hands.

"Did what?" John asked.

"Instigated that attack that nearly got Kelly killed when she was just a girl! You fucking knew an animal attack like that was likely to kill her!"

"Win-win," Kelly said smugly and then seemed to remember she hadn't won. Her smug smile became a glare.

Richard said, "Did the boy agree to try again?"

"He would have but my fucking father kept me in the goddamned hospital waiting room for three fucking days and by the time I got back Brandon was gone!"

Mark said, "Of course he was, you dumb fuck! He'd almost killed a girl! What did you think would happen? That he'd sit around waiting for the police to find him! It wouldn't have mattered if he'd intended his dog to just bite her to get you into bed and not almost kill her. It was still an attack! He'd have been charged and done serious time. You both would've! You're goddamned lucky the police thought it was just a random dog attack! You'd have been arrested then and there if they knew you'd arranged it!"

John said, "Your sister almost died!"

Stacy leaned back, crossing her arms and glaring at John. "Would you rather it had been me?"

"Fuck no!" Mark said as John said, "It didn't need to be anyone! You encouraged that kid to attack her!"

Stacy glared at him as if he'd said yes.

John said, "You were always jealous of Kelly, wanting her toys and whiny when we paid attention to her, but I hadn't realized you didn't like her, not to this

129

degree. You were willing to see her killed... and for what?"

John sat back, rubbing his face like he still couldn't believe it.

Stacy said, "Kelly was a whining brat always following me around and getting me into trouble. But I didn't hate her until then. She could've told me, but she didn't."

Richard said, "There wasn't anything for her to tell."

Stacy pursed her lips. "I thought it hadn't taken because I sat up for nights watching her when she came home from the hospital, but I suspected when she disappeared that night." She turned to smirk at Mark. "I still wasn't sure, but when you persisted in following her around, I knew. And you might have fooled Kelly, but I knew you'd kill to keep your secret. I saw you had the hots for her. Your crush was pathetic and creepy and everyone saw it, except her. But I could see she trusted you and I needed her to fight for me. You'd have done anything she asked. Is all I needed was for her to tell me the truth and then tell you that she had. It would've been a win-win, she'd either have to bite me to keep me safe from you, or you would have to bring me wherever you came from to keep me safe for her. And I figured once I was there someone would bite me. I'd almost convinced her to trust me when you disappeared and I didn't know who they'd sent to replace you or how she was being watched.

"Brandon had told me if the wolves suspected I knew the truth that they'd kill me, so I was really careful, but I finally saw her out running with her wolf shadow that she didn't seem to know about.

"And then you came back, and she had the fucking nerve to rub it in my face!"

Mark said, "You're delusional! This is all in your head! Did you really think screwing every boy in her school would make her like you?"

Stacy's eyes glittered. "She should've helped me. I was dead broke and you were giving her everything! Why shouldn't she pay if she wasn't willing to give me the money I needed to live on?"

John said, "Kelly didn't owe you a thing. Those were all your own decisions!"

Stacy smirked. "She owes me now though. If she wants me to keep quiet, she better pay up." She leaned forward, glaring at John, "And don't think you can help her welch. She pays or everything I know goes public. You can kill me and it wouldn't matter. I have friends, good friends, and they'll fucking kill her, the brat, and my fucking mother for good measure!"

"You're a fool if you think anyone would believe your lies," Richard said. "She doesn't know a thing. We're wasting our time here."

Stacy jerked against the chain that held her, her furious gaze on Richards's back as he strode to the door.

"You truly are an evil person," John said as he stood.

Stacy sat back, smiling as if he'd said I love you. "I'm practical. I need insurance and you're a fool if you don't think they'll kill us all to keep their secrets! I'm saving your fucking life!"

John banged on the door.

Mark stood, "I'll never forgive what you did to her and our children."

"I didn't do shit to your brat! I was locked up in here!" she called after him, laughing as if she hadn't a care in the world.

The officer closed the door and Mark could still hear her laughing.

"I'm still your sister-in-law. Whether you like it or not we're family!"

Mark winced, rubbing his forehead, hoping it was only his wolf hearing that let him hear her so clearly through the closed door. He'd thought the thick walls and metal door would have muffled sound better.

The officer said, "She's a raving lunatic!"

Richard said, "You heard that, *huh*?"

"Some of it. The shouted bits."

John said, "Let's get out of here."

Stacy continued to curse them but only a few of the words were clear. Mark followed Richard, expecting to be accosted and stopped any second but they reached the entrance with no more than pitying glances following them.

Reporters and news crews waited on the sidewalk and they all shouted questions when they appeared.

Richard put his hands on his hips, saying angrily, "As you can imagine, my family is grieving! If you could have the decency to respect our privacy, please!"

The shouting didn't abate a whit.

Richard held up a hand, waiting for the shouting to die down to say, "I realize the community is concerned and wishes to show its support to the family. The funeral will be private and we plan to scatter the ashes. We're asking that donations be made in lieu of flowers and that gifts of toys not be left at the gate at our home but be brought to Midland Hospital and donated to the children's ward there. You can contact the Henderson Olsen Wildlife Sanctuary for further details."

Police officers cleared a path to their car while reporters shouted more questions. Mark closed the door with a sigh of relief.

John said, "This is a nightmare."

Mark muttered, "I need a shower."

The stink of Stacy's perfume seemed to linger in the air.

Richard clasped Mark's knee. "He's a fighter."

Mark said, "How can I talk him down when he's just a baby?"

"We won't give up," Richard said.

"What are you talking about? The puppy?"

"He's my son." Mark's words caught on a sob.

Richard said, "Werewolves mate for life. We don't survive the death of a spouse, but we *can* survive the death of a child."

"You know he's going to take us with him."

"I don't know that and neither do you!"

"I don't know what to do here, Richard. My daughter could die if we go to the woods and my son will die if I don't."

"You could leave her with us," Richard said hesitantly, and Mark moaned.

Tears burned his eyes. "I know I should."

John said, "Alice and I would take her. Is she human? Is that the problem?"

"Werewolves normally don't manifest their secondary forms until puberty. She'll become a wolf then and she needs the pack around her to teach her how to be a wolf."

"But…"

Richard nodded grimly. "Marcus shouldn't be able to shift. He'll have no control at all and a feral werewolf is very dangerous."

"You'll kill him?"

"Of course not. He's just a baby!" Mark glared at John. "What kind of father do you think I am!"

"I have no idea what you—people—will do. You seem pretty ruthless. Four men have been killed and just as many have been shot and it was all a ruse!"

Richard said, "That's true, we did kill four men, but they had it coming. They weren't innocent humans. They were kidnappers who'd have let your daughter be murdered to make a buck. Don't kid yourself about that. They all knew Kelly wasn't walking out of there. Do you think Stacy would've released her when the sun rose or tried something else?

"You think those assholes were just going to apologize and let her go? And what about the babies? What do you think they'd have done to them to try to get them to shift shapes? Imagine what they'd have done to her if she *had* shifted... And how many of them do you think truly believed she could shift? I mean, I know they wanted her to, but do you think they really believed she could?

"They let drugs and greed influence them. It was a game for them, nothing more. They didn't think they had anything to lose. Her death wouldn't have made them lose a wink of sleep! So yeah, we fucking killed them, and their own friends and family aren't surprised by how they died. The world believes they were killed while trying to kidnap a baby. And these are the men you're so worried about!"

"But they weren't."

Richard shrugged. "Because we caught them first." He sighed hard, pinching the bridge of his nose, taking a few slow breaths before releasing his nose and saying calmly, "If the police killed you during an attempted abduction of a child that you'd intended to sacrifice, every single person you know would be shocked. The men we killed were rotten enough no one was shocked. What does that tell you?"

"That you think murder is an option."

"I guess I do. I'd do anything to keep my pack safe!"

"Including kill my grandchildren?"

Richard smiled wryly. "Even if I wanted to, wolf biology prevents it. No wolf could harm a werewolf child. At least not until they lost their baby scent. Or maybe if they were really crazy, but I've known some very scary wolves and not one of them had ever harmed a child. We just can't do it."

"So they're safe with you? I mean if I believe all this shit?"

Mark said, "We haven't lied."

"You lied for years!"

Mark winced, turning away from John's accusing glare.

Richard said, "Werewolves have an amazing sense of smell. We can smell when people are nervous and afraid of us. You need to get a handle on that or Kelly will know it and we want her calm. Werewolf children can smell our unease and will react to it. "

Mark said, "It doesn't matter because I'm taking them away!"

John said, "She'll want to speak to us."

"She can't speak. She's a wolf and I don't know if she's coming back!"

Chapter 13

Mark said, "For the love of God, Audrey, stop crying. I'm not angry. No one was hurt. It's over and no big deal. I'd have had to say something to John anyway."

She'd been giving him false smiles and had reeked of misery since they'd left Richard's, which he'd done as soon as they got back. He'd ignored the tears because it was clear she was trying to contain them, and he'd hoped she'd feel better if he spoke normally to her, but tears continue to trickle from the corner of her eyes.

Audrey sniffled and rubbed her face on her sleeve and Mark felt bad for yelling.

"Look," he said in a kinder tone, "I trust you with them because I know you'd never let anyone hurt them. I *want* you to protect them ferociously."

"I still can't control my wolf, Mark. I'll never be able to control it."

"And it hasn't been a problem. We handle it, don't we?"

"I hate it!" She snapped her mouth closed and picked up her pace.

She carried a pack that had to weigh at least two hundred pounds and both children. Mark carried a much smaller pack and Kelly. They'd driven into the hills on the quads but the trail had grown too steep for the heavily loaded vehicles and the vehicles upset both Kelly and Marcus as evidenced by escalating breathing and low moans. Carrying them seemed to be better and they'd been hiking for an hour now. It was starting to feel secluded enough to please him.

He lifted his head to scent the air.

Audrey grinned wryly at him. "Water to the left, coming from that hill."

Mark examined the hill, liking what he saw. Cedars and pines grew in a thick profusion around rock outcroppings. The lower part of the hill was covered with shale, boulders, and low scrub.

Mark said, "I'll clear a place right on the tree line and we'll have good lines of sight."

"I'll bring some tools when I come back."

They hit the stream and followed it. The water was icy cold and moving fast. It had cut a deep channel that reached Mark's thighs, but it was almost narrow enough to step across. He set Kelly down on the opposite shore and offered Audrey a hand to balance on.

The stream widened as it crossed a small meadow, burbling over the rocks. Mark stepped over the deeper channel into the shallower water that reached his ankles.

"This will be a good spot. We can fish if we want and I saw plenty of game signs."

"I'll bring fresh meat every few days."

"It's a long walk. The others will help—"

"There's no one around for miles. I don't mind the walk and I can take a dirt bike most of the way."

Mark set Kelly in the grass and dropped his pack beside her. He took the children from Audrey and laid them beside Kelly. Audrey began unpacking the pack, handing Mark a sandwich and taking one for herself as she sat cross-legged beside him.

"This is a nice spot."

Mark said, "If we go feral, I want you to be my daughter's guardian."

"Richard—"

"Will be her Alpha. You'll be her mother."

"Kelly could recover."

"I hope so." Mark shrugged, lifting his face to the sky. "The pull to join them is growing stronger. My wolf wants me to be with our son. My daughter helps me resist it and I'm trying to hold on, but if I let go, you take her, even if it means fighting us to do it."

He opened his eyes to see hers had filled with tears again.

"If I think I can't hold out, I'll give her to you. This is just worst-case scenario stuff."

"I don't want to fight you..."

"You could try tranquilizing us. Whatever the hell Matti gave us worked."

"WBGDP13 isn't a real tranquillizer. It wouldn't knock you out."

"It felt like it would."

"It's a blend of wolfbane and marijuana with a ketamine kicker. There's stronger versions though. WBGDP22 would knock you out even if you were already in wolf form." She pursed her lips and said thoughtfully, "We could try it on Kelly and see if it works. Marijuana, well, specific blends of marijuana mixed with wolfsbane will suppress the wolf. Matti has been experimenting and she might have a better idea of what to give Kelly to bring her back."

"Ask her, but I'm going to wait a few days before doing anything. She might come back on her own if we let her sleep undisturbed."

Audrey stood. "Let's get your den built."

Mark crammed the rest of his sandwich into his mouth as he jogged up the hill.

Audrey frowned at the worn tarp that they'd stretched over a newly cleared piece of earth.

Mark had pulled out enough rocks to make a comfortable bed, but he'd need tools to remove the remaining ones. He'd spread another canvas tarp over a loose pile of freshly gathered bracken and laid his children and Kelly on it. All slept peacefully with relaxed muscles and slow breathing.

He said, "I'll hollow out the hill more when I get a shovel."

"You'll need a pickaxe. I'll bring one and a saw and a regular ax. If you cut back these two trees you could wedge some limbs there to form a wall and then attach a tarp to that. It will give you plenty of room out of the weather, and if you put some brush over the tarp no one will notice you even if they flew over."

"Good idea. I'll need a bunch of blankets for the baby and something to store the extra ones in so they don't get wet. And maybe my guitar…"

"I'll bring blankets and clothing and diapers. She'll need to be washed. I'll bring you a camp stove to heat water on so you won't have too much smoke to give you away."

"Bring extra diapers—like a lot extra. I plan on just letting the river clean them."

Audrey laughed and bent to kiss the babies. When she straightened, she said, "Are you sure you have enough food for a few days?"

"Yes. And I can always hunt. Give us four days before coming back. Don't let anyone disturb us." Mark set the cooler of meat in the shade. He opened it to check on the ice, which was still frozen solid. Audrey placed the canned and dried food beside the cooler and gave him a hug.

"I'll be back," she said, releasing him and heading down the slope.

"We'll be here!" he called after her, hoping they would be.

He laid beside Kelly, putting an arm around her and pulling the light blanket over them. His wolf urged him to shift but ceased pressing when he laid a hand on his daughter's back.

If he could remain in control, they had a shot.

Chapter 14

Mark set three thicker branches atop the smaller kindling pieces that he'd laid in a carefully constructed firepit.

He hadn't bothered cook anything since they'd arrived a week ago. Kelly preferred cooked food though and he hoped the odor of cooking meat would be enough to pull her from her slumber.

She hadn't moved an iota since he'd settled her on the soft bracken bed, not even to defecate or urinate. His son slept as deeply with a heart stopping sort of stillness. His daughter woke every four hours or so, drank amid loud complaints, and fell back to sleep quickly.

She was due to wake again soon and he planned to let her cry a few minutes.

He lit a small fire, using green wood to skewer and hang the steaks above it to grill.

The smells made his stomach rumble. The fire didn't appear to be very smoky but he ran partway down the hill to better judge if the smoke was too visible, A small trickle of smoke was mostly obscured by the trees it wafted through. The smell of cooking was stronger but would only be of interest to passing predators.

He ran back to his camp and settled beside his wife to stroke her silken fur. His children were snuggled between her forelegs with her tail partially covering them. His daughter began to fuss, making small sucking sounds that warned an angry cry would be imminent.

"Wake up, sweetheart," he said as he reached to brush Kelly's tail back. It worried him that his daughter would choke on the fur if she tried to gum it.

To his surprise it was Marcus who was waking. Excitement made his voice tremble when he said, "Kell, wake up, sweetheart. The kids need you to wake.

The sharp scent of urine suddenly laced the air and he knelt to gather the babies. He placed them both behind him and covered them with a blanket, which woke his daughter who began to cry.

"You can do it," he said encouragingly as Kelly's paws began to twitch.

Marcus began to whine and Kelly growled then moaned. Her paws scrabbled as if she'd forgotten how to stand and her growl grew loud and angry. Her eyes opened as she lurched to her feet, ignoring his outstretched hands to nuzzle the children. She licked them both then picked Marcus up by his scruff and retreated beneath the nearest trees where she flopped to her side to nurse him, growling warningly when Mark approached.

He retreated to gather his now screaming daughter who he feed and changed, dressing her in a clean onesie before sitting in front of the trees.

He waited for an hour before speaking again. His wife was so still that if he couldn't smell her, he'd have thought she'd run.

"Kell, want to hold her? I'm sure she'd like you to feed her too. Maybe Marcus will come back if you do..."

He slowly pushed the branches back to see her grooming their son and his heart plummeted. She was deeply meshed with her wolf if she was willing to lick him clean. He hesitated, it was a risk to reach for Marcus when she was so clearly bonded with him, but he did it anyway, moving slowly and talking softly.

"Whose a good, boy?" he crooned as he gently picked up his son. "Come on, sweetheart, it's much more comfortable in the camp. Our daughter can't sleep beneath the tree here. I need to be able to see her. Come lay down with us."

Kelly huffed and snorted, growling softly as Mark backed away but not as if she was angry, more in a grumbling confused tone. She emerged from the brush and stretched, raking deep furrows in the ground.

She surprised him by running suddenly and he jumped to his feet, not sure what he meant to do as he couldn't leave the children undefended to chase her, but to his relief she just ran in widening circles about the camp with her nose to the ground.

He poured her a bowl of water and placed one of the steaks on a plastic plate.

"Come eat, sweetheart. You must be starving."

She ignored him, still sniffing diligently. She slowed to a walk and circled again following the path that Audrey had taken when she'd brought him supplies six days ago. Mark cleaned Marcus and remade the bed, using most of their blankets to make a soft pad for the children.

It took her almost an hour to satisfy herself, and Mark was glad only Audrey had come and not recently. He'd make sure to leave a note saying not to approach until Kelly was more settled.

She grumbled as she returned with her ears flicking and her nose twitching. Her gaze traveled from the steaks to the kids and Mark chuckled as she leapt to grab the meat he'd left over the firepit. He'd let the fire die out but the coals were still warm and he hoped the meat wasn't hot enough to burn her.

She bolted it down and then drank all of the water, ate the other steak, and then used her paws to rip into the plastic container that held the dried meat and canned goods.

The plastic was no match for her claws. She tore through it as if it were tissue paper, scattering the canned goods to reach the packaged fish.

"Wait," he said laughingly as she tore through the plastic with her teeth to get at the dried fish inside.

He opened the cooler and before he could offer to cook the meat it contained she snarled and snatched it from him, eating so quickly he was afraid she'd choke.

"I'm sorry, sweetheart. I should have had more waiting for you. Give me a few minutes and I'll make you more."

He only had a few canned goods that he hurriedly opened and she ate everything and then licked the last scraps from the cans.

He knew she was still hungry by the way she eyed the remaining plastic bin, so he opened it to show her it only contained baby clothes.

"I should go hunting."

She lay beside the children and began grooming Marcus again.

"Will you be okay here alone if I go hunting?"

She didn't look up.

"Kell, can you shift back and talk to me a minute?"

She continued to nuzzle Marcus.

"Kell!"

She lifted her lip, placing a paw across Marcus.

"I need you to shift back just for a minute."

She returned to grooming but her ears were back and she shot him nervous glances as if unsure if she trusted him. It made him really uneasy, which he knew she could scent by the way her nostrils flared.

She rose to peer about, growling low in her throat as she slunk into the trees.

Mark sighed in annoyance as she circled, sniffing and slinking, clearly confused as to why he was nervous.

"I'm sorry, sweetheart. Come back and rest."

He grabbed his guitar and began to play, more to distract himself than to soothe her.

She returned and settled beside the children, curling around them and covering them with her tail. Her golden eyes stayed on him and her ruff never fully lowered. He was careful to move slowly and talk softly when he laid his guitar back down.

"I'm not sure if I should stay with you or go for food. I'm afraid you'll try to hunt for yourself if I don't go but I'm also afraid you'll try to hide the kids if I do go. Our daughter needs to stay here. You can't pick her up with your teeth. The woods are too dangerous for her. She can't lie on the cold ground. She has no fur to protect her from bugs or cold. She needs care only a human can give her. Do you understand me at all?"

Kelly's expression hadn't changed while he spoke. He didn't think she'd understood him.

He stared at her unsure what he should do and she lowered her head to her paws, her eyes half closing. She was clearly tired and that decided him.

"I'll be back in two hours if not sooner."

He backed away slowly and her eyes opened and her head lifted but she remained laying with the children. He waited until he was deep in the trees to undress and

148

shift and then he ran for the quad, cursing himself for not thinking of bringing writing materials.

He used his claws to gouge 'Leave it Here' then urinated on the bikes tires, which he was sure Audrey would notice.

He slunk on the way back, sniffing and listening, hoping he'd smell a deer but he didn't spot anything except rabbits and squirrels that he passed without chasing until he was minutes from his campsite.

He hated the idea of his family there alone. Kelly was more than a match for smaller predators but a real pack of wolves or a bear would be dangerous and both roamed the hills here.

It took him longer than he liked to catch even one rabbit but he lacked the patience to hunt. *It would have to do*, he decided as he transformed back and grabbed up his clothing.

Kelly had dug into the hillside in his absence but hadn't moved the children although it was clear she wanted to.

He lay the rabbit down to check the children, both of whom were still sleeping.

She snatched up the rabbit and ate it completely, fur and bones.

"I'll help dig out a snug den. You rest."

He grabbed the shovel and began to dig. He'd feel more secure when she did. A snug den would be easier for her to defend, and he wouldn't worry so much about leaving her to hunt.

He talked while he dug, telling her about past hunting trips and tales other wolves had told of their wives after giving birth, making sure to keep his tone light and the subjects unworrying.

He wasn't sure if she was asleep or just resting but he thought she slept. This was a real sleep not the deep unmoving hibernation of earlier and he hoped she'd be more herself when she woke, but his hopes were dashed the next morning when she ignored his greeting.

She ran to the brook and returned within minutes. It was clear she was hungry but she was more concerned with digging out a shelter. She pushed past him to use her paws, digging furiously until she'd made the hole deep enough that she could stand and turn all the way around. It was clear by her grumbling and laid back ears that she wasn't really satisfied but she grabbed Marcus by the scruff and settled to the dirt.

"Come out a minute and let me make it more comfortable."

She ignored him, nudging Marcus to her side to nurse.

Mark waited until Marcus fell asleep to place him with his sister. "Come," he said, feeling slightly ridiculous but patting his knee and making kissy noises.

She lifted her lip but left the den and he hurriedly made it as comfortable as he could, moving the dried bracken he'd gathered and placing the blankets on it.

She licked his cheek when he placed Marcus and their daughter inside and he laughed as he rubbed her head.

"Stay here. I'll go get us some breakfast and no more eating the fur. You'll be sick."

He waited until she settled and backed slowly away.

His daughter would wake soon but he had time to set some snares out. He'd hear her crying and maybe Kelly would tend her if she thought he wasn't close.

With a heavy but hopeful heart, he went to find food for his family.

Chapter 15

Kelly followed her son as he took his first fumbling steps from the den. She growled at her mate, warning him to stay back. Her mate said something she didn't understand, except for the amusement in it.

She sniffed deeply, ensuring there were no dangerous predators nearby.

Her mate approached and she lifted her lip in a soundless snarl, warning him away again. He was a distraction she couldn't afford. The noises he made, his scent, all might distract her and let an enemy approach unnoticed.

When she rose her hackles and showed all her teeth, her mate desisted and returned to the den and her other child.

She huffed an annoyed sigh that he was so stubborn and ran ahead of her son to sniff the long grasses that hid him from sight.

She smelled rabbit and rodents, birds, and the green undergrowth. Faint traces of her and her mate abounded. The day remained sunny and calm with no signs of danger. She kept a sharp eye out for the shadow of birds. Some of the hawks that lived close by would be a threat to her son.

He pushed through the grasses sniffing and strutting, intrigued with every new scent and she followed close on his heels.

He ran around her, barking in happy excitement, dancing around her feet a moment before darting forward clumsily. He could barely walk, and she wasn't even certain he could see more than a few feet. His eyes still held a hint of baby blue.

She barked a sound that meant come, the one she used when it was time for him to eat, and he turned back to her.

A rabbit jumped through the grass, startling him and he whimpered as he fell. She nudged him with her nose, making the small noise that meant all is well, I'm here, and he playfully batted at her at moment before he seemed to remember the rabbit and scrambled gracelessly to his feet. He lowered his nose to the ground and followed the scent.

Kelly put her paw on his back, lightly pressing him down when they reached the edge of the high grasses.

She lay beside him and they both stared out over the rocky ground that abutted the brook.

She made an exaggerated production of sniffing the air before leading him to the water edge.

Her tongue lolled in doggy laughter as her son splashed in the shallow edge. The sun shone down brightly, and the water was warm and moved sluggishly. It wasn't the fast-moving stream of a month earlier, but it still teemed with delicious fish that swam slowly through the shallow depths.

Her son had spotted one and stared in fascinated interest.

He yipped happily and jumped forward and before Kelly could blink, her son was a fish swimming beside the other fish that darted away.

She stared frozen in shock for a moment then began barking the bark that meant come. She added a growl and ripping snarl, standing over his now scaly form and snapping at the water.

He stuck his head out of the water and she barked harder.

Her mate called to her in obvious distress but she didn't dare even turn to see what had upset him when her son could be swept away at any moment.

She barked again as urgently as she knew how, and her son resumed his wolf shape with the same shocking suddenness as he'd become a fish.

She snatched him up and ran for the den, her heart pounding at the nearly diverted disaster.

Her mate greeted her laughingly.

She dropped her son to snarl at him.

To her annoyance, he persisted, trying to take her soaked son, so she lunged at him, not meaning to connect but trying to show him how serious she was. Her heart still pounded with fear.

Her mate jumped away looking shocked and angry, but she didn't have time to comfort him. Her son whined at her feet and she grabbed him again and carried him to the den where she groomed him and let him nurse.

She'd been lax but no more. She'd teach her son that no meant no and to come when called. She'd have to teach her mate to respect her rules too. She laid her head on her forepaws, sighing deeply as she considered her options.

Chapter 16

Mark slunk through the grass, sniffing the air to pinpoint his prey. They'd been here almost two months now so he knew right where the rabbits made their burrows. It took him no time at all to slink in close.

He gathered himself and leapt. The rabbit squealed once then stilled. He shook it hard to break the neck then used his claws to rip it open. He ate it all and went to the stream for a drink to wash it down. Rabbits abounded in the meadow. His snares caught one almost daily, but hunting was fun and he allowed himself one hour a day to do it.

Reminded of the time, he glanced at the sky and headed back to his camp.

Soft summer air brought him the scents of the forest. He could smell his old kills but no other predators or people. The sun was warm on his back and he was tempted to nap but he had things to do. He crawled beneath a bush on the edge of the stream and shifted, emerging as a man and running the rest of the way to his camp.

Kelly had dug farther into the bank in his absence.

"It would be easier to use the shovel," he said.

She sneezed at him and flopped to their bed. Her tongue lolled in a doggy smile as she began to groom Marcus.

"Are you digging it out because you want more room or are you just bored? Audrey brought some books."

Her ears twitched, so he opened a plastic bin and withdrew a stack of books. "Want to read your economics book?"

He laughed when she wrinkled her nose.

"Me neither. How about a classic? We have Huck Finn and Robinson Caruso. Or maybe you'd like to read this one?" He placed an erotic novel on the ground beside her.

She huffed, laying her head on her paws.

Marcus mewed and she opened one eye then used a paw to nudge him closer.

"He's getting big. He'll be catching his own food soon."

Mark reached for him and Kelly growled low in her throat.

He ignored it and picked up his son, sitting beside her to pet them both. He picked up his guitar and played softly. Marcus lay with his head on Mark's thigh with his tail wagging until sleep claimed him. He adored music and would happily listen as long as Mark played.

Kelly opened her eyes when he laid the guitar down.

"She needs you too, Kelly. You could be a wolf when he needs it and a human woman for her."

Kelly sighed deeply, closing her eyes again.

Mark cuddled his son for another minute before laying him beside Kelly.

"If we're going to be here a while, I guess I'll work on the wall."

He cut tree limbs and pounded them into the ground for the rest of the afternoon. Marcus woke from his nap and explored under Kelly's watchful gaze. Their daughter woke and Mark changed her and fed her. She cooed happily while he cut more branches.

When the sun began to set, he fed his daughter again and put her pajamas on her while Kelly nursed their son. She nuzzled their daughter, using her paws to gather both children to her chest.

"I'm going out for a few hours." He hefted the cooler, opening it so she could see it was empty, then loaded his forty-five and placed it on the rickety table he'd made. "The gun is here if you need it, but I'll be back soon."

He squatted in front of her. "Could you please just shift for a few minutes and talk to me?"

She closed her eyes, turning her head away, which was her usual response but it still made him sigh deeply.

"I love you."

He didn't look back until he reached the meadow. *The brush he'd cut and laid around the outside of their den would need replacing soon*, he noted. It had begun to brown on the edges. A casual observer wouldn't notice his home but an alert one might.

He sniffed deeply and only smelled the familiar scents of forest. The woods teemed with life and sound at night and he ran surefootedly through the trees to his hidden dirt bike.

He was tempted to leave it and shift to a wolf, but it would take too long to run back with supplies.

He paused three times on the way back to Richard's to stop the bike and sniff the air, but he never smelled a thing out of place, and he didn't catch the scent of man until he reached the foothills behind Richard's house.

Lights glimmered in the distance. Houses and cars were on the road on the hill across from him, but he lost sight of them as he got lower.

A wolf waited on the path when he reached it. They'd heard him coming.

"Arny," he said as greeting. The wolf ran alongside, veering off into the woods when Mark reached the cleared fields behind the house. He drove to the shed, gassed up, and left his bike.

Richard, Leah, Matti, Audrey, Star, and Alan sat on the back patio. He smelled more of his pack in the woods and could hear someone playing a guitar by the barn.

He missed them but was glad Richard had kept them away. Kelly would be alarmed by their scents when he returned. It was better for her if there weren't many scents for her to sort although the food smells never bothered her. He sniffed appreciatively.

The delicious smell of barbecue was making Mark's stomach rumble.

Richard stood, opening the grill, calling, "Matti made her famous chicken and it'll be ready in a minute! How's the family?"

"The same. I think it's time to try one of Matti's concoctions."

Star said, "I'll get your supplies," and she headed for the patio doors.

"She hasn't tried to shift back on her own?" Matti asked.

"No. I'm not even sure she understands me. She still growls when I pick up Marcus. His eyes are open now and he's starting to explore and chew things."

"Oh, Mark," Leah said sadly.

A lump grew in Mark's throat. He said, "He's healthy and happy."

Leah stood to hug him. He felt the love in her embrace and told himself it didn't matter if he never spoke to his child if Marcus felt his love, but he hated that his son would never know the richness of life as a human.

Matti said, "I'd like to be there when you administer it."

Richard said, "Is this scientific curiosity or could there be complications?"

Leah patted his shoulder when she stepped away.

Matti said, "Both. I've never seen this condition before so I can't know what the drugs will do."

Alan stood and headed to the picnic table where he began filling plates. He said, "It does different things to all of us. It needs more testing."

Mark sat beside Audrey and gave her a hug.

He said, "I don't know if she'll let you get close."

"I'm willing to try it. If she chases me away, I'll go. But my presence shouldn't antagonize her like Richard's would."

Leah said, "I'll come too. She might listen to me."

Matti said, "She might feel compelled to fight you, Leah."

Leah said, "But not to the death. Her wolf would accept my surrender and let me leave."

"Maybe, but it's a risk."

Mark said, "Everything we do is a risk, but we need to do something!"

Richard said, "I've put the police off but any day now they're going to come with a warrant for Kelly to appear in court. I can tell them you've run but that means you'll really need to disappear. At least until we get all these legal dealings worked out. They could file charges on her. The disappearance might need to be permanent. We can't risk her having to spend even one night in jail."

"I'm not worried about disappearing, but will it get you into trouble?"

"I doubt it. They won't be able to prove I helped you and there's no warrant out on you or anything."

Leah said, "We should preempt them and call and say you left a note. We can say you went to Alaska to see your parents.

"Tony will love that," Mark said sarcastically.

Richard shrugged, grinning a hard grin. "We're also giving them Stacy."

Mark said, "Do you hate them or something?"

Matti said, "Bennet has brought his pack back into the Alaskan hills already. It shouldn't matter at all if anyone goes looking for you there. Stacy could breed as easily as Kelly. It might be a genetic trait. Bennet will pick out a strong wolf for her. He'll keep her in line, and she'll be way out in the boonies living in their cave."

Leah smirked and said, "We said we'd try to make her a wolf. We never said she'd like it when she was one."

Mark said, "I should call John."

Richard handed him his phone. "I still think you should take a satellite phone."

"Maybe. Let's see if Matti's potions work first. If she'd just talk to me we could go to one of the cabins instead."

"Give her time, Mark," Leah said. "It was hard for me to leave my den too. I know you're worried about colder weather and your daughter but that's still months away."

Alan handed him a plate and Mark began to eat as he dialed.

"Yes, Mr. Henderson," a man said.

"It's Mark. Is John handy?"

"I'll get him, sir."

"Discreetly," Mark said.

"Of course, sir."

Richard said, "You could probably call openly."

Mark winced. "I don't want to have to speak to Alice."

Leah said, "She's a nice lady. You can't blame her for being worried. You'd be worried too if your son-in-law institutionalized your daughter and wouldn't tell you where or let you speak with her."

Mark said, "The longer this goes on, the harder it is." He was going to say more but John asked anxiously, "Mark?"

Mark winced again. "There's been no change. We've decided to go ahead with one of Matti's drugs."

"Should we come?"

"Maybe. How's Alice?"

"Angry, confused, and worried. I'll have to tell her soon if Kelly can't speak to her."

"I trust you'll do what's best for our family."

"*Ha!*"

Mark pinched the bridge of his nose.

"I'm doing the best I can here, John."

John heaved a heavy sigh. "I know it, son. Sometimes I forget, you know? I get busy and the day passes and I forget and think, I should call Kelly, and then I remember and it feels like a dream. I can hardly believe that this is all real and I saw it with my own eyes. I'm afraid Alice won't believe me without seeing for herself and I'm scared to death that seeing will kill her."

"Her heart?"

"She's always had a mild arrhythmia. The doctor has just put her on medicine for it though."

"Have you given any thought –"

"Constantly! But to go through with it... What if only one of us makes it? What if neither of us do? How the hell would Kelly cope with that on her conscious?"

"I don't know. It's something the three of you need to talk over. Bring Alice. She should be here if she's sickly."

"I'm afraid I'll make her suffer for nothing. To try and fail... all the years we might have had will be lost. She could live another forty years with this condition, Mark."

"I don't know what to do either. Alice's presence might be enough to bring Kelly back, or she could try to kill you. The wolf has a mind of its own and if Kelly isn't strong enough to guide it, the wolf will do what it wants. If the wolf is frightened of you it *will* attack. Kelly would be horrified if she hurt you and it's a common problem with made wolves."

164

"Audrey called me to apologize and explained. I hope she knows there's no hard feelings between us. Her burdens are more than anyone should have to bear."

Mark said, "You should know I've asked Audrey to be my daughter's guardian if Kelly and I can't do it. She'll need to be raised in the pack to be safe. Richard will ensure she gets to see you and Alice, but she'll have special needs that you won't be equipped to deal with."

"I've spoken to Dr. Sorenson and Richard about what to expect, and frankly, I was relieved she'll be so normal."

"Wolves today *are* pretty normal but female ones need protecting. Werewolves don't have many children. Male werewolves still outnumber female ones by about five to one. My daughter can have a normal life if we can keep her hidden. Most wolves run in packs and stick to their own territory. We'd smell them if they entered ours. She can go to school and have human friends when she's old enough to protect herself. She'd smell a strange wolf and know to call for help or hide.

"The problem is everyone knows she's a werewolf. It wouldn't take a genius for another wolf to figure out I'm part of Richard's pack. Even with friendly packs we generally keep the births in the pack secret until the children reach puberty and are old enough to decide for themselves whether they want to join their parents' pack or not. Other wolves would know right where to look for her now. Small packs would be very tempted to steal her. When she's with you, you need to be certain there are guards, ideally from the pack, because a wolf wouldn't hesitate to kill a human to get to its mate."

John said, "Richard and I spoke at length about that. Alice and I are still discussing selling the farm."

He sighed hard again. "Alice needs to know these things to make a good decision. She doesn't think the human werewolf wannabes are that big of a worry. I agree for ourselves but she doesn't know about the potential dangers of men hunting their mate and my insistence on selling is confusing her."

Mark said, "I sincerely regret how hard this is on both of you."

John said, "Alice wants to send the guards back. The cost of hiring all these men is way beyond us and I agree that it isn't right for Richard to have to pay it."

"If you were kidnapped, all of us would be at risk. It isn't a chance we could take."

John said, "I know we should sell; I just hate giving the place up. It's been in the family for five generations."

"Then don't sell it. We can hire a caretaker. Richard could build you a shell corporation to hide who owns it. Maybe someday my daughter could live there or her child..."

"I'll speak with Alice again. I'd hoped to have good news... I have no idea what I'll say."

"You're always welcome here."

"Call me when you can."

John hung up and Mark handed the phone back to Richard.

Richard said, "That was a good idea. I'll see about getting some wolves in their house. Maybe we can catch some of these pesky smaller packs."

Alan muttered, "Silver lining," and Richard laughed.

Mark smiled although the thought of his pack fighting without him made his head hurt.

He rubbed his temples and said, "How are things here?"

"Quieting down some. "We've reopened Howls and donations are way up."

Leah said, "As are visitors."

Richard waved dismissively. "Don't worry about it. We're taking advantage of it. We're thinking of holding a Halloween party, a dusk to dawn blowout."

Mark set his plate down. "That's too risky. Someone would be bound to notice you weren't there all night."

Richard winked at Matti. "We will be there."

"You're going to use the drugs and stay?"

"We'll do a test run first and see if we can manage it. If we can't, there's always body doubles and costumes."

Leah said, "Don't worry about that either. That's months away."

Star returned with the cooler and a net bag of clean bedding that was surprisingly heavy when he took it.

She said, "I put two bottles of gas in there for the stove."

Richard dumped the rolls from the basket onto the table and filled it with chicken hot from the grill. "Don't kill yourself eating and driving."

Mark gave him a hard hug, breathing deeply of his scent.

Leah said, "We'll be there tomorrow at noon."

Mark began to jog to his bike, calling over his shoulder, "Bring some oranges. She likes fruit!"

Chapter 17

Kelly curled her lip at her mate, turning her back when he laughed.

He spoke, the words noise that meant nothing. He persisted, his voice gaining volume and a timber that pulled her attention and she strained to understand his meaning. His body language gave her no clues. He was kneeling but not by their cubs. No tools were in reach of him and he'd eaten the last of the delicious meat. Reminded, she curled her lip again and licked the basket for the last traces.

He pulled the basket from her. Another unintelligible spate of sound followed but she managed to puzzle out one of the sounds and approached like he'd asked.

He smiled but shook his head and she could tell by his scent he was becoming upset.

She listened harder but his words made no sense. She understood the word for no and the one for come but the rest was just a babble of sound.

Her girl cub made the sound that meant the boy was bothering her and Kelly growled at her mate, angry that he'd distracted her from her duty, grabbing her son by his scruff to pull him away.

He knew he'd disobeyed. Urine trickled down his leg when she dropped him. She put her paw on him, not to hold him, he wasn't trying to run, but to keep him submissive and licked him clean. When she released him, he ran to the new basket and began to chew it.

She lay beside him, warning him softly to slow down and he obeyed. With her nose and paws she showed him the parts of the basket, the rough edges to avoid, the metal staples that would hurt, the delicious juices caught in the corners.

Her son was happily absorbed when she smelled wolf.

Her mate and the girl cub had gone to the stream. She pressed her son to the ground, warning him to stay with a sharp growl and bounded from the den.

Her hackles rose when she saw the two wolves approaching. She slunk through the long grasses on her stomach.

"Kelly!" her mate called. "Come…" the rest was a meaningless babble, but she ignored his calls even though she knew he wanted her.

She crept closer slowly, sniffing hard.

She knew these wolves, and her mate was unafraid, but she didn't want them near her daughter.

She stood and snarled, warning them to leave and knew they understood her. Her snarl gained depth when they persisted in coming closer.

Her mate headed to her and she ran forward, getting between him and the others.

She snapped at his hand when he reached for her and growled, warning him he should back away.

They all spoke. She understood only a few of the words. She quieted to listen hard, confused by their presence in her territory.

Her ears pricked as she caught the scent of the cloth her daughter used as coverings and her fur lowered as she realized they were the source of the food she ate.

"Leah," her mate said, and Kelly remembered his name was Mark.

Shock rooted her in place. She knew Leah. Leah was Richard's mate. She'd been kind, a friend, someone Kelly trusted. Leah had a son and Kelly could picture his face. She was Aunt Kelly.

Leah crouched in front of her and spoke again, and Kelly heard and understood. Leah had come for the babies. Fury instantly consumed her, and she leapt for her enemy's throat.

Her mate yelled at her to stop, but it was white noise lost in her rage. Blood coated her tongue and she snarled in savage triumph as her enemy fell to the ground.

Her mate pulled her off and stabbed her shoulder and the world grew hazy. She scrabbled frantically, growling and barking, trying to warn him, trying to tell him to save their children. Words, she needed the words and she almost had them, but the world darkened before she could remake herself to say them.

Light and motion came to her slowly. It took her a moment to realize it was leaves blowing in the wind and not herself moving.

Her mate spoke, a long litany of sound fraught with angst that made her hackles rise but she couldn't force her limbs to obey her. Two wolves appeared and she wanted to growl and bite but try as she might, she couldn't manage more than weak thrashing and low whimpers.

Her mate held their son— was handing him to the other. Her son whimpered and the sound made her insides quiver in a deeply disturbing way. Her son needed her, and she was failing him.

Part of her strained for understanding while another part raged. The light grew brighter becoming strands of color, each one different. The colors held information, but she couldn't smell anything and it terrified her. Without a sense of smell, she'd be unable to find her son. With all of her might she strained to see him through the piercing light. The light expanded, engulfing her with the force of a blow.

Her sight returned but with an odd perspective. She knew she was looking at grass even though it was just a glow of flowing green. Her paw wasn't a paw but shades of orange and red with a cool blue undertone. Her chest was a crystal orb surrounded by a bright light encased in a viscous shiny liquid. The sight was somehow terrifying. Her panic made that shiny liquid flex. Her panic would crack the crystal and it would destroy her. She didn't know how she knew it but she was certain of it.

Turning her attention to it caused it to gain depth but the act of examining it threatened to shatter it too. She ceased trying to make sense of what was happening and instead strained to reach her son before he was swallowed up by the brightness.

"It isn't going to work," Mark said. "She's terrified."

Matti nodded agreement. "I'll leave you a shot and maybe you can try again without us here."

Leah said, "She seemed to be listening."

Matti said, "I'm not sure how much she understands but I'm certain she understands the word babies."

Mark grimaced as he said, "I'm so sorry, Leah. I didn't think she'd just attack like that."

Leah placed the empty water bottle with the other empties and took another full one. "I'll be right as rain in another hour or so. I just need some water. I wasn't expecting it either and I should've been. I'd attack anyone I thought was after my child too."

Matti said, "He looks good. They both do. We need to be patient. We should try again but not like this. I'll speak to Audrey and see if she'll be willing to camp in the meadow for a few weeks. Maybe if we give Kelly time to get used to us, it would go better."

Mark said, "Let's give Kelly some time to get over this. I don't want her to take him and leave."

"She won't leave you," Leah said reassuringly.

Matti said, "She might if she thinks Marcus is in danger. She'd come back to you, but her wolf could compel her to hide him until he was big enough to take care of himself. It might be smarter to wait a few more weeks until he's at least weaned. Her instincts should settle down and your daughter should have the stronger pull then."

Mark said, "He'll never get to have a childhood. He'll only get a few short years..."

Leah hugged him, saying sadly, "They can be happy years and there's hope. He was a human. His body knows the shape. We just need to make him remember it and want it."

"God, if only I could make her understand!"

Kelly is in there and she knows. She loves him too, Mark. If she's staying a wolf, it's because he needs it."

"Or she's forgotten how to be human too. She was as terrified as him. Maybe she just doesn't want to come back..."

Chapter 18

Kelly glared out from the cover of the trees, not sure if she trusted her mate. He'd stabbed her without warning again. The sneak attack had shocked her as much as the realization that she'd forgotten who she was again.

Lethargy slowed her. Within moments she was too weak to even stand. The world became odorless with bright colors and sudden sounds that made her skin jump making it hard to concentrate on the revelations.

Her wolf had been guarding Marcus, making certain he didn't shift from his wolf form. It was a constant effort that took her total attention when he was awake. From the moment his eyes had opened he'd been learning to mimic every animal he saw but as her wolf she was able to force obedience. She wasn't sure she'd have the same control as a human.

Her human self was horrified with the deadly danger her son was in. She'd have screamed for Mark to let her be if she could have but whatever he'd given her made speech impossible. She had no idea where Marcus was. She tried to call for him but only managed a stifled whimper.

Mark crouched in front of her. "Our daughter needs you too," he said.

Guilt made her feel nauseous. She'd totally neglected her daughter.

Marcus whimpered and her heart fluttered. He needed her. He'd die without her.

Mark continued to beg her to return and she wanted to. She wanted to curse but lacked the strength. He thought he was helping but her inattention could be the death of their son. Marcus hadn't the wit to know that becoming a bird or mouse could be deadly. The first time he'd transformed it had almost killed him. If she'd been one second later, he might have been eaten or swept away in a current. It still made her feel sick to contemplate him being trapped in the form of a fish.

Whatever Mark had injected her with made the colors meld and flow and left her unable to control her body. She could become neither a human nor a wolf. This time she didn't see the crystal center of herself but she felt fragile as if her form was on the cusp of a monstrous change.

Mark screamed a sudden terrified shout.

Panic seized her and she began to hyperventilate. She gasped in air until her throat burned. The pain of it was reassuring that she still had a corporal form.

Marcus whimpered again and her wolf surged. She would have cried in relief if she could have when she resumed her wolf form and felt Marcus's nose touch hers.

"You were coming back! I know you could fight this if you wanted to! Come back to me!"

The distress in Mark's voice pulled to her but it was no match for the soft whimpers of her son.

She was tempted to fight her wolf and speak with him, but Marcus needed her to be a wolf. Ever since Mark had injected her that first time, she could see the lines of light that connected her to Marcus. She'd learned how to pull them to force his obedience. He was learning as she was and soon he wouldn't need her so much and she could resume her human form.

She let herself drift on the swirling colors and sought the safety of her inner wolf. The wolf would protect Marcus and felt no shame about that. It was perfectly content.

She wasn't ready to be a woman again. She had so much to teach Marcus and so much to learn.

Chapter 19

Kelly grabbed Marcus by his scruff and shook him lightly. His ears flattened and he looked chagrined when she released him and placed a paw on him to hold him down.

She lifted her lip in warning, lowering herself to her stomach to creep through the ferns beside the brook. When she reached her target of grass bordering the burbling stream, she glanced back and tapped the ground beside her.

Marcus's tailed wagged with excitement, but he stayed low as she'd taught him and moved slowly as he stalked through the grass to reach her side.

She nodded and licked his cheek quickly, placing a paw on his back lightly in warning, staring pointedly at the far shore.

She pressed him down hard and released him. He understood that she meant for him to stay. She hoped he'd understand what she was trying to teach him.

Mark was upstream. She could smell him and the rabbit he'd just killed, and she smiled a doggy smile when he threw the offal into the water as she'd thought he would.

Marcus's ears pricked and his nose twitched, and she knew he could smell it too, but he remained motionless as she'd commanded.

She nudged Marcus with her nose when she saw a bird shadow over the water.

The offal had attracted fish, which had attracted the bird. The sharp cry of a hawk was immediately followed by the bird swooping down with claws extended. It grasped the fish and Kelly pounced.

Marcus barked excitedly and jumped after her.

She snapped at him, warning him to back away as she let the hawk fall into the water and grabbed the fish it had released when she'd killed the hawk.

She brought the fish to the bank and dropped it with the growl that meant wait and went back for the bird.

It had floated away but she found it within moments and she returned to find Marcus waiting impatiently.

She licked his cheek and dropped the bird, growling softly as she nudged Marcus back.

She stared at him intently until she was certain he was paying attention and then extended her forepaw, elongating one claw to delicately traced the puncture wounds the bird had made on the fish.

Marcus watched with wide eyes, his tail quivering in excitement. She showed him the bird talon and then remade her paw to pick up the talon and press it against the fish's wounds.

Marcus cocked his head, his gaze darting from the bird to the fish, lingering on her malformed paw.

She spread the talons and then reshaped her paw, making her claws long and sharp and placing it beside the outspread bird talon.

Again, she showed Marcus the wounds the bird had made on the fish. She let him sniff them both and then gently scratched across his paw, flexing her claws exaggeratedly.

He whined a small, excited whine and his claws elongated.

She shook her head, huffing the sound that meant no, letting her paw revert to normal and barking for him to follow.

He glanced back in puzzlement but followed her willingly. She led him further down the brook until the water grew shallow and carefully pointed out the minnows swimming along the edge.

She reformed her paw, scooped out a handful of minnows, and dumped them on the shore. Marcus whined and sniffed the minnows, clearly not understanding what she was showing him.

She left him splashing in the shallow water, snapping at the minnows as she ran back for the dead fish.

It didn't take him long to understand the minnows were small fish the same way he was a small wolf. He stared with an intense expression as she continued her mime and she knew the moment he understood her that small things were easy prey to bigger ones. His eyes widened and he began to bark excitedly as he darted from her to a nearby tree. Birds roosting in the tree flew away with aggravated squawks and he returned with his tongue lolling in a doggy grin.

He slashed at the fish and she barked in approval. Barking in encouragement, she ran back to the bird. Marcus placed his paw beside the dead bird's talon, barking in excitement.

"Having a good day?" Mark asked.

She growled, warning him not to interrupt. She knew he understood her, and it angered her when he ignored her warning and picked Marcus up to cuddle him.

She was tempted to snap at Mark but was afraid it would confuse Marcus. He whined anxiously, so she licked his cheek and flopped down at Mark's feet.

Mark said, "Is playtime over?" He kissed Marcus's forehead and set him back down. "I don't like him by the brook like this. It's dangerous."

Kelly snorted, using a paw to pull Marcus closer. Mark had no idea how dangerous the stream was for Marcus. She had no idea if there were others able to assume multiple shapes like Marcus could or not, but she knew a child who could become a fish was in mortal danger. She began to groom her son.

Mark said, "I know you can understand me."

She narrowed her eyes at him.

"I need you too," he said.

She turned away. She couldn't come back until she knew Marcus would be safe. He was learning quickly but she couldn't take the chance on resuming her human form until she was certain he had his shifts under control. Marcus would assume whatever form she did, she was sure of that, and she needed him old enough to have the intellectual capacity to understand how dangerous it was. A three-month-old baby who could transform into a fish wouldn't live out the day. She needed Marcus to be a wolf. Tomorrow she'd take him far enough she was certain they wouldn't be interrupted.

Mark called a greeting to Arny who dozed in wolf form on Richard's back patio. Arny sat and Mark waved him back, "No news. I just came to tell Audrey not to come for a while."

Arny lay back down, resting his head on his paws. His expression said clearer than words that he thought having a mate was more trouble than it was worth.

Mark knocked on the back door and entered before anyone answered. He headed to the kitchen phone. "Anyone home?" he called but the house was silent enough he didn't think anyone was.

Richard answered on the second ring.

"It's Mark. Tell Audrey not to come. Kelly has been avoiding me and she's really unhappy. I can't try that drug again any time soon."

"Damn, I was really hoping it would work."

"It did work. She lost wolf form. I think it almost killed her though. She didn't become human shaped."

It still made his pulse pound with dread when he thought of it and he had to take a moment to collect himself.

"She wasn't a wolf or human but something… monstrous."

"She got stuck halfway?"

"No. Or maybe… I don't know. It was hard to make out. She was insubstantial. A huge greenish black cloud. I thought at first she'd disintegrated into dust but I could see an enormous gold eye."

"Maybe you imagined it?"

"I wish… I really think it was real, Richard. It wasn't anything I've ever heard of or seen before or want to see again. It was as if she was trying to become something deadlier than a wolf. For a split second she had an enormous, scaled paw with talons as long as my arm. And she was scared to death. She whimpered for hours and still whimpers sometimes when I get close. She's more obsessed than ever with Marcus. Maybe the drug made her imagine whatever that shape was into existence. She can reshape parts of herself. I'm terrified she'll hallucinate some hideous form and get stuck like that."

Richard said, "I'll talk to Matti. Don't give her anymore of it. I'll tell Audrey to wait a few more weeks before moving closer. But don't give up. Sometimes it takes a few months for the human half to get the upper hand. Mark, as hard as this is, you and Kelly can still have a long life together. Losing a son will be hard but if you can stay human, she might come back when he's gone."

"Twenty years without her." His breath caught on a sob. "Twenty years to love him..."

"Your daughter—"

"Needs me, I know. I'd wait a million years for Kelly, but she won't outlive him. She won't be able to let him go. She can barely let him out of her sight..."

"You never know, Mark. He'll be fully grown in one year and she might come back to you then."

"It just kill's me, Richard. He should have had such a long life."

"I know. I'm so sorry."

Mark hung up and ran back to the bike.

Chapter 20

Mark laughed and laid his guitar down as Marcus pounced on his mother's tail. She opened one eye, lifting her lip and Marcus slunk away, heading for his sister.

"Oh no you don't!" Mark said firmly as he scooped him up.

Marcus licked his face making Mark laughed again. He set him down in the grass, shaking his finger as he said, "Stay there! Your mother and sister are napping!"

Marcus barked once and then ran through the grass to investigate the water. Kelly barked a sharp yip of sound that Marcus answered the same way. Mark expected her to follow but she lay back down. Mark sighed, laying the axe aside in order to follow Marcus, casting a quick glance back to be sure his daughter was securely enclosed.

Their hillside den was growing slowly as he added on to make room for the baby supplies that seemed to multiply daily. Bugs and mice infested everything that wasn't sealed and Kelly would growl savagely at him if he killed the mice in their den. She'd let Marcus hunt them, but they were off limits to him. So Leah had brought him more plastic containers to store the baby's clothes, bedding, diapers, and food. His tools were also growing. He had an axe, a pickax, a shovel, a gun, a saw, and a bucket, but hardly any time to use them. They lay in a jumbled heap on his table slash workbench.

Taking care of an infant in the wild was a fulltime job. He'd fashioned his daughter a playpen of sorts, using wood he'd cut but he worried about the rough edges even though she hadn't learned to roll over yet. She didn't seem to mind sleeping outside, but he worried she'd get sunburned or learn to crawl while he was busy. He worried constantly.

He stopped to tuck the camp stove, which he hadn't used much because he'd been hoping the raw food would bring Kelly from her wolf—beneath his makeshift table. Kelly had taught Marcus anything under the table was off limits and so far he'd been good about respecting that.

He took an orange from the cooler and waved it beneath Kelly's nose. "Want one?" he asked cajolingly.

Kelly seemed happier as long as he kept his tone light. If he let his temper get the better of him, she'd whimper and hide in the bushes. If he approached with anything except food, she'd take Marcus and run, so he made a real effort to be cheerful while in camp and never came near either of them with the tools.

She huffed and put her tail over her face, burying her head and he laughed and placed the orange in the center of the table, glancing around for Marcus.

He spotted him at the edge of the stream and headed for him.

A sharp yip and splash hurried his steps. *Marcus kept him busy enough for five people,* he thought irritably as he yanked his son from the stream. Baby teeth showed in a puppy grin as Marcus tried to lick his face. Mark kissed his nose and set him on his feet. He was surprised Kelly hadn't shown up to investigate and it heartened him that she was trusting him.

Marcus headed right back to the water. Mark sat on the bank and let his son wade as he debated the best way to keep him away from the stream.

The water moved at a sluggish pace now and was a much narrower stream than it had been in the spring. It barely reached Mark's ankles except for a few deeper knee-high spots in the center. A man could easily step past the deeper parts or pull himself away, but the current was strong when it rained and a puppy wouldn't be able to reach the bottom.

"No!" he said firmly when Marcus headed to the deeper center.

Marcus returned to the shallows and sniffed the brush, biting at the waving grass heads and pouncing imaginary foes in the shallow water. Mark lay back on his elbows and enjoyed the sun on his face. Kelly joined him thirty minutes later. She drank deeply before wading into the water and Mark sat to watch as she growled at Marcus when he ran to her.

She'd been weaning him slowly and it both worried and relieved him. Mark hated when she disappeared into the forest for hours at a time almost as much as Marcus did. Marcus had howled for her the first few times Kelly had left but he'd eat the meat Mark gave him now and would amuse himself by exploring their home or gnawing a bone.

Kelly walked the length of the brook until he lost sight of her in the trees. When she returned, she called Marcus with a soft yip and pushed him with her nose, growling low in her throat.

Mark wasn't sure how much either of them understood but the baby seemed to realize she meant keep away from the center. He backed away immediately and sat on the shore when she crossed the stream. Mark patted his lap and got a disdainful look.

Kelly ran to him and put her wet muzzle on his shoulder and he hugged her a moment before she bounded away. Marcus followed her and the two of them played in the grass, running and rolling.

He wished he could join them, but his daughter would be waking soon and he didn't like to leave her alone, and Kelly didn't like him to play with Marcus as a wolf. It gave him hope that it disturbed her, and he contemplated remaining a wolf for a few days to see if that would encourage her to shift. He'd have to give his daughter to Audrey though and worried it would make his wife leave him.

Kelly returned to him and stretched out. Marcus followed and was asleep in seconds. Mark picked him up and brought him to the play pen where he laid him beside his sister.

Kelly leaned over the rickety stick fence to sniff them.

"She needs you too, Kelly. You have to come back. It's been three months. Marcus can eat solid food now."

She flicked her ears and glanced at the cooler.

Excitement made Mark's voice rise. "That's right, we're talking about food. I'll feed Marcus and you feed her. We haven't even named her yet. She needs us too! Wouldn't a cooked steak be good? How about mashed potatoes with butter and sour cream?

"I miss you so much. Come talk to me. I'm sure your parents want to speak with you too. I know you can hear me. Come back!"

For a moment he thought she would. Her ears lowered and she hunched but his daughter whined and woke Marcus who barked his, 'I'm awake come feed me call.'

"I'll feed him." He pushed her aside and picked Marcus up. "You feed her."

She followed him to the cooler and licked the bone he removed but she let him give it to Marcus.

"Will you let her cry? She's hungry too and you could feed her."

His daughter's cries grew angry and Mark's wolf urged him to soothe her with a feeling of pressure beneath his skin that grew stronger and more painful as the baby cried.

He sat beside Marcus to offer him small bits of cheese.

Kelly growled and snapped at his fingers, lowering her ears when he laughed.

"She needs you. I've been patient but enough is enough." He jerked back when she snarled, there was real anger in it, but she wasn't looking at him, she was staring past his shoulder.

He jumped to his feet as she began to run and he followed.

Marcus ran after him. The scent that had caught Kelly's attention wafted to him and all the hair on his body rose.

"Stay," he snapped. He didn't know this person.

Kelly had reached the thicker trees and he could no longer see her. Mark ran back for the gun he kept in the cooler.

He'd just plopped the cooler on the table when a twig snapped to his left.

"I could kill you before you take one step," a man said.

Mark lifted his hands and took a deep breath, but the wind was against him and he could only smell the familiar camp smells.

The man laughed a harsh bark of laughter. "Or maybe I should kill your kid and the pup. A son for a son after all."

Mark peered over his shoulder.

"Did I say you could fucking move? You even twitch and I'll blow your head off."

Marcus had sat where Mark had told him to stay. His ears and nose twitched. Mark hoped with all his soul he would disobey and run to his mother.

"It's just a dog," he said.

"Shut that brat the fuck up. I can't hear myself think."

"She's hungry. Her bottle is here in the cooler."

"Leave it," the man snapped. He was aiming not at him but Marcus and Mark let his reaching hand fall.

He kept his hands up and walked slowly to his daughter. She sniffled and snorted against his shoulder. He knew she'd resume screaming if a bottle wasn't forthcoming soon.

The man was sweating now and pale, his gaze riveted to the baby.

"She's innocent," Mark said. "Leave her alone and just take me." If he could get within reaching distance, he could rip the gun away. He'd survive a shot or two. In thirty seconds he could transform into his wolf-self and rip the man limb-from-limb.

"You're not even going to try to deny it?"

The wind stirred the trees and the man took a step backward. He glanced over his shoulder and when he turned back his jaw had hardened.

Mark assumed this man was the father of one of Stacy's confederates that the pack had killed. He hoped he could just talk him down because he didn't look up to killing.

"Give her to me," the man said.

"No."

"Give her to me or I'll pry her from your corpse."

Mark took a step backward. "You can't hurt her, can you?"

His muscles tightened. This wasn't a man but a werewolf.

"I'm not going to hurt her."

"If you kill me, she'll die."

"Not if I take her with me."

"Richard will hunt you to the ends of the earth."

"I'll take my chances."

"You're Brandon's father," Mark said with certainty. "From the Delmont pack.

"I'm a Delmont alright. Frank Delmont, and I'm surprised you remember his name."

"He was feral. I had no choice."

Frank laughed bitterly. "Like your son?"

"My son hasn't killed anyone!"

"Yet."

"We won't let him roam free. He isn't a danger. He's a baby. Marcus, come!"

Marcus scampered to him.

A gunshot sounded in the distance and Frank smiled a grim satisfied smile that made Mark's palms sweat.

Frank snapped, "Get him the hell away from you!"

"Afraid to smell him?"

The shot took Mark by surprise and knocked him to his ass. He hadn't thought Frank would risk hitting the baby Mark held. She screamed when he fell but the shot had taken Mark low in the gut and missed her. Marcus began to bark and Frank fired again.

Mark screamed, more to warn Kelly than because the new shot hurt. He hardly felt it although he knew it was a serious wound and would hurt like a bitch any moment. He rolled to his feet, hunching over his daughter and reaching for his son.

Marcus whined now and was sticky with blood when Mark scooped him up. He placed both babies behind the cooler on the table and called for his wolf.

Distant snarls ended abruptly.

Frank said, "Your bitch is dead, and you will be too but I'll spare the children." The snarls had distracted the man, or he was being sporting and letting Mark finish his transformation.

Mark dropped to the dirt and rose as a wolf, snarling as he charged forward.

Another shot took him in the shoulder and knocked the wind from him. He rolled with the force but urged his wolf on. Kelly was fighting close by. He could hear the snarls.

Frank shot again, he assumed at Kelly because the bullet came nowhere near him. Mark leaped forward, intent on the gun.

"Run!" Frank yelled and fired again.

Kelly let out a sharp pain-filled yip.

"You were supposed to shoot her from the blind!" He shot again and Kelly snarled. The shot knocked Mark down, pain and fear leaving him breathless. The wolf Kelly fought was bleeding from a long gash on her side and was missing an ear. One of her eyes was crusted with blood and dirt, and she limped as she circled, looking for an opening. Blood coated Kelly but Mark couldn't see any obvious wounds.

"Run!" Frank yelled again and shot at Kelly.

He blew her front foreleg off, leaving it dangling obscenely by a thread of skin, and Kelly yipped again, rolling away from the other wolf. Her form shimmered, becoming an indistinct shape as if she stood in a furnace and heat billowed around her. When she got to her feet, she had all four legs.

She circled the other wolf, looking for an opening then darted at Frank.

She was trying to reach the gun. The other wolf rushed in and bit her leg, dragging her back. The two wolves rolled in the dirt. Frank hesitated, unwilling to hit his own wife.

Mark pushed through the pain and lunged for the arm holding the gun.

It went off again and Kelly snarled. Mark knew she was hit by the scent of fresh blood but hoped she could again shift quickly to mend the damage.

"What the hell are you?" Frank asked shakily. "We should've bought the fucking silver bullets!"

He shot again, hitting Mark in the back. Mark was falling when Frank shot again and missed. The bullet hit one of the gas tanks under the table. It exploded with a force to ruffle Mark's hair. He bit Frank's leg, clamping down as hard as he could.

"Run!" Frank hollered. "I can't hold her off long!"

The other wolf snarled then yipped and Kelly growled and barked.

Frank hit Mark with the butt of the gun, knocking him loose. Mark struggled to get his feet under himself.

Kelly and the other wolf bounded past. Kelly caught her prey and rolled, and the wolf whined a long moan of sound.

"I'll fucking blow his head off if you don't back off right now!"

He hit Mark again with the butt of the gun. Frank was likely out of bullets if he wasn't shooting. Mark called for his human form with real hope they could win this if he could tell her and she could understand him.

"Sheila, we're going!"

The smell of smoke had joined the smell of fresh blood and Mark glanced over his shoulder. He didn't

know it were planning or accident but the table his kids
lay on was burning.

Chapter 21

Kelly either didn't see or didn't realize the danger because she continued to fight.

Frank dropped to the ground, hunching as the change took him.

"The kids," Mark gasped as soon as he could talk.

The shift left him weak and panting, too dizzy to stand. He could barely force the words out, but he tried again, yelling as loud as he could, "The babies are on the table and it's on fire! Get them and the gun! Go, Kelly!"

A package of diapers he'd left on the table had caught and burned hotly. The tarp above them was old and dry and covered with drying branches, it wouldn't take much for it to burn.

Mark hoped Frank would go for the kids himself, but the scent of smoke was hiding their newborn scent and Frank's wolf ignored them.

Frank bounded past him as Kelly jumped forward. Her body flowed into her human shape as she ran and she snatched up both children, knocking the cooler beneath the table.

The two wolves ran past Mark, heading for the trees as the spare gas tank exploded. Bits of metal and wood rained around Mark. He rolled to his side, throwing an arm over his face.

Kelly lay on the ground, hunching over the babies, using her body as a shield. Both babies cried. Marcus ran to him and began licking his face and whining piteously.

Mark flopped to his back, taking deep breaths trying to force air into his aching lungs.

"Get the gun and get the babies out of the den!" he yelled as he dragged himself backward with his hands.

"Kell, can you get the fire out?"

He sniffed hard, scanning the woods but couldn't smell anything over the smoke and the scent of blood. Frank and his mate had left a blood trail so one of them was seriously injured. The brush was still but they could be regrouping. Shifting would heal them too. They'd be weak until they ate and drank but they could have supplies with them.

The thought of water made Mark moan. He'd never been so thirsty in his life. His blood felt thick in his veins. Each beat of his heart sent a wave of pain through him as if his blood burned. He tried to force himself to his feet.

Marcus hampered him with his mewling and anxious pawing.

"Go to Mommy," he said.

Marcus yipped and continued to paw at him.

Mark turned to examine Kelly. She hadn't moved. Their daughter still cried and now lay in a puddle of blood. He was close enough to see Kelly was breathing but she wasn't moving. Her hair hung down in front of her face and her posture was tense and he couldn't see much of their daughter.

"Kell, is she okay?" he groaned as he tried to pull himself faster.

"Marcus, can you get Daddy a water bottle? Daddy needs water."

Marcus yipped and jumped away, his gaze going to the stream and then to his mother.

"No, stay with us," Mark said, sorry he'd asked. "Stay with me, son."

Marcus ran to Kelly and licked her face.

She moaned and Marcus dropped to his stomach and whined. The smell of blood bloomed, and Mark opened his eyes, cursing as he realized he'd closed them and had stopped moving. Marcus had crawled to his sister and was licking her now.

Kelly's arm's shook and her muscles strained, and she screamed as she fell forward, landing awkwardly on her face.

Bile rose in Mark's gut. The pickaxe was stuck through her lower back, pinning her to the ground.

"Just hold on a few more minutes!" A distant sound of a motor made him moan. It would take him a few hours to recuperate enough to be useful in a fight and he didn't have a few minutes. Kelly needed that metal out so she could shift before she bled to death.

His wolf was frantic and wanted to manifest but he needed his hands. He groaned as he rolled to his stomach and pushed himself to his knees to grasp the handle of the pickaxe. She screamed when he yanked it loose and he vomited, choking and gasping as he fell to his side.

A flurry of gunshots sounded in the distance.

Marcus howled and pawed at Mark's face. He began barking shrill terrified barks. Kelly's body was reverting to wolf in slow motion. It was the slowest shift Mark had ever seen and he realized she was unconscious and not in control of herself when she didn't respond to Marcus's frantic barks or the renewed screams of her daughter who she lay across. He'd never seen or heard of a werewolf manifesting when its human host was asleep or unconscious, but he didn't have time to ponder what it meant.

One tiny hand waved from beneath Kelly, all that was visible of his daughter. Marcus darted from him to Kelly and back then howled right in Mark's face.

"I know, son," Mark gasped out.

Tiny teeth dug into Mark's shoulder. Marcus whined and panted as he tried to drag him. He gave up within moments and grabbed Kelly's wrist in his sharp teeth.

The smell of burning plastic tickled Mark's throat and stung his eyes. He reached for his son and missed.

"The fire will die out in a minute. Daddy just needs a minute."

Marcus growling in his face made him open his eyes and he realized he'd fallen asleep or unconscious. Embers floated through the air, catching and burning the tall grasses, which sent off clouds of smoke but burned so quickly the flames weren't spreading far. But the grasses outside of their den were thicker and one spark would set it all ablaze.

Mark realized the motor was much closer. His gun was only three feet away beneath the table. But it might as well have been ten miles. Black smoke gusted from the burning clothing and blankets in the plastic bins, the heat of it ruffling Mark's hair. He worried one of the embers would land in Kelly's fur.

His daughter's pain-filled cries were nails on a chalkboard, but Mark was relieved she could still cry at all.

It took him two tries to roll to his side. His body shook, his limbs refusing to obey. He gave in and let his wolf take him.

He was less shaky when the transformation was complete but weak as a kitten.

His daughter had stopped crying and the silence felt ominous. The motor had stopped also. The hill was too steep to drive up. He was certain someone was still coming.

He managed to nudge Kelly aside with his head enough to reveal his daughter's face.

She blinked up at him looking angry and scared and he realized Marcus had stopped barking.

Mark licked his daughter's cheek, and she sobbed a weak stuttering breath. Neither he nor Kelly had the energy for another fight. That gun was his only hope.

He struggled to his feet and stumbled into the fire.

His fur began to burn, the delicate skin on his ears and paws blistering. His new wall had caught fire despite the greenness of the wood.

He still had hope that the fire would burn out once the flammable goods in the plastic buckets had burned. The cooler where he kept the gun had landed on its side, scattering the meat.

His jaws were closing on the handle of the gun when hands grabbed him and yanked him from beneath the table.

He snarled and snapped, thrashing weakly. A heavy weight knocked him to the ground and rolled him. He pushed back with all his strength, urging his transformation to human but knowing it wouldn't help. He was too weak to reach the gun.

Black combat boots were the last thing he saw as a hank of material covered his face.

Chapter 22

Kelly woke with a blinding headache. It took her a moment to remember what had happened. Every joint in her body throbbed in time with her heartbeat, making it hard to concentrate. Marcus snarled and snapped right beside her ear, but she lacked the strength to push herself up. Her daughter coughed weakly and she realized the air was laden with smoke. As soon as she noticed it, her throat and eyes began to burn.

Shapes had weird halos, confused by both smoke and her wavering vision. A flurry of gunshots and men shouting made her labored breaths come harder.

Marcus snarled again. She could feel him shaking against her side. His claws slashed past her face and she turned to see a stranger stood mere steps away.

Two other men were wrapping Mark in a blue tarp. Blood coated his face and the remains of his clothes, but she assumed he was still alive because of the gingerly way they handled him and the restraints,

"He's heavy as fuck," one of the men said.

Steve said, "He's worth his weight in gold. Get him to the truck and get the hell out of here. We'll bring her and meet you at Howard's. Mike, get the fire out."

"Who cares? Let it burn!"

"I care, asshole. We don't want to alert the rest of his goddamned pack! Put it the fuck out!"

Kelly's daughter yelled shrilly.

"And someone put the kid in the crate! And be fucking careful!"

A growl escaped Kelly despite her efforts to hold it in. She was regaining her strength but in no shape to fight.

One of the men heard her and said, "It's coming to!"

Steve said, "Who has a tranq?"

"I'm out."

"Me too,"

"I got one."

"Well, shoot her ass! And grab that puppy!"

Kelly scrabbled weakly, trying to force her leaden limbs to obey her.

Steve said, "Kyle, Teller, get the mut and get going." Frank is still out there somewhere. See if you can catch up to Pat but stay alert!"

Steve leaned over her then knelt on her side, using his body weight to hold her down.

Marcus lunged forward and Steve backhanded him, sending him rolling.

Kelly strained to warn Marcus off but she couldn't manage more than a ragged whine.

Steve shifted his position to press on her neck.

"Cut the shit or we'll kill him. We don't need him, only her."

Kelly couldn't turn her head enough to see Marcus, but she could hear him growling.

"Feisty little fucker," a man said laughingly.

"Just get it caged and get out of here before Howard's boys show up."

"Mike, you got the brat?" Steve asked quietly a minute later.

"Good to go."

"Tranq mama wolf and get her tied."

The pressure on Kelly's neck eased and she gulped in air.

Steve said, "Hand me the tape."

Kelly lunged at the hand that crossed in front of her face. She connected solidly and bit down as hard as she could while the man shrieked and kicked at her.

"Shoot her!" Steve yelled. He fell across her back, pushing her hard to the ground. Kelly didn't release the wrist until black spots danced before her eyes.

The man was screaming. She'd almost bitten his hand off. Two men were speaking to the screamer, Helping him wrap the wrist and injecting him with something.

"Shut the fuck up!" Steve said. "We wanted her to bite us and she did. You should be thankful! Now help me tie her!"

"They're tough as shit," another man said as he yanked her front paws.

She snapped at him, but she was slow and weak, and he avoided her easily.

Steve punched her in the side of the head and knelt hard on her neck again.

"Give her the damned tranq!"

A needle jabbed into her side right as a man swore and a gun went off.

The pressure left her neck and she tried to push herself up. A man holding a wire cage containing Marcus was running along the far edge of the meadow. He'd be in the woods in moments. Her daughter yelled then fell silent so suddenly she knew she'd been hurt and she redoubled her efforts to get her feet beneath her.

"Fuck!" a man yelled, and a wolf growled. Blood splattered Kelly's face but before she could feel relief, she realized it was Frank, not Mark or the pack.

A body thudded to the ground and another shot rang out followed by too many shots to count as the men yelled at each other.

Kelly staggered to her feet, but the ground felt as if it was bucking and swaying and she didn't manage more than one step before falling hard to her side.

Colors were darkening as if night were falling but she knew it was the drug. Her gaze landed on Frank. He raced for the woods, dragging a metal cage that contained her daughter while bullets thudded into the grass around him.

"Stop, you'll fucking kill her!" Steve shouted angrily.

The men continued to shoot. Another body fell, shot by Steve, and the gunfire stopped.

"I said fucking stop! We'll get her back. He'll call Stacy. He isn't going to wait for it to grow up. He'll want her or maybe this one now that his bitch is dead."

Chapter 23

Pins and needles rapidly escalated to cramps that made Mark moan with the pain of it. It took effort to pry his eyes open and once they were open it took him a few minutes to puzzle out what he was seeing.

He'd been tied tightly and lay on a cement floor with his face just inches from a metal grill.

He closed his eyes to sniff deeply but he heard people approaching before he smelt them. He couldn't smell anything over his own drying blood and a musty rotten odor from the hay he lay in.

"Awake, I see," Steve said cheerfully.

A man Mark didn't know said, "Is it safe to go in?"

Steve said, "What's the fucker going to do? He can't even turn over."

Another man said, "Who knows what they can do?"

Steve said, "Don't be a pussy, Mike. Just leave the damned water."

As Steve spoke he was unlocking a metal door. Light preceded Steve into the room.

Mark lay still, focusing his senses on what he could hear. By the shuffling footsteps and low mutters he knew there were three others with Steve.

Steve kicked him in the back. "No use pretending. We know you're awake."

He fisted his hand in Mark's hair, yanking him to his back. A fresh wave of cramps made Mark moan and Steve laughed as he slapped his face.

"You still feel pain. That's good to know." He jerked Mark's head up and pointed to the corner near the door. "We've got audio on you and the door is alarmed—"

"You shouldn't tell him," Mike said.

"Shut the fuck up!" Steve snapped. He dropped Mark's head and stood, putting his hands on his hips to glare at Mike. "I'm in charge here. You don't know shit about werewolves."

"You don't know shit about them either," one of the other men said in a mocking tone.

"I know more than you fuckers do," Steve said. "He needs to know he can't break out. Or did you want him to try to break down the fucking door?"

Mike said, "I don't think he could. It's reinforced steel."

"Whatever. This is my fucking plan!"

"Fine, have it your way."

"Damn straight!" Steve squatted by Mark's head. "As I was saying, the door here and every other one is alarmed. Don't bother trying to break it down. It would just piss me off. You can cooperate and make my life easier, but I don't really give a shit if you wanna do things the hard way." He patted Mark's cheek, sitting back on his heels to examine him. "If you cooperate and don't give us any crap, I'll untie you or you can lay here in your own shit."

A commotion in the distance made Steve jump to his feet.

"Finish this later," he said, gesturing impatiently for Mike to exit.

The other men had already headed to the stairs. Mark counted as they climbed and knew he was just one story below ground. When the cellar door opened a wave of fresh air brought him the men's scents and the faintest odor of his wife's blood.

The scent energized his wolf who roiled beneath his skin with a feeling of pins and needles. It sharpened his senses and he breathed deeply trying to clear his head.

Steve slammed the cell door and ran up the stairs. Mark strained but all he heard was an indistinguishable mumble of sound.

"Kelly!" he called. "Kell, are you down here?" he was going to call again but the cellar door opened and a group of men approached.

Lights came on and Mark examined his prison, his heart plummeting when he saw there were no windows, just a metal grill in the wall that was too small for him to fit through. Metal cages encased the light on the ceiling, an intercom, and a camera. A row of metal rings was above his head. The walls appeared to be cement, except for the wall that the door to the cell was on. That wall was wood covered with chain link. The wall had claw marks and tufts of fur in it. Mark sniffed deeply trying to sort out the smells. An animal had been caged here recently. He could smell feces and urine and a harsh musty scent that reminded him of panthers and bobcats although it was slightly different. He knew it was a big feline of some sort. The floor beneath the hay had been recently cleaned. It was still slightly damp and smelled strongly of cleaning products.

The cell door looked new. It had a small window blocked with a wire screen that opened and closed from the outside and a narrow passthrough obviously meant to be used to slide food through. The gap on the bottom was barely big enough for a mouse. He'd never get his hand beneath it. A covered five-gallon pail was to the left of the door and a case of water bottles was to the right. He eyed the bottles longingly.

A man said, "You're certain it's a werewolf and not just a wolf?"

"Dead certain," Steve said.

"And it's alive? It looks dead."

"It's alive."

"What about that?"

"That's the money right there. It's just a pup. We can raise it and it won't matter at all if the others don't cooperate."

Mark's heart began to thump hard enough to make hearing difficult. They had Marcus and likely Kelly.

A new man accompanied Steve into his cell and Mark knew he was looking at the money behind the operation. The new man was clean shaven and wore an expensive suit, a Rolex, a fake tan, and a manicure. He carried a cell phone that he slid into his suit jacket pocket as Steve gestured expansively.

"So...." Suit waved Steve away. "Give us a few minutes."

Steve glowered but left.

Suit waited for the door to close to say, "I'm sorry we're starting out on the wrong foot like this. I hope you can see past our introduction and can appreciate what I'm willing to do for you."

"Let me see my wife, please."

"In due time. Let's get to know each other a bit first."

He frowned around the bare room then shrugged. "I admit, this setting makes negotiations difficult but it's prudency. We can't take the chance you won't hear us out."

"I'm listening," Mark said dryly.

"I've spoken with your wife's sister. She's an unpleasant person and I'm not certain how much she really knows or even if she spoke truthfully."

Mark said nothing.

Suit stared at him a moment, clearly debating how to proceed. He finally said, "I'd hoped we could reach a mutually beneficial arrangement."

"You aren't making friends by caging me like this."

Suit flicked his fingers dismissively. "Is Richard Henderson a werewolf?"

Mark said nothing.

Suit sighed hard. He tapped his fingers on his thigh a moment than said, "Stacy claims speaking of werewolves is a death sentence, and I agree it's a prudent precaution, but since I know of you already, what could it hurt to speak openly?"

Mark said, "There's no such thing as werewolves."

Suit's eyes narrowed. He'd clearly angered him. Mark said, "I don't even know who I'm speaking with. This room is under surveillance. Steve told me pointedly he was recording audio and I have no idea who else might be listening in. I'm not saying shit until I see my wife and you can assure me our talks are private."

Suit nodded thoughtfully as he gazed about the cell again. He turned and banged on the door. It opened immediately and Steve smirked at Mark.

Suit said, "Let him see his wife and turn off the listening devices."

"How the fuck—"

"You brought him in here, didn't you? How hard could it be to drag him out or her in? Jesus, just get it done. And bring me in a chair. Shackle him so we can have a more civilized talk."

"He can transform and slip free from shackles."

"Not before I can shoot his ass and get out the door. Stacy said it took the wolf a minute or two—"

"He was faster."

"Maybe but I doubt he's faster than a bullet."

"Whatever you say," Steve said.

It was clear by his tone that Steve didn't care if Mark killed the man.

Suit shook his head and strode from the room.

Steve yelled, "Turn off the security for a minute, Mike!"

Small red lights that had been blinking on the devices in the corners of his cage darkened.

"Have you fed it?" Suit asked.

Mark strained against his bonds but couldn't see more than Suit's feet through the open doorway.

Suit was leaning forward but he jerked back as Marcus growled and metal rattled.

"Damn it!" Suit snapped.

"It's not safe to go near it," Steve said smugly.

"Bring it upstairs."

"Let me see my wife!" Mark called, but the men all ignored him. "Please, my uncle will pay good money. If you let us go, I won't even report this. Please, just let me see her!"

214

None of them had mentioned his daughter. It made a cold sweat break out on his face and his stomach flip to think they'd killed her. He was afraid to mention her and give Suit ideas. Maybe Suit didn't know about her and Steve hoped to ransom her. He had to know how rare female werewolves were and Kelly's daughter would be worth a fortune. He gulped back his nausea as he struggled futilely with his bonds.

Chapter 24

teve returned within minutes bringing a chain and two sets of handcuffs. He cut Mark free and used both sets of handcuffs on him while Mike pressed a gun to Mark's temple.

Steve took the gun from Mike when he was finished and tugged the chain. "Give me any shit and your bitch will pay. I'll make her wish she'd never been born."

Mike said smugly, "Stacy told us she's scared as shit of dogs. We got her a nice surprise if you try anything. Even if you killed one of us, you won't get by us all and I'll make sure you see what we do to her."

Marcus began to whine. Men outside Mark's cage door spoke in low laughing tones, calling to Marcus.

It took Mark two tries to get to his feet. Steve laughed as he tugged him forward by his shirt and dropped him in front of the wire cage that held Kelly.

It was clear by her limpness that she was unconscious. Marcus began to bark when he saw him.

He wished he could cuddle him but the best he could do was rest his forehead against the metal so Marcus could lick his face.

"Let me see my wife, please."

Steve hit him hard enough to knock him to the floor.

"Cut the shit. You know that's her!"

Mark bit back his groan as he turned to stick his bound hands against the cage. Her cage was chain link and didn't fit the décor of the room that looked as if it had once been a fancy wine cellar. Another nearly identical, empty, chain-link cage was across from her. Hoses were coiled neatly by a row of water spickets and two shovels and a broom leaned against the paneled walls.

A fancy wooden table and four chairs were to the left of the stairs with a rack holding wine bottles behind it. There was a stack of wooden kegs beneath an oil painting that was lit by discrete lighting. A built-in shelf beside the alarm pad held glassware and a small sink.

Scuff marks on the tile floor showed where other racks had been recently removed to make room for the cages. His cell was also paneled along the front, the door hidden behind paneling and another oil painting. A cursory search of the room wouldn't reveal it.

He examined the marks on the floors and walls again and realized they were marks from brackets that could be used to rearrange the chain link. The accoutrements of a wine cellar left behind were props. They likely had shelves and cases of wine somewhere that they could place here and further hide his cell. Whatever this room was, it was clear it was used frequently to hold either animals or people.

"You're all fucking crazy," Mark said.

Steve nudged him with his foot, grinning as he dropped the key to his cuffs in his pocket. "You seen her. Let's go." He yanked Mark away and Marcus barked shrilly.

Suit said, "Cooperate and we can all be friends."

Mark snorted and Steve laughed.

"Yo!" a new man called, and Suit turned to the stairs.

Suit said, "I'll feed the pup after I've spoken to his father."

One of the men said, "What did you want us to do with the drone?"

Suit returned to the stairs and Steve glanced over his shoulder and then leaned closer to whisper. "There can only be one alpha dog and that's me."

A cold sweat sprang up on Mark's brow. Steve knew there was no way he and Stacy could ever be friends.

Chapter 25

Steve shackled Mark to the wall of his cell and kicked his feet out from under him.

Mark said, "How'd you get out of jail anyway?"

"I'm out on bail, if you can believe that shit." He snickered as he jerked a thumb at the door. "Howard is an asshole but an asshole with real pull. He's got connections and all the toys."

So, Suit's name was Howard, Mark thought as he said, "You're going to kill him though."

Steve laughed again. "That's what I like about your kind. You're pragmatic."

A cold sick feeling settled in Mark's gut. Steve was working with Frank; he was sure of it. He wondered if Howard knew.

Mike stuck his head through the doorway and said, "He's having his men make her a room upstairs. The stupid shit is going to get us all killed."

Steve said, "Get Ed and Henry and tell them to have their crew standing by."

"Right 'oh, Boss."

Mike left.

Mark was certain the recordings in this room were off by the way the men were speaking. He said, "She can't shift. Neither can he."

Steve smirked. "We know."

"My daughter?"

Footsteps on the stairs warned the others were coming. Steve glanced over his shoulder and his expression hardened.

Howard said, "Leave him alone."

"We're just chatting," Steve said.

He turned back, grinning an evil grin. "She burned. Roasted like a suckling pig. Squealed like a pig too."

Mark began to shake. He gagged and retched, his daughter's cries seeming to ring in his ears.

"I said leave him alone!" Howard snapped.

Steve shrugged. "He's not going to cooperate, no how."

Two men brought in chairs from the main room that they placed before the cell door.

Another brought in a table and another a small cooler.

Howard had them move one of the chairs beside Mark and he sat in the one at the table.

"Give me your gun," Howard said, snapping his fingers at Steve.

Steve glowered but placed his pistol on the table.

"Leave us alone," Howard said briskly.

Mark knew the new men were Howard's men by their professional demeanor. They wore combat gear and carried rifles with flashlights and silver knives on their belts, and all of them had a handgun either sheathed beside the knife or in an ankle holster or both. Steve's men by comparison were scruffy. All four of the ones Mark had seen so far wore leather jackets and silver crosses. They carried the same weapons but also had spray bottles in their back pockets, except for Steve. He carried two knives, one of which was big enough to be considered a machete.

Steve left, closing the door behind himself, and Howard sat.

He appeared to be unarmed. If Mark could get his hands free, he could kill him in moments, but he was weak, shaky and nauseated. His pulse pounded hard and he had to drag his gaze from the water bottles. He stared at Howard's feet and tried to breathe shallowly. Mark's wolf wanted this man dead with a fury he'd never felt before.

Howard said, "My name is Howard Cirillo and I have connections that can make your life much easier. I'm sorry about your daughter. I know that's no consolation, but I really had nothing to do with her death. That fire was none of my doing."

"You do know Steve and his friends are crazy, right?"

Howard laughed a moment and nodded. "But useful. They had connections I needed. Steve's overstepped his bounds and he'll be dealt with."

"He's going to kill you. You're a fool to trust him."

"I assure you, I have the situation well in hand."

Mark snorted.

Howard said, "Let's ignore all that for the moment. I want us to be friends, comrades even. I have a lot to offer you and your pack, and I sincerely regret the way we're meeting. I'd intended to approach in a more civilized manner…"

"Then why didn't you?'

Howard pursed his lips.

Mark said, "My uncle will pay you whatever you ask to get us back."

Howard flicked his fingers. "This isn't about money. I have plenty of money and I'm willing to use my funds and connections on your pack's behalf. Is all I ask for in return is access to some, shall we call them test subjects? I'd like a few volunteers or if you have criminals, I could use them."

"You want to experiment on us?"

"Nothing too invasive. I assure you, the tests can all be performed with a minimum of discomfort."

"Sure, do whatever tests you like on me. I'll cooperate with anything you want just let my wife go home."

"I'm afraid that isn't an option. At least right now. Stacy was under the impression that female werewolves are very rare and that few women survive the transformation if they're bitten."

Mark shrugged and nodded.

Howard's eyes narrowed. "Frank confirmed her information in almost every regard."

It shocked him that Howard knew about Frank, but he shrugged as if it didn't matter. "Frank is a liar and a sociopath. I wouldn't put much credence in anything he has to say."

"He tells me that your cousin Richard is the alpha of your pack."

Mark snorted. "Are you special needs? Seriously, think about this logically for a minute. You just said female werewolves are rare and yet Richard is married and I have a sister. Or do you think it's just Richard, Kelly, and I?"

"You're saying he isn't?"

Mark said, "I'm saying I'll cooperate in any test you want to perform. I don't know what horseshit you've been sold but werewolves aren't real. Her sister is crazy. The only true part of her tale is that my wife was bitten by a dog years ago. Do some research and you'll see Kelly never did anything at all odd. It was Stacy who was crazy and made all this shit up. Stacy hates her sister and would do or say anything to make her life miserable. Did she tell you that she used to blow guys for ten bucks at Kelly's high school games? Did she tell you how Kelly worried about her and gave her money? Kelly would've done anything for her sister."

"Not, I think, told her that she'd been made a werewolf. That very love would have stopped her." Howard spread his hands on the table. "We won't get anywhere if you persist with these lies. We have your wife and son—"

"My son was murdered," Mark said harshly.

"Then how do you explain the wolf and pup in the next cell?"

"How do you explain having these cells? Look at those scratches. This cell has been used in the past to hold animals. Who the hell knows what you crazies are up to!"

Howard said, "If you persist with these lies, we'll have no choice but to take extreme measures."

"I'm cooperating! I said you could do your tests. What else do you want from me?"

"Talk your wife into cooperating. Answer my questions honestly and I mean full disclosure. And in return, I'll keep Steven and his men away from both of you. I'll speak with Richard and he and I can work out a mutually beneficial arrangement. Think how much better I could make your pack mates' lives."

Mark snorted in disgust. "Richard is doing pretty well. What makes you think he needs your help?"

"He is and it's admirable but he's wasting opportunities—*your* opportunities. There's no need to scrape by in your tiny homes working nine to five at low paying jobs. The world could be yours—cars, women, anything you wanted! And I can make that all happen. I can get you passports and ID's and you'd never have to worry another moment about being found out."

"Are you government?"

"No, nothing as ineffectual as that. I'm talking real power."

"How did you find us?"

Howard grinned and nodded, leaning back in his seat. "It was easy actually. We thought you'd be close by and it didn't take more than two weeks to find you with our drones."

"You're lying."

"I admit, Frank helped narrow the area but he only cut down the search time. We'd have found you eventually."

"Why not just go to Richard now?"

"If I want to negotiate, I need to know what the pack wants, how they operate—what their weaknesses are."

He folded his hands, smiling his smug smile that Mark wanted to rip from his face.

"You're going to tell me everything. Why not make it easier on her?"

Mark slumped against the wall, closing his eyes. "They want my wife. If you hurt her, Richard will never deal with you."

"She's special like Stacy said or is it just because she's female?"

"She's special. There's never been anyone like her before. She's not as strong as a regular werewolf though. She could be killed much easier than me.

Female werewolves are always delicate and she's very fragile. Werewolves have a hard time breeding but not Kelly. In that respect she's much stronger than the rest of the females in the pack."

"How many female wolves are there?"

"Twenty-seven in our pack but only a few have had children. There's over a hundred males."

Howard's eyes narrowed.

Mark said, "Everyone at Howls is one of us. Most are very weak. The strong wolves need to be outside most of the time. Caging us like this will kill us."

A distant howl from Marcus made Mark cringe.

Howard acted as if he couldn't hear it and continued speaking, "*Ahh*, I'd wondered why he worked as a game warden."

Mark nodded. "We won't last more than a week or two without fresh meat and fresh water. We need to sleep on live plants too, but even that won't prolong our lives by much if we're caged indoors."

Marcus continued to howl and bark and Howard's brow wrinkled. Mark almost smiled. It was clear Howard hadn't counted on how stubbornly Marcus would insist on seeing his mother.

"How come one of your offspring was human and the other not? Which one of them was flawed?"

Mark lunged forward, the chains jerking him back. He fell to his knees and panted hard a moment.

Howard said, "I don't mean to be insensitive. It just seems very odd."

"Go fuck yourself," Mark shouted hoarsely.

He let himself fall to his side.

Howard stood and picked up his cellphone. "We can continue this discussion at a later date. One of my technicians will be in shortly, and if you do cooperate, I'll take that as a sign that you can be trusted. Meanwhile, I'll see to your wife's comfort."

A howl built in Mark's throat that he held back by gritting his teeth so hard he heard one crack. The pressure from his wolf made him writhe on the floor and he vomited without warning. He retched and gagged until only dry heaves remained.

When he finally pulled himself together he crawled to the wall to tug on his bonds.

Chapter 26

Mark allowed two men in white coats to shackle and hobble him and he followed without complaint as they led him up the stairs.

The house was much bigger than he'd thought. The cellar they were in must have been built after the house was finished because the stairs came out in a closet built into an exterior wall. The cellar wasn't under the house at all.

The room's windows looked over a small garden and a graveled drive that led to a barn. If his wife and child weren't trapped, he'd have jumped through the window, shifted in the brush, and ran for it— but they *were* trapped. He might get away, but he doubted Howard would leave her there long enough for him to come back with help, be it pack or the police. He hoped Richard knew they'd been taken and was already tracking them, but he doubted that Richard even knew they were gone yet. Richard wouldn't begin to worry until Mark didn't show up for his weekly supplies and he wasn't due to do that for two more days.

The next room had a twenty-foot ceiling and wide windows with decorative trim. It was furnished with antique furnishings, leather furniture, and an assortment of animal mounts, including one of an elephant.

The two men led him through that room, another room that wasn't quite as large with less taxidermy mounts and plusher furniture, and a library that was three stories tall with curved walls, window seats and the biggest mahogany desk Mark had ever seen.

One of the walls proved to be a hidden entrance to an elevator shaft.

They went down one level and exited into a white tiled room with bright lights and an assortment of medical apparatus. Glass walls separated the different workstations in the center of the room, most with drawn shades. He could see five men and two women were busily at work in the cubicles without the shades drawn. The corridor went in a square around the center glassed workspaces with closed doors around the outside edge.

This cellar was also an addition built under the front lawn. Mark estimated it was slightly longer than the house he'd seen.

One of his guards paused to examine a computer screen right inside the door and said, "Good, we can go right in. No one is scheduled for another hour."

He led Mark passed an alcove that contained shelving holding photographic equipment, an assortment of lights and an array of printers, a few shelves of paper, and two computer workstations, at one of which a woman was working. Backdrops hung from a pole, only two of which Mark caught glimpses of. One appeared to be the sort police used in lineups and another was of a hotel lobby. An open door to the left of the woman led to a bathroom and another door to her right led to a dressing room of some kind. An assortment of clothing hung on moveable racks and a countertop was strewn with makeup.

His pack had a setup very like this one, albeit on a smaller scale, that they used to change their identities.

They passed a closed door labeled '*Suite One*' and Mark slowed to sniff deeply.

A man exited the next door and Mark's guards stopped. They didn't move forward until the man entered a room two down from the one that he'd exited.

Every doorway was labeled with a suite number and had an alarm pad on it. Only one had open blinds. The suite appeared to be an empty hospital room.

"What do you do here?" Mark asked.

The man shrugged and used a swipe card and punched in a code on a keypad beside a door to enter an empty glass cubicle. A hose was coiled in a corner and the floor had a drain in the center. Lights in the ceiling brightened when they entered, and the door closed with a whoosh of air that made Mark think it was sealed.

Only one of the men had accompanied him into the room and he pressed on a tile beside the door that slid open to reveal water controls.

"If you'd remove your clothing, please?"

Mark lifted an eyebrow, glancing around and the man shrugged again.

Mark sighed hard but began removing his clothes.

The man said, "I'll be right back with a key for the restraints and some soaps. You'll be able to hear us through the speaker there" –he pointed to a grill in the ceiling— "We can vent the room, so don't be a dick."

No one working in the neighboring glass cubicles paid him any attention, which made him believe they were used to people being brought in wearing shackles.

The man returned and removed his restraints, replacing them with plastic cuffs that connected to retractable metal cables that were hidden behind the tiles.

Mark washed as he was ordered and then he was taken to another cubicle. This one had a plastic table and a variety of machines. It smelled of disinfectant, blood, perspiration, and fear.

"Sit here, please."

Mark said, "What's your name?"

"You can call me Hans and that's George." Han's said, indicating the other white coated man who now stood in the doorway holding a cattle prod.

"That won't be necessary, George," Mark said.

George winked, grinned sardonically. "I'll be the judge of that."

Hans shook his head at George and waved Mark to a seat on a table that was surrounded by what Mark thought were x-ray machines.

Mark said, "Can I get a robe or something?"

"The x-rays shouldn't take long. I'll position you and if you'll just hold the position until I say, we'll be done before you know it."

Mark held his arm as the man wished and was told to hold his breath. "Is this safe?"

"No talking, please."

Hans stepped into a small booth to observe a screen, ignoring Mark's questions. He was turned and repositioned for an hour and then taken to another machine where he had dental x-rays and then a CAT scan and then he was given something vile to drink and led to another machine. They took blood, hair, skin, and urine samples, and did a rectal exam. Finally, he was weighed, measured and photographed and asked about every bruise and laceration, which were also measured.

Hans handed him a plastic cup and said, "We need a sperm sample."

"You expect me to jack off here in front of everyone? No fucking way. I'm not here for your fucking amusement."

George said, "Do it or—"

Hans cut him off with a sharp wave of his hand. "The doctors will decide appropriate methods. Mr. Miller is being very cooperative and that test can wait!"

George pursed his lips but snatched the plastic cup from Mark.

Mark frowned as he considered his options. It was clear by the way men spoke and acted that his cooperation meant shit to his predicament. It only made their jobs easier, but he needed time to get the lay of the land here. Every man and woman here would need to be killed and the equipment and recordings destroyed, and he needed to know who'd seen them and where copies were kept. More importantly, he needed to know how many of them believed in werewolves and why they did.

Hans gave him a bottled water and a ham sandwich and left him in the shower cubicle to eat it. He could hear Hans and George talking although it was very muffled. They were complaining about missing their weekend off and arguing about going into town or not. Apparently they needed a pass of some kind to leave this compound and passes where difficult to get.

A man wearing a suit carrying a briefcase and trailed by four younger men in white lab jackets passed. The suited man paused to examine Mark and one of the lab-jacketed men gave Hans an irritated glower and touched a panel beside the door that darkened the glass.

He said, "I'm sorry, sir. I'd no idea anyone was being processed. I'll see that it doesn't happen again, but I assure you, he's nothing to worry about."

"Is he the source of my kidney?"

"I believe your donor is already in theater three."

Bile rose in Mark's throat. The sandwich he'd just eaten felt laden in his stomach. Howard was trafficking in human organs. Sweat broke out on his brow when he considered why Howard would want werewolves. If Howard thought they regenerated he could harvest them indefinitely.

They were letting him see too much. They had no intention of ever letting him go.

Two hours later, Hans led him back to his cell. Kelly was curled in a tight ball in the back corner of her cell. He was careful to do no more than glance at her. Someone had left a blanket on the moldy straw in his cell.

Hans said "Thank you for cooperating. Someone will be back to get you in four hours. Sleep if you can and I'll have a meal brought to you and this room arranged more for your liking."

It felt as if he'd just fallen asleep when George poked him with the cattle prod.

"Fuck!" he snarled as he jumped to his feet.

George snickered as he backed to the door. "It was on its lowest setting. If you feel it again, it'll be on high. Don't give me any shit. Let's go—and leave the blanket."

He was led to the same lab and told to shower. George led him to another cubicle, this one with a door that led to a small office.

The man at the desk said, "Restrain him but use the padded restraints." He smiled at Mark as he said, "It's just a precaution. My name is Doctor Fisher and I thought we could go over your test results."

Mark said, "Making me walk around naked isn't making me feel very warm and friendly toward you."

"My oversite completely. George, fetch him a hospital gown if you'd be so kind."

George said, "I shouldn't leave you alone with him."

Mark said, "I'm cooperating."

George grunted and Mark shrugged.

Fisher said, "Well, on your way out then." He turned his computer monitor so Mark could see it too. "You're in very good shape and I find it a bit odd. You've never had a broken bone or a cavity, no surgeries, no medical records that I could find."

Mark shrugged again. "Good genes, I guess. I have medical records, not many but there are some. I was raised in Alaska and we didn't get to town much."

"You were home schooled?"

"If you can call it that…"

"Are your parents still living?"

"Yes."

"Yes?" Fisher paused with his pen raised, obviously expecting that to be a no. "Really?"

"Why does that surprise you?"

"I suppose it shouldn't. They'd likely be living if you were born a werewolf, but I assumed you'd be unwilling to give their names."

"Well, first, there's no such thing as werewolves, and I am unwilling to give their names but it's public record and easy enough to find out."

"So you're claiming now you're not a werewolf?"

"I wish I was. I'd tell you everything to save my wife. I could claim to be one but have no way to fake it. I'll give you anything I can. If you let me call my uncle, I'm sure we could work something out. He'd pay to get us back."

"*Ahh*, Richard Henderson." Fisher leaned back in his seat, tenting his hands. "You claimed earlier Richard the younger was a werewolf."

"Howard claimed it, I just agreed. I'm trying to be agreeable."

"Lies won't help you here."

"I figured as much, which is why I'm telling you that you're misguided with this."

Fisher shrugged and Mark realized this man didn't believe. His disbelief wasn't going to stop him from doing as he was told though. It was also clear that to Fisher, Mark wasn't even a person but a job.

"George, take him to Doctor Smith."

George snickered quietly as he unlocked the restraints holding Mark to the chair. He snapped a pair of cuffs on Mark and took a pole with a noose on the end from a cabinet beside the door and put the noose around Mark's neck.

"It's like that, is it?" Mark asked grimly.

"Let's just say I doubt you'll be cooperating long."

Chapter 27

"Can you take me to see my wife first?" Mark asked.

"No."

"Because she isn't here?"

George shrugged and tightened the noose, tugging Mark forward. The shrug made Mark think George wasn't a believer either. Mark still planned to kill him though.

The lab was emptier now. Only two men were still at work and George went out of his way to pass the room they were working in.

Mark's breath caught in his throat and he stumbled. A wolf was being dissected on a metal table. The parts were being measured and weighed and for a moment he thought it was Kelly, but the blood-soaked fur was a darker shade of grey and the faintest whiff told him it was Frank's wife, Sheila.

"Gross," Mark said, and George laughed again.

"You're a sadistic fuck, aren't you?"

"What can I say—I love my job."

He tugged him harder, making Mark gag as he led him down the hallway.

"Here you go, Doc, as ordered," he said as he thrust Mark into a new room.

Smith pointed to a chair in the center of the tiled room. The room had a drain in the center and sealed the same way as the shower had. It was bigger though with a low counter and a few machines in the corner.

"Restrain him and then you can go."

George snickered again.

"Enough of that. I don't want my results biased. Restrain him and go!"

Smith began hooking electrodes to Mark's body. When he was finished, he draped a thin sheet over his lap and pulled a wheeled cart forward.

"This is a simple lie detector. Yes or no answers only."

He asked Mark a series of questions that Mark lied about whenever he thought Smith wouldn't know the truth. His wolf raged within him. He was concentrating more on holding it back than the test.

Smith frowned at the results. "Well you didn't appear to lie but the readings are suspiciously similar." He stood and rummaged in a cabinet a moment, withdrawing a cattle prod similar to the one that George had used.

"Let's try this again." He turned a dial on the prod and tapped Mark's shoulder.

Fire licked along Mark's nerves. He only managed to mutter an oath as he jerked against his bonds.

This time Smith asked the questions faster and repetitively, shocking Mark if he hesitated in answering or if Smith didn't like the result.

Mark's wolf roiled beneath his skin more painfully than the shocks at first.

"You're going to kill me," Mark said when he could catch his breath from the latest round of questions. His skin shivered and hummed and his muscles ached from the force of his contortions.

Smith said, "It appears you're telling the truth—or perhaps your werewolf biochemistry allows you to manipulate the results." He took a cell phone from his pocket and made a call, saying, "George, clean him up and bring him to exam room one. Tell Doctor Fisher to finish his tests and preform a hearing test, the olfactory test, and get a base line on his sense of taste. He can feed him if he wishes but I want records on when he eats and defecates."

George arrived a few minutes later and led him back the way they'd come. A woman stood at the door of the autopsy room arguing with the men there.

"I'm not cooking that," she said angrily.

"Tell the boss that. Our job is to give it to you. Sign for it and it's your problem."

Mark gagged on the bile that rose in his throat.

She said, "I'm not a butcher. How the hell can I make steak tartare from that?"

The man shrugged and handed her a white plastic sack. "Organ meat all labeled but the rest is up to you. We saved the blood as requested. I'll bring it down after I clean up here."

"This is just ridiculous. We need a butcher on staff if he's going to keep doing this."

She flounced away, tugging the cart that still smelled of Sheila beneath the bloody meat odors.

Sweat streamed down Mark's brow but his bound hands prevented him from wiping it.

George thrust him into the shower room and hosed him down with cold water and then gave him a hospital gown.

He brought him to another cubicle and shackled him to a chair.

Fisher entered and George said, "As ordered."

"Take a break," Fisher said. He waited for the door to close to say, "You don't look at all well."

"You're going to kill me and eat me, how am I supposed to look?"

Fisher winced. "I've received no notice of that. As far as I know, we're just trying to determine if you're a werewolf or not."

"You know I'm not."

Fisher shrugged, saying, "I don't make the rules."

"Bullshit. You could get us help. None of you are turning a hair when you see a naked cuffed man being tortured. What kind of sick fucks are you?"

"We do good work here. Important work. I'm sure Mr. Cirillo will tell you all about it if you join us."

"Ha! You know he's going to kill me. Sooner or later he'll realize I can't give him what he wants and then what? I figure I have until the next full moon, but I don't even know when that is," he lied.

"Two weeks. But there's other ways you could make yourself useful."

"Work for him, you mean?"

"I'm sure—"

Mark interrupted with a harsh bark of laughter. "Seriously, you think he's going to give me a job? What about my wife? What about my daughter that he murdered? You think none of that matters? She was three months old for Christ's sake!" Mark took a deep trembling breath and wiped his stinging eyes. His head pounded with the worst headache of his life.

"I have nothing to do with any of that. Let's just get this over with."

Fisher performed his tests quickly and gave him a ham sandwich and a bottled water. He left him in the cubicle, shackled by one hand for two hours. Mark debated not eating. Food would speed his healing up. If he fully hydrated his injuries would mend within a day or so, much too fast for a human. His room was

241

monitored, which would make it really difficult to hurt himself purposefully but if he were too weak he'd be useless in a fight and he didn't have the willpower to turn away the water completely. The best he could do was sip it slowly.

Smith finally showed up with a stack of folders that he was browsing. "Let's see if we get the same results."

This time the hearing test knocked him out. He came to with George slapping his cheek. George hauled him up and grabbed his jaw.

"Open your mouth or I'll fucking break your jaw."

Smith dabbed something in his mouth that made him vomit and George slapped his cheek.

"Expected response," Smith said mildly. "Let him rinse and we'll try the next."

"Fuck you! I'm done cooperating with you assholes. You know I'm just a regular guy and are torturing me for the fun of it. You're never going to let me go or see my wife!" He bit George's hand and George screamed and jumped away.

"He fucking bit me!"

"Let me see," Smith said.

George swung at Mark and Mark ducked away but his bonds wouldn't allow him to avoid the blow entirely. He was almost smug about it. The new injuries would mask the older healing ones.

George continued to hit him until Smith yanked him back.

"I said let me see it!" He grabbed George's hand and dragged him to the counter. "It's bleeding. I want some swabs and to see it beneath a microscope."

"I'm going to fucking die!"

"Maybe not. Some live. You'll have the best care we can give you."

These men truly believed, Mark thought worriedly.

"You've got to be kidding me," Mark said. "He isn't going to turn into a werewolf. Don't be ridiculous!"

Smith pursed his lips and said, "Go to my office and send me Hans."

George hit him again before he left, and Smith said, "There's no point in denying what you are. We know all about you. There's a man in the next room who your wife bit. I don't think he'll live but we'll see. We'll certainly see in a few weeks. Why make these weeks harder than they need to be?"

"My wife doesn't bite people. If you mean that wolf downstairs bit that guy, maybe the bite is just infected or the wolf is rabid or something."

"They saw you shift!"

Mark rolled his eyes. "Sure they did. I bet I was with Big Foot when I did it too and had just gotten off the mothership."

"These are trustworthy men."

Mark laughed so hard tears came to his eyes. "Oh my God, that's rich. You're a bunch of lying thugs who'd sell your own mothers for a buck. Seriously, I wouldn't believe a guy like George if he said the sky was blue. I bet they *forgot* to film it or their cameras malfunctioned or some shit, right?"

Smith's expression darkened. He pointed to a black globe on the ceiling. "The camera's here are recording everything. When we're ready to show the world, we'll have inconvertible scientific proof!"

"Sure you will." Mark smiled smugly certain by the doctor's anger that they hadn't caught him or Kelly shifting on camera.

Smith said, "I think it's time we did that pain tolerance test now."

"Go fuck yourself," Mark said.

Smith gave him a shot in the arm.

Mark wasn't certain what the shot was supposed to do. He felt no different. It wasn't until Smith grabbed his arm that he realized the shot was intended to slow him, maybe even put him to sleep. It took effort to move his arms and doing so made the doctors eyes light so he stopped moving.

Smith shackled both of his hands and then his feet. The bar he'd been shackled to lowered, forcing him to hunch over.

"I'll know if you're faking," Smith said pleasantly. "Just answer honestly and it will be over quickly."

"Go fuck yourself," Mark said the words emerging with a drunken slur.

Smith laughed.

What felt like a hot coal touched Mark's back.

He yelled even though it hadn't actually hurt that much.

"Ah…" Smith said in satisfaction.

Fuck, Mark thought as he realized he'd jumped. He steeled himself not to move but still jerked a bit at the next hot pain.

The heat lasted longer the next time but it didn't actually hurt much. He was able to hold still.

Smith increased the length and duration then began slicing lines across his back.

Mark screamed as if they hurt, and they did hurt but not as much as he was acting as if they did. He knew from Matti's testing that werewolves didn't feel pain like a human did. Even serious injuries would only hurt for a short time and then be a manageable pain. Richard had taught all of them how to fake human reactions. They were taught to recognize when injuries should hurt and the usual human response. He was careful not to jerk away but moaned and cried out as if the cuts were truly painful.

"I suppose we'll need to do this again," Smith said cheerfully. "Now, let's see what this does."

He placed a plastic bag over Mark's head.

Mark fought his wolf as he gasped for air. *He isn't going to kill is. They need us,* he thought desperately. His wolf retreated suddenly and completely. Mark slipped into the dark, barely feeling the sting of a needle.

Mark lay motionless, unable to even open his eyes. The shot he'd been given had worked but not, he was certain, as Smith had intended. It had knocked him out but only his body. Smith left and Josh and Hans entered.

It took Mark a few minutes to gain the upper hand on his wolf. The wolf was focused on attack, cataloguing what it could hear and smell, ignoring the words the men spoke. Mark was able to shift his attention once his wolf realized it was still trapped.

Josh was saying, "—no idea he really believed in all this."

Hans said, "Mr. Cirillo is convinced. We've never found any conclusive proof but he's more certain than ever this time."

Josh snorted. "Fools and their money are soon parted."

Both men laughed.

Hans said, "Give me a hand with him. We'll soon know all about Mr. Miller."

Josh said, "What a waste of time."

Mark would have smiled if he could have. Medical tests had never shown any differences. Matti had been doing them for years. Hearing tests were easy to fool when he knew what his wolf was reacting to. And as dehydrated as he was his injuries would heal slowly. He'd just have to keep himself dehydrated and encourage them to make new injuries. A sperm test might show differences or might not. He wasn't sure but he had no intention of cooperating with them.

Josh said, "The fucker's probably going to die if we don't treat his wounds."

Hans grunted agreement. "I've been ordered to measure and catalogue injuries and keep track of the rate of recovery but not to interfere unless it's deemed the wound is immediately life threatening."

The two drew closer as they spoke and lifted him.

Josh said, "Well, I don't like these recordings. Our company has a good reputation and if these were leaked…."

"The recordings are necessary. Mr. Cirillo is entirely aware of the delicate nature of our work and keeps the recordings under tight security."

"Well, I still don't like it. It gives him too much leverage on us."

"You're being paid very well and he's on the tapes himself."

"True…"

The two men threw Mark back into the shower stall, not being gentle about it. They hosed him down and it brought him around enough he could stand but he lay there as if he was still incapacitated. They left him alone, which was worse then their experiments. It gave him to much time to consider what they were doing to his wife and son.

Chapter 28

Kelly lay perfectly still, trying to sort the scents and sounds as she catalogued the pains in her body.

Marcus grumbled softly, his body a spot of warmth against her aching ribs.

The paw that had been shot off ached a bit as did her lower back. Her throat burned and she fought the urge to cough until it burst from her.

"She's coming around, I think," a man said.

His voice made her headache throb.

"Get out of there," another man said.

Marcus barked, sending a shaft of pain through her head, making her whine, which made Marcus whimper. She nuzzled him weakly. The small effort made her pant.

"That's disgusting," Stacy said.

Kelly snarled and Marcus began to bark. Kelly yipped the bark that meant no and placed a paw on him.

248

She kept her eyes closed, opening them worsened her headache tenfold. She licked his face and continued to groom him while he whined and cowered against her.

A man said, "Miss Anderson, I'll thank you to speak civilly."

"She's disgusting."

"Henry, take Miss Anderson upstairs, please."

Stacy said, "Fine, whatever. I'll go."

Kelly sniffed deeply. Wherever she was there was live plants close by and water and meat. She smelled numerous men and the stench of Stacy's perfume that she'd hoped to never smell again.

Only three scents were strong and fresh enough to be men near her. She cracked her eyes, whining at the pain in her head but kept them open enough to examine her cage.

Wire enclosed her on three sides. The fourth was a paneled wall. She lay in hay between potted ferns. A dog bed was in the far corner. Potted trees and shrubs lined the back wall of her eight-by-eight cage.

She crawled to the back and wedged herself behind the plants.

Marcus followed.

A man in a fancy suit said, "Make sure her water is fresh and keep the cage clean. There's nothing to be afraid of, Mrs. Miller. My name is Howard Cirillo and I'm a friend. The cage is just a precaution. Your husband is here and cooperating with us. We'll let him visit shortly once our preliminary tests are done. If there's anything we can do to make your stay more pleasant just ask."

One of the men standing beside him laughed, quickly coughing to cover it.

Howard said, "Keep everyone out. Let's give them a nice peaceful night to think about their new circumstances."

The men left and turned off the lights.

Kelly examined her cage again and then the room beyond. She spied two cameras with small red lights behind wire cages, searching carefully for more but didn't spot any.

She growled softly, warning Marcus to stay then slunk from the meager shelter of the bushes to examine the water and food.

The water smelled fresh and she drank until her stomach felt bloated. It refreshed her, lessening her headache considerably. She examined her cage again, sniffing along all the edges looking for weaknesses.

A rattle warned her someone was coming. She thought the noise emanated from the cage across from her so wasn't surprised when the back wall swung open to let an ATV pulling a small cart enter.

Two men tugged Frank from the back of the cart, letting him fall.

"Get the food and water while he's out," the older one said.

The younger one stepped through the open door to hit an alarm pad. The door of the cage clicked. He let himself from the cage and filled a bucket at the bar sink while the older man set out a covered bucket that Kelly thought was meant to be a toilet.

The door to the cage had relocked by the time the bucket was full.

The same sequence of sounds opened the door. She was able to see three of the five numbers he'd pressed and had an idea of the other two. By the time they'd finished cleaning Mark's cell, she'd learned the sounds for all of the numbers on the keypad.

The two men hadn't mentioned her daughter. She was hoping they'd leave the recorders off and she could question Frank but they turned them back on when they left.

She was still debating what to do when she heard the door at the top of the stairs open.

A whiff of blood—her husband's blood—made her growl.

Marcus barked shrilly but stopped when she growled. She slunk back behind the potted trees. Marcus followed and huddled against her. It took all of her willpower not to growl or throw herself against the bars of her cage like she wanted to.

She began to groom Marcus, steeling herself not to react.

She didn't dare do a thing that would make them believe that Stacy was right.

Chapter 29

Mark stopped dead at the bottom of the cellar stairs. Frank was in the cell across from Kelly. He looked older, drawn and pale with white in his once coal black hair. He reeked of fear and Stacy's perfume.

"So, Stacy sold you out. It couldn't happen to a more deserving man."

"Fuck you, asshole! I hope they torture you to fucking death!"

Hans pushed Mark forward.

Mark said, "Everything that happens is your fault. You know that, right?"

"You fucking murdered my son!"

"I had nothing to do with it. Your son was as twisted as Stacy is. He fucking killed himself! You sold out your family for nothing! What the hell did you tell her anyway?"

"That I'd find you and kill your sorry ass!"

"How's that working out for you?"

"Shut the fuck up!"

Hans said, "You both shut the fuck up. Get in your goddamned cell."

Marcus yipped and ran to the cage door. Kelly barked and Marcus growled but returned to her.

Frank said, "I'm sorry about the kid though. I never meant for the kid to be hurt."

Mark stomped into his cell, and Hans kicked the back of his knees, knocking him down. He slipped the noose from Mark's neck and ran from the room. Mark staggered to his feet and thrust his hands through the slot to let Han's unshackle him.

He barely had the energy to stand never mind fight. He was covered with fresh bruises and his back twinged at each small movement. Smith had cut long scratches across his entire back, supposedly to measure the regeneration rate and his pain tolerance, but Mark thought he was getting off on it. He could still smell his own blood so he knew the cuts hadn't healed much.

At least the amount and placement of injuries would make it easier to hide his regeneration rate, he thought in annoyance. It worried him though because Kelly and Marcus would be able to smell his injuries as well. Knowing that it would scare them made him furious.

Hans thrust another ham sandwich and water bottle through the slot and Mark took them both to his bed to eat. It wouldn't be enough for his werewolf metabolism. He doubted he'd heal much by eating it. He was just glad they didn't try to serve him Sheila.

He shuddered as he contemplated that and wondered if Frank knew. He hoped not. He ate his sandwich as he pondered what Frank's plan was. Frank was a strong wolf. It would likely take him a few weeks to die. It must be hard as hell to hold back his wolf though. He'd have to kill him before he wolfed out and revealed himself as a werewolf, but how?

Chapter 30

Hans came for him four hours later. He thrust a water bottle into the cell that Mark could smell had been tampered with.

Frank yelled, "I'm not drinking this!"

"Drink it or I'll shoot you!"

"Go ahead. Or maybe you'd like to come in and force me!"

Marcus began to bark, and Kelly whined.

Mark yelled, "Just drink the fucking water! I'm sick of hearing you!"

Hans said, "You drink it too, asshole! It won't knock you out just make you a bit sluggish so we can get the restraints on. The alternative is a tranq dart but those can kill you and they hurt like hell, but it's your choice."

Frank said, "Guess you better tranq me then cause I ain't drinking this shit!"

Hans swore and Frank laughed. Marcus continued to bark while Kelly whined and growled at him. Mark knelt to peer through the slot.

Frank had thrown his water, splattering Hans, and he began kicking the cage.

Mark turned to face the camera and drank his water. He sat with his back to the door and his hands behind him. Kelly's low whines were fingernails on a chalkboard. He didn't think she could control herself if he fought them here. It was better if he went calmly.

Kelly called for Marcus again, grabbing his scruff and shaking him lightly when he returned to her. He lay beside her and they both watched as Hans called for backup. Josh and Eddy arrived a few minutes later.

Frank had managed to dent a big section of his chain link and she hoped they'd put Mark in the cell across from her and Frank in the other cell although that might be harder on Marcus.

Frank said, "Mark, tell your wife that I'm truly sorry that I involved her in this. You're right, I should've handled my son myself but Sheila... I still fucking hate you, but I never intended this. No one deserves to die like this..."

Josh shot him and he let out a loud oof, staggering back, plucking the dart from his shoulder and throwing it.

"I tried to make amends. Make these fuckers pay and kill that goddamned bitch! Tell my father I never—

He fell face first and lay motionless.

"Give him a jolt," Josh said.

Eddy said, "He's fast as shit. Keep me covered."

Frank didn't move when Eddy tapped him with the cattle prod. Josh called for more men and they carried him and Mark out.

Kelly couldn't help her low growl but none of them paid her any attention.

Josh called after the retreating men, "Kyle, tell them we're cleaning the cages and turning off the door alarms while we do it. The alarms are as annoying as fuck. Tell Hotchkiss I want that fixed ASAP. We need to be able to put these doors on a time delay or something without turning everything off."

"Will do!" one of the men yelled back, and Kelly put a name to the man. She had most of the ones she'd seen named and she'd know their scents, which were more distinct to her than their faces.

"We shouldn't do this with her in here," Eddy said as he withdrew a set of keys from his pocket.

Josh rolled his eyes. "What's she going to do—tell them? Besides, you need the code to open it."

Kelly watched carefully as Josh punched in a code on the keypad beside the stairs opening the door in the back wall of Frank's cell. Every time someone came in or out they punched in a code. Each number had a distinct tone that she'd memorized so she knew which buttons he'd hit even though he'd blocked the pad with his body. She knew the codes that turned off the alarm and the one to open the door. She didn't know the code to her cell yet but even if she did she had no way to reach the alarm pad even if she shifted, which she didn't dare do while the security was on and recording.

A whoosh of cool air brought the scents of hay and a meaty musty odor that she thought was dried dog food or something similar. The opening was wide enough to drive through, and the men made short work of raking out Mark's cell.

A minute later a loud clanking was followed by the low sound of an engine and Kelly jumped to her feet, growling softly to warn Marcus to stay.

A golf cart drove up to the opening and the men loaded the dirty hay into a cart it pulled.

Josh said, "Dump this and bring back a couple cots and two of the toilets."

The driver of the cart grabbed a hose from the wall of the new room and handed it to Josh. He leaned closer to whisper, "Macy is still looking but there's no sign of this drone footage."

Josh said, "Maybe it doesn't exist. This whole fucking thing is a scam. I wish I'd thought of it first."

"Still, I'd like to get my hands on it. Howard can't be the only gullible nutcase."

"Steve probably still has it. I've checked Cirillo's office both here and at his home. I even checked his safe. There's a ton of cash in it. We should set up a hit."

"Not until we've milked this dry. I hear he's got three men scheduled for facial surgery and another two revenge cases. If you keep copying that footage, we'll have enough blackmail material we can all live like kings for the rest of our lives. Get Macy looking for a buyer for the pup. I figure he's got to be worth three figures easy."

"He's going to notice if it goes missing."

"We don't need this pup. We need *a* pup. I have Owens looking into Frank's background. There's bound to be someone we can snatch, and it'll be child's play to convince Howard it's a werewolf. Is all we need is another wolf."

"Fucking genius."

"We need this done fast before he realizes he's been duped. Mark's a pussy. He'll tell Howard anything he wants to hear. We need some alone time with him to drop some clues. Maybe we can get him to tell Howard that female werewolves have to stay a wolf until the kid reaches puberty or something and males have to stay human."

Eddy said, "I'll get Macy researching the myths."

Josh said, "We need Steve's crew out. Let them go a little overboard. Howard won't put up with his pets being abused."

"Maybe we can make him think they snatched the pup."

The two men bumped fists.

Kelly used her claw to draw a circle around a mouse she'd just caught and killed. She touched its nose lightly and then tapped Marcus's nose while whining the sound that meant good boy.

She wasn't sure how well he could see. The room was dark and she was crouched over him.

She tapped the mouse and then him and then the planter beside her. She did it again and this time picking the mouse up and tucking it beneath the leaves.

Marcus yipped in excitement and she growled low in her throat, warning him to be quiet.

He licked her cheek and she licked him back then drew the circle and touched his nose.

She whiffled softly in approval when he took his mouse form.

She rubbed her nose with her paw and then gently tapped him and he became his wolf shape.

She made happy noises at him and ran with him around the cage until he tired of it. Again she hunched over him and circled her paw.

He transformed again and she let him explore as a mouse for a while before calling him back. She wasn't sure how safe it was to let him remain a mouse, if it was hard for him to let the shape go as it was sometimes hard to push back the wolf, but she knew it wouldn't be safe for him in this cage much longer.

Frank would be able to smell the doorway in his cell, she was sure of that, but she didn't think he'd be able to open it before they noticed and stopped him. He was on a ragged edge and she didn't think he could hold out much longer. She couldn't hold out much longer.

She could open the door though if she could get out of her cage. And she could get out of the cage if they'd turn off the surveillance and get within reaching distance.

Is all she needed was for one of them to clean the cage again and turn off the cameras.

Chapter 31

Mark stumbled to his feet, Kelly's low whine pulling him from his bed before he'd consciously registered it. The room swam and he fell to his knees. He was surprised to be unfettered. The room had been cleaned in his absence; the straw replaced with a bed with a portable toilet placed in the corner.

"Well, well, you don't look happy to see me," Stacy said smugly.

Shock rooted Mark in place a moment.

Kelly growled again and Stacy laughed.

Stacy said, "Still pretending, I see. What about you, Mark? You still pretending to be human?" She slid the grill open and grinned at him.

"Why don't you come in here and see?"

She laughed again, shaking her head making a tsking noise. "You don't look at all well. Captivity not agreeing with you?"

She turned away and he rushed forward to press his face against the grill.

Kelly had backed into the farthest corner of her cell behind the potted trees and was looking not at Stacy but the stairs.

Stacy glanced over her shoulder and winked at him. "She smells my little surprise. Steve, bring them down!"

Stacy took off her jean jacket and dropped it atop her huge purse. She squatted to rummage and reapplied her lipstick, smiling smugly the entire time.

The door at the top of the stairs opened and Mark caught the scent that had alarmed Kelly.

Stacy slid the table Howard's men had moved back into the main room in front of Kelly's cage and rested a hip against it, her smile growing as Steve herded Alice and John downstairs.

"You've got to be kidding me," Mark said.

Stacy turned to glare at Kelly. "You'll admit what you are, or I'll fucking kill them both!"

Alice said, "Stacy, honey, it's clear you're unwell. Please, I know this isn't the real you—"

Stacy turned to glare at her mother. "Ha! The real me! You never could see what was right in front of your face. You're the stupidest woman I ever met!"

Mark said, "Jesus Christ, you can't seriously think your sister is that wolf?"

Stacy pulled a forty-five from her waistband and pointed it at him. "Shut the fuck up. I'm fucking sick of your lies!"

Mark said, "Seriously, why do this? Richard will give you everything you want. He'd give you *anything* you asked for if you just let us all go."

John said, "She wants to murder us. Look at her. This has nothing at all to do with Kelly or you or anything else. This is her twisted fantasy."

Mark knew he was speaking for Kelly's benefit. Stacy did too. She jumped to her feet and slapped him.

Steve laughed.

Mike said, "Where do you want them?"

"Tie them to the chairs." Stacy nudged one of the chairs forward with her toe. Her smile returned as she leaned against the cage. "Put them close enough she can reach them."

"That's a dangerous animal," Alice said in a quavering voice as Mike pushed her into the seat he placed in front of the open cage door.

"It sure as shit is," Mike said.

Stacy took a gun from her waistband as she said, "She could bite you and save your life. A small nip is all it would take."

Mark said, "That wolf is wild." He stared hard at Kelly, willing her to understand his warning, "It would kill them," he said to her.

Stacy shrugged as John said, "Let your mother go upstairs. You know your mother has a bad heart. There's no need—"

Stacy hit John with gun, interrupting him. His head snapped back, the chair he was in rocking from the force of the blow.

"Damn it," Steve muttered as he grabbed it to stop it from toppling over.

Stacy had hit John so hard Mark feared she'd broken his neck but John shook his head a moment later and picked his head up.

Stacy placed the gun on the table to put her hands on her hips, turning to face Kelly who hadn't moved or made a sound since her parents had come down the stairs.

"Everything that happens here is your fault and you know it. If you weren't such a selfish self-absorbed asshole none of this would've been necessary."

John said, "Kelly is a daughter to be proud of. I know how hard her teen years were. Mark told me everything. I know all of the terrible shit you've done, everything that Kelly was afraid to tell me. She wanted her sister back. She's nothing like you—will never be anything like you. You've never done anything for anyone except yourself! Your sister on the hand did the hard thing—the only she could do for you."

"Ha! She never did shit for me! And don't pretend you give a damn about me."

"You're right. I don't. But your mother and sister do. I gave up on you years ago. I saw who you really were and I hated that person."

John turned away from Stacy, not facing Kelly but Mark knew he was speaking to her when he said, "I love the woman Kelly's become. She's an amazing woman and a brave one. This won't break her. She'll do what's best for her family—even you. I don't know why she loves you, but she does—she'd help you if you let her."

"I don't want her fucking help!" Stacy screeched. She spun to lean over John and yell in his face. "I want her to admit what a lying whore she is!"

"You're the whore," John said.

Mark cringed, expecting her to hit him again but to his surprised she laughed a harsh bark of laughter and returned to the table where she perched on the edge and swung one foot.

Alice said, "Your father is understandably upset but we do love you too, honey."

"Save it. I'm not buying and I don't care."

John said, "She doesn't care, sweetheart. She'll do or say anything to turn your affections from Kelly. She's poisoned with jealousy."

Stacy said, "Tell her to turn, Dad, or I'll blow your fucking head off."

"There's no such thing as werewolves," John said enunciating each word clearly.

"Are you sure you want those to be your last words?"

266

Alice gasped and began crying, "You can't mean this! You can't! We're your parents! Not even you could be so evil."

Stacy stood, lifting the gun, cocking an eyebrow.

John said, "You're going to do whatever you want to do. No one has ever been able to stop you. I can pretend to buy into your bullshit but nothing I or anyone else says to that wolf will make it your sister. It's just a wolf. There's no such—"

The gunshot was deafeningly loud in the confined space. Alice screamed once shrilly than gasped and moaned, her head falling forward.

The scent of fresh blood covered all the other scents.

Mark yelled, "This isn't your sister's fault, you sick fuck! This is you, you fucking evil bitch!"

Stacy laughed, wiping the spatters of blood from her face as she leaned over to feel her mother's pulse.

"She's alive but barely. Going to let her die too?" she asked challengingly as she stepped away from Alice's bound body, gesturing to her with the gun.

"Get her medical help! She's your mother for Christ's sake! You can't really believe a bite would do anything except kill her! It wouldn't work! Please, for the love of God! Please!"

"Tick tock," Stacy said.

Steve said, "Call Henry and the boys and throw this meat to the tigers."

Kelly whined the barest breath of sound and Stacy laughed.

Mark squeezed his eyes closed, resting his forehead against the grill. "Please don't do this. There's no need. Get Alice medical care and I swear on my soul Richard will give you anything you want—anything!"

Stacy said, "Throw her in too."

Kelly charged the open door, growling savagely. Two gunshots coincided and Marcus yipped a high painfilled sound that was almost lost in the sounds of breaking pottery.

Steve had been ready for it and kicked the door closed.

Kelly crashed against the bars of the cage, snarling savagely.

Booted feet thundered above them. Steve was yelling for Stacy to stop as they struggled over the gun.

Stacy fired again but Mark couldn't see if Kelly were hit or not. He couldn't smell her over the scents of gunpowder and John's blood and fresh feces. Alice hadn't twitched. He thought she was dead already. He hoped she was because Stacy wouldn't hesitate to throw her to the tigers and the thought of Kelly seeing her mother eaten alive made bile rise in his throat.

"Stop, you're going to kill her!" he screamed hoping Howard's men were coming.

Josh ran down the stairs followed by five of his men.

"Drop the fucking gun. You know the fucking rules! No one fucking shoots the goddamned captives, wolf or not!"

"If we feed her fucking puppy to the tigers, she'll talk!"

Kelly barked a sharp spate of sounds and Mark tried to puzzle out what she meant. She was hunched in the corner again. He recognized she was speaking to Marcus, telling him to stay. He strained for a better view, but the room was crowded now and more were coming. He could hear running footsteps above his head.

"Get the fuck out of here!" Josh yelled.

Steve said, "Keep your knickers on."

Josh lifted his rifle. "Drop the fucking guns and get the fuck out or the cats are having a fucking feast!"

Steve snorted and holstered his gun. Stacy hesitated and then did the same. Mike had already dropped his and stood with his hands raised.

Josh said, "Take the fucking corpses with you and send some men back to clean this shit up." He gestured at Stacy with the gun. "You get back to your house and don't leave it again without Mr. Cirillo's permission."

Stacy leaned over to feel her mother's pulse again and kicked the chair when she stood. "Damn it! I'd hoped to feed her to the tigers!"

"Jesus you're a cold bitch," Josh said.

Stacy smiled, shrugging as she said. "I wanted to record it so Kelly could see it, but I guess recording her dead body being eaten will have to do."

"We aren't fucking doing that. There's no way I'm compromising my men by having that shit on a recording."

Stacy shrugged again. "The zoo is under surveillance, dumb ass. You're already compromised."

"Only the outer perimeter and the areas open to the public, and I control who sees it. I don't trust you one fucking bit! Those tiger pens are off limits! You go making a recording and it gets seen, hard questions are going to be asked."

Stacy grabbed her bag and coat and headed to the stairs, pushing past the men who'd gathered. They all backed away from her, and by their expressions Mark knew they thought her crazy.

"Stay the fuck away from us," Stacy said as she exited.

Steve and Mike both grabbed a corpse and followed.

"With pleasure," Josh muttered. He waved his men to leave.

Hans said, "Get this place cleaned up before Mr. Cirillo gets back. I was supposed to run some tests on the wolf, but my results will be off while it's so riled."

Josh said, "It doesn't appear to be hurt."

"Leave it alone and let it settle down. I'll run my tests tomorrow."

The two men headed to the door still speaking,

"What sorts of tests?"

"Pain tolerance and reaction to stimuli. We'll do an amputation of a paw to see if it regrows."

The closing cellar door cut off the men's laughter.

Mark rested his forehead against the bars and stared at his wife's hunched back. She was curled into a tight ball behind the shattered remains of the pot that had held one of the larger trees. Marcus was nowhere in sight and neither were making a sound. His jaw ached he was clenching it so tightly on the words he wanted to shout but there was nothing he could say to ease her even if they weren't still recording. He stared at her until men returned with buckets of water and mops.

"Please God, don't let my wife hate me when she finds out what her sister did to try to get me to talk."

Kelly hunched further, flattening herself as much as she could.

"The bitch is crazy," one of the men said.

Mark said, "Whatever they're paying you, my uncle will double. Please…."

He slumped when the man glared at him. He slid gracelessly to the floor where he rested his head in his hands.

Chapter 32

Mark backed away from the door when he heard footsteps running above him. An argument above him was rapidly escalating.

George and Hans ran down the stairs followed by Howard. Two men from Josh's team and Josh followed and they all headed directly to Kelly's cage.

Mark's pulse began to pound.

"Get her out," Howard said. He turned to glare at Josh. "If she's injured, there's going to be hell to pay. What were you thinking letting that crazy bitch down here?"

Josh said, "You said let her confront her!"

Howard waved dismissively.

George opened the cage door while Hans readied a pole with a noose on the end. Hans entered slowly but with confidence.

He whistled sharply, "Here, girl!"

Kelly picked her head up and he used the noose with practiced efficiency.

Mark held his breath, but Kelly made no effort to rip the pole from his hands. She jumped and whined but settled down quickly and let herself be pulled from the cage and thrust into the empty one across from it.

Mark wondered where Frank was and hoped they weren't still torturing him. He couldn't hear him screaming but he thought that lab might be soundproof. He hoped it was and that Kelly hadn't been able to hear him either.

Hans released her and threw her a dog biscuit that she ignored. She paced, growling softly until she settled into the farthest corner and lay with her tail half covering her muzzle, leaving just her glaring eyes visible.

"Where's the puppy?" Howard asked and Mark tore his gaze from his wife to scan the cage.

"Did it run past you?" George asked.

"Search the cage!"

Josh took out his cell phone and made a call, "Everett, send a full team to Stacy's quarters. She stole the damned pup. Search every building, all of them, even our own men, and pull the security footage. I want a list of everyone who's left the compound within the last five hours. Send another team to the tiger pens and take all of their damned cell phones!"

Howard said, "How did she get it past you?"

"I have no idea but we can find out."

"You think she fed it to the tigers?"

Mark moaned, jerking back from the open grill to cover his eyes, but it didn't help. He couldn't stop the images that the word tigers had invoked. Marcus wouldn't last a minute.

Kelly barked the bark that meant stay and he gritted his teeth and straightened, rubbing his cheeks briskly. *Stacy wouldn't have killed Marcus, she'd have him somewhere,* he told himself firmly. And if Kelly could control herself while her parents were killed and their children were murdered to keep their secret, he could control himself until he found Stacy and ripped her apart.

Hans and George began hauling out the potted plants.

"Clean this fucking mess up and I want to see that footage in my office now!" Howard snapped.

"What about him?" George asked.

"Do your damned tests!" Howard stomped up the stairs.

Hans peered through the grill on the door, "Going to give us any trouble?"

"You fucking murdered my in-laws! I thought we had a deal?"

"Mr. Cirillo had no hand in that."

"They're still fucking dead and under his watch!"

"I'm sure he'll make whatever amends he can."

"Call the fucking police! You're all guilty as fuck in this. You have to know that!"

274

Hans turned to speak to someone. "Tranq him. It's clear he isn't going to cooperate."

"Fuck you!" Mark stepped to the side of the door, pressing his back against it.

Kelly again barked the bark that meant stay.

Mark's cell door opened, and he grabbed at the man who entered.

"Fuck," Hans gasped and dropped the needle he carried to hit at Mark.

Mark banged his head as hard as he could against the wall as he punched him with his free hand. He let the man fall and reached for the needle.

Two men rushed in. Both carried guns, one a pistol and the other a tranquilizer gun. He knew neither of them and wondered if they'd hired new men or if the usual guards were all out hunting for Marcus. He didn't have time to consider it long.

"Drop it or I'll shoot," one of the men said.

Mark laughed as he ran at them. "Go ahead and they'll feed you to the tigers too." The man with the pistol backpedaled. Mark ignored him, heading to the one with the tranquilizer gun.

That man shot and Mark growled as he ripped the dart from his chest.

He reached the man and got his hands around his neck. The man began hitting him with the gun. Mark used his body weight to push him to the floor. The other man hit him with the butt of his gun, grabbing his arm and trying to pull him off. The room swam, a combination of sedative and blows making him dizzy but he laughed as the man's neck snapped and he reached for the other man. His hand wouldn't cooperate.

"Don't kill him," George said warningly.

The other man grabbed at Mark's arm.

The room wavered and spun and he groaned a wordless angry shout as he fell back.

"Let the ketamine do its thing," George said.

"Mother fuckers," Mark gasped. "I'm so sorry," he said to Kelly.

She barked the bark that meant stay, sounding really angry.

"I'll stay alive as long as I can," he tried to say but darkness swallowed his words.

Chapter 33

Mark forced his gummy eyes open. The lack of water was affecting not only his ability to heal but his ability to concentrate. The room spun and it took Mark a moment to realize the high-pitched shrieks he heard were a woman screaming. He could smell multiple people near him and thought the screamer was in a nearby cubicle because of the muffled nature of the shrieks.

He was strapped to a table with wide cloth cuffs on his wrists, ankles, and across his chest and legs. He thought he could probably rip a hand free but didn't think a human could. While he debated his options, he craned his neck to examine the room.

Three terrified women were right behind him, staring at him and the glass wall to his left. The women had been cuffed together and to a ring in the wall. One was obviously pregnant. One didn't appear pregnant, but Mark could tell by her scent that she was. He looked but couldn't see the screaming woman. He could see the lights and camera crew though and wondered if they were making snuff films.

"What are they going to do with us," the pregnant one asked shakily.

"Nothing good."

Mark was instantly sorry he'd said it. The woman moaned, cradling her stomach and the sharp scent of urine laced the air.

"Don't look, Amy," the woman beside her said.

"Fucking animals!" the other woman shouted and began yanking on the chain.

Doctor Fisher entered and tapped the controls on the wall that made the glass between the rooms darken. "That has nothing to do with you. You shouldn't have been brought in now. There's no need to be afraid."

"Fucking liar," Mark snapped.

Fisher said to him, "Why terrify them?"

"Why do whatever the fuck you're doing?"

George tapped him with the cattle prod. His body contorted and the women screamed.

"Enough of that," Fisher snapped.

Mark wasn't certain if he spoke to George or the women, but he supposed it didn't matter. The women quieted to low sniffles.

Fisher said, "Cooperate and this will be quick and painless."

Mark said, "Why pretend you're going to let them go?"

"We *will* let them go if they don't give us any trouble."

"Sure you will. You'll let them just waltz out of here after seeing all of this."

"They have no idea where they are. What could they say?"

"Your names. Your descriptions. You tell us this shit to keep us cooperating to make your life easier, not because it gains us anything."

"That might be true for you, but not for them. Unless you plan on telling them details they shouldn't know, there's no reason they can't be released once we're done with them."

One of the women said, "What are you going to do to us? Why were you cutting her tits off?"

"Jesus," Mark said in disgust.

"I'm sorry you saw that. That woman doesn't have a thing to do with you. Her husband requested the procedure as a punitive measure. I assure you, it sickens me too."

Mark said, "And yet you help them. You're crazy. You're all crazy!"

"George, I think it best that you gag him."

"With pleasure," George said and laid the cattle prod on his thigh. When Mark's body stopped contorting, he was gagged and Fisher was inserting an IV into his arm. Sweat streamed down his cheeks as he realized what the women were there for. He had no idea what a transfusion of his blood would do to them or the unborn children they carried.

He wished he could apologize to them because he knew they'd never be released and it was all his fault.

Kyle entered and took the pregnant women away when Fisher was finished, and he and George cut the clothing from the last woman as she screamed and hit at them.

Fisher took his vials of blood and left, and Smith entered.

"Hans?" George asked.

"Dead. And so is Hamilton. He killed them both."

"Mother fucker!" George hit Mark on the side of his head.

Smith said, "Enough!" He yanked the gag from Mark, grasping his jaw hard to turn his head to the remaining woman. "She's your new mistress. You'll fuck her daily until she becomes pregnant."

"Like hell I will!"

"George, give him incentive."

"With fucking pleasure!" He snatched a scalpel from a tray on the counter and slowly sliced Mark's pinky off.

Mark grit his teeth, concentrating on containing his furious wolf.

The woman began to sob.

Mark debated screaming, he'd been putting on a show for them but she was already terrified.

"Nothing they do will make me rape you," he said.

George began slicing another finger off, cutting the skin and muscle away slowly and then using snipers to break the bone. Mark had suffered more painful wounds in the past and knew he'd heal even this after a few shifts and enough meat.

George snipped off another finger.

"Enough. Maybe try her."

"It won't work," Mark said. "Nothing you do will make me cooperate—nothing!"

"Please," the woman said in a trembling voice and Mark didn't know if she were begging him or them.

Josh banged on the window and they all turned.

He opened the door to say, "The boss is pissed! He authorized one amputation! Get the specimens you need another way!"

Mark laughed, sneering at George. "Going to suck me off, George?"

George hit him and Josh grabbed his arm. "I said fucking enough! Bind his fucking wounds and put him back in his cage! Give the girl one of the nice suites and get her to fucking cooperate!" As Josh was speaking, he was rummaging in a cabinet. He emerged with a small vial and filled a needle that he took from a drawer. He injected Mark and tossed the needle to the floor.

"Let it take effect before moving him."

"He should be kept here."

"I agree and I'll speak to the boss about it."

"Fine." George slapped the cuffs on tightly.

The room began to spin, colors and sounds growing insubstantial.

"Get this room cleaned and don't try this shit with the wolf. One paw, that's it!"

Mark whimpered, struggling weakly, cursing himself for not ripping his bonds loose when he'd first woken. He wouldn't waste his next chance. He'd kill them all and to hell with the recordings.

Chapter 34

Kelly paced by the door to her cell as Kyle and Josh carried Mark down the stairs and put him back into his cell. He'd been gone for three hours and the wait had been agonizing. She'd hoped they'd turn off the recordings again to speak to him when he was brought back and that would be her chance, but Mark was clearly unconscious.

Kelly sniffed deeply, growling softly when she smelt the fresh blood on him.

Kyle said, "Think he can hold out much longer?"

"With incentive. He'll hold on if he thinks we have her. Do what we discussed." He shot a meaningful glance at the alarm pad beside the door.

Kyle said, "He'll be out an hour or so."

Josh headed to the stairs, calling back, "Clean up this place a bit and see if you can get that wolf to eat the treats. Howard will be happy if we can tame it a bit."

"Sure," Kyle said in a laughing tone. He grabbed a broom and turned off the alarm.

Kelly hesitated and then growled warningly at Marcus. He peaked from beneath a pile of leaves in the shattered planter.

Stay, she barked warningly, adding the low growl that meant I mean it.

This might be her only shot and it was clear they thought Mark would wake soon. She headed to her food bowl and pawed at the meat scraps, sniffing them all over and growling and then grabbing a chunk that she swallowed almost whole.

She retched and gagged, and Kyle said, "Slow down or you're going to choke." She staggered and snarled for Marcus to stay, adding a whine to her repertoire as she circled and drooled. She fell to her side in front of the door, waving her paws feebly.

"Jesus Christ! She's been poisoned!" Frank yelled.

Kyle ran to the keypad and hit the switch to open her door. She bounded out and leapt at him as he was punching the number to turn the alarms back on.

He shrieked, his eyes widening as her elongated claws cut a deep furrow across his neck. His eyes widened further when she transformed, and he gurgled, trying to speak and skitter backward while holding a hand to the blood spurting from his neck.

Frank ran to grip the bars of his cage. "Let me out!"

"Go to Daddy, Marcus," Kelly said as she punched in the numbers to open the back door in Frank's cage, saying to Frank, "Like hell! Get yourself out! And if you can't get away, have the fucking decency to kill yourself before you bring us all down!"

She kicked Kyle's hand away from his belt and fell across him, letting her muzzle reform but keeping her human torso, except for one hand that she left a paw to use her claws. He gasped weakly as she savaged him.

Gunshots sounded in the distance and she knew she didn't have much time. Frank had been spotted and they'd be on their way. She'd spent longer than she'd meant to mauling the corpse and she muttered swears as she rose to run to Mark's cage.

A hand gently patting Mark's face woke him. The light seemed bright and at the same time muted and cast odd shadows about him. A small boy was staring at him from inches away. The boy was smiling a sunny smile as he leaned forward and licked his cheek, and for one moment Mark was overcome with joy. But the boy stood and a moment later disappeared and he knew he'd dreamed him.

Gunshots and distant yells faded and grew as did the smell of smoke. Kelly barked her come to me call, the sound so lonely and painfilled he wished he could unhear it. He hated this dream. It was a nightmare. He'd never see his son and his wife was likely being tortured and there wasn't a thing he could do about it.

Tears burned his eyes. He let the darkness pull him back.

Kelly resumed her wolf form, barking for Marcus to come. He scampered from beneath the door of Mark's cell and trembled at her feet.

She resumed her human shape to pick him up and cuddle him a moment. Her son was so fragile in this shape. His form as light and defenseless as a butterfly. It made her sweat contemplating how easily he could be killed but she didn't have a choice.

She could smell his terror over the fresh scent of blood and she wasn't sure if it was her actions, the situation, or that Mark wouldn't wake.

"We have to go, sweetheart. I'll get Daddy out. Be quiet as a mouse." She resumed her wolf form leaving the hand that held Marcus human to place him on the back of her neck.

She hoped he'd hold on and be hard to see in her fur. The cameras were off down here but she wasn't sure if they were off everywhere or not.

Another round of gunfire made her grin a wolfish grin as she ran up the stairs. Frank must still be at large and fighting them if they were still shooting.

The door opened easily. She raced down the hall following the scent of cooking food. A quick glance through the closest window had shown a lot of men milling about a burning car right outside. She didn't dare use those windows. But kitchens had windows too.

An alarm began to ring and more gunshots followed.

A man was in the kitchen talking on his cell phone. He screamed as Kelly ran in. She ignored him to throw herself against the screened door. Her claws shredded the netting and she was out.

She headed at her top speed to the nearest bushes where she hunkered, panting hard while she got her bearings. The house where she'd been held was bigger than she'd imagined it being. A curving drive led through a thick planting of firs in one direction and to a row of low barn-like buildings in another. Chain link cages were visible in the distance as were much higher cages made with thick metal bars and cement. They looked abandoned with heavy overgrowth.

To her right, a swath of forest was broken by low rooftops and another smaller group of empty chain link cages. To her left, a much bigger barn was teeming with people. Vehicles filled the small lot in front of it. Smoke drifted in lazy plumes from the barn roof. Frank apparently wasn't done setting fires and she blessed his quick wits. She hoped the entire place would burn.

Three cars headed up the drive toward the main house and very distantly she could hear a police siren.

She kept her nose low, sniffing for the reek of Stacy's perfume. No one seemed to notice her. Whatever they were fighting about was happening at the bigger barn.

She caught a whiff of her target and veered to follow it.

Stacy had come this way recently, she was sure of it.

A musty earthy odor lifted the fur of her ruff and she slowed. She slowed even more, dropping to her stomach to crawl forward when she heard men arguing.

Josh was saying, "Get back to the house and stall them as long as you can. We need a few minutes to clean this up. If you catch that bitch, make sure you take all of their cell phones. We can't afford for the police to see that shit!"

"Yes, sir," the men he was speaking to said. They jumped into two golf carts and drove back toward the barn.

A tiger growled softly, and Josh slapped George's hand down. "Don't shoot the fucker. We don't want the police to hear it and come to investigate this."

"How the hell will we get the bones away from it?"

"See if you can entice it with its food or something. I better get a shovel and some sacks! And hurry the hell up!"

Josh headed to the only remaining golf cart and Kelly leapt.

He saw her and whirled, his eyes widening as he reached for his pistol.

He got off one shot. A sharp crack of pain in her shoulder staggered her but she reared on her hind legs, swiping for his face with claws she'd elongated. Marcus barked shrilly darting to bite Josh's ankles. She snarled as she snapped at Josh's face, coming away with a glob of bloody flesh that she spit out.

A tiger roared and Josh fell back. She followed him down, pawing at his face, ripping deep furrows in his skin. She went for his throat, biting into his jugular and tearing it loose. She whirled from the corpse, but George had run.

Follow she barked at Marcus and she ran to the tiger's gate where she resumed her human shape to open it. She opened the next three for good measure and then darted for the woods as her wolf, following the faint scent of Stacy's perfume.

She'd just reached the treeline when a loud shout from behind her was followed by the crack of a gun. Someone had seen her. She snarled as she changed direction and headed back to the thicker trees by the houses. Stacy could wait. Marcus was the priority.

The woods were thin and bordered a dirt road. The first two buildings were obviously bunk houses. The next six that she could see were small but well maintained. Each had a small covered front porch and two windows on the front and two on the side facing her.

The road curved and she couldn't see if the houses there were bigger or not. Two of the six smaller houses had cars in front of them. She headed to the first one that didn't.

When she reached it she resumed her human shape. Marcus danced around her feet as she slid a window up.

289

She pushed the curtain aside to plunk him inside and crawled after him, closing the window behind herself.

The inside reminded her of Mark's house. It was one room with a small kitchenette, a couch, television, and chair, and a doorway where she could see a wrought iron bed post and nightstand.

A sweatshirt jacket lay over the back of a chair beside a small dining table and she knew it was Josh's by the smell. The entire place reeked of him.

He'd left his laptop on the counter, which she ignored as she examined a row of monitors showing scenes from inside the house. None of the cameras seemed to be focused on the tiger pens and she heaved a sigh of relief. Nothing inside the house looked at all amiss but men were arming in a white tiled room.

She averted her gaze from a woman who was strapped to a metal table bleeding profusely from mutilated breasts, and clicked on an image of Mark, realizing it was old footage when she saw herself in the next cage.

She searched the desk quickly, looking for a phone and found a drawer full of USB drives all marked with dates. She grabbed them all and stuffed them into a plastic bag she found in one of the kitchen drawers.

There was no wall phone in sight, so she ran to the bedroom and searched it quickly. Josh had left a duffle bag in the corner of his closet under a blanket that held wads of cash, a passport with a different name, three guns, two knives, two changes of clothes, hair dye, duct tape, zip ties and a disposable phone. She'd found his go bag.

Marcus was busily sniffing the room and she let him be as she flipped open the phone to call Leah.

The phone rang three times before Leah answered. Kelly peeked from the curtains. Blue and red lights strobed through the trees. The cops had arrived and she could hear firetrucks on the way.

"Leah?"

"Kelly?" Leah asked, sounding amazed.

"I don't have a lot of time. Mark and I are in a zoo of some kind. I have no idea where. It's partially deserted and likely owned by Howard Cirillo or a company that he owns. He's here now and comes frequently enough people should know where it is."

"Are you—"

"Listen," Kelly said urgently, cutting her off. "We haven't said a thing but there are surveillance tapes, drone footage. The head of Howard's guards had a laptop here and I'll hide it, under the couch maybe, but it doesn't have that footage." She was lifting the couch as she spoke to see if the laptop would fit. She wedged it and the bag of USB drives up into the springs. "He's been searching and hasn't found it. I don't think it's anywhere on this compound or in the main office. Josh had access to that and would have found it, I think, but I could be wrong. He thought Steve has it.

"The police are here now. I think I can get Mark out but they're going to have questions. The recordings will say there was a fire…" Her breath caught hard and she forced words past the sob that wanted to catch in her throat. "Frank took my daughter, but they know about the fire. Mark thinks she's dead, killed in the fire, but I saw Frank grab her."

"We have her."

"You do?"

"Frank brought her to Ezra Delmont his pack leader, and he brought her to us. She's okay."

"Thank God…"

Kelly began to cry and had to breathe hard a moment to compose herself.

Leah said, "Frank was supposed to call and arrange a meet with Stacy, but we haven't heard from him."

"He's here too somewhere. I released him."

"His wife is dead."

"Good," Kelly snapped.

"Your son?"

"Marcus is with me. He's—"

Shouting drew closer and Kelly tensed.

"Someone's coming. I have to go. But we need an address to tell the cops where we were, somewhere that burned four days ago."

A man banged on the door. "Josh, you in here? We need you at headquarters!"

"He won't be joining you," Stacy said, and she fired.

Kelly dropped the phone and called for her wolf shape, barking the bark that meant hide to Marcus.

"She's inside," Stacy said excitedly.

"Let's just go," Steve said.

"Fuck that. She's a coward and I know that fucker has money in there."

"Fine, get yourself killed or arrested. I'm out of here. We can try again."

Stacy kicked the door open and ran inside firing. Kelly jumped forward, catching two bullets, one in the arm, the other grazing her shoulder.

Stacy screamed as Kelly's claws connected, cutting through the jean jacket she wore and into her arm. Kelly shifted to her human form and yanked Stacy's injured arm hard.

Marcus growled and snapped at Stacy's ankles.

"No!" Kelly yelled, but Marcus continued to bite at her.

Kelly formed her hand into a paw and swiped again, trying to rip Stacy's throat out but Stacy jerked back and fired, the shot pushing Kelly to the floor before her claws could do more than scratch Stacy's cheek. The pain of the gunshot left Kelly breathless a moment.

Stacy kicked Marcus and he yelped once then thudded to the floor where he lay unmoving.

"Die bitch!" Stacy yelled as she fired again, knocking Kelly to the floor before she could get her feet under her.

Kelly shifted and leapt. Stacy screamed as she backpedaled, firing without aiming but hitting Kelly again and knocking her back.

Kelly hit the closed door with a thud that dazed her.

She whirled but Marcus was up already, shaking his head.

Stacy was gone.

She barked her furious you've been bad bark and told him to hide again.

The police had to have heard this commotion and would be there any minute.

She ran to the bathroom and shifted twice while standing under the shower and wetting a towel. She rinsed off quickly and ran back to clean up as much of the blood as she could. She used four towels but managed to clean most of it. She dumped all the towels she'd used into the small washing machine in the bathroom, poured in all the bleach and turned it on.

Two police cruisers pulled up outside the house and someone shot a rifle. Kelly peeked from the window to see a tiger run by. The police were focused on it but were bound to notice the blood on the door and porch any minute.

She ran back to the bedroom and yanked out the zip ties and duct tape from Josh's pack. Marcus followed her into the bathroom in his mouse shape.

The bullet wounds had healed but she was bruised along her left shoulder and thigh. A lighter bruise below her right breast still had a red pucker mark. She formed her hand into a claw and made a quick slash over it.

"Be quiet and stay hidden until I call you."

Kelly picked Marcus up and dropped him into the pocket of the sweatshirt on the chair. She wasn't sure he understood her words or not but hoped he'd remain still enough no one would notice if he shifted back. How she would explain wanting to keep a wolf pup if he did, she didn't know, but it was the best she could do.

She ran back to the bedroom, winding the duct tape over her mouth, wincing as it pulled her hair. She zip tied her hands and feet together and then to the bedpost and was just pulling the last one tight when the police kicked in the door.

Chapter 35

A police officer ran inside, nudging the radio on his shoulder. "We have a tied woman here. I need medical." His partner crouched and ran past him to push the bathroom door open with his foot.

"Clear."

He entered the room to check the closet as the other officer said to Kelly, "Is anyone here?"

She shook her head and he holstered his gun and knelt beside her.

"Sorry," he mumbled as he pulled the tape from her mouth, ripping strands of hair off with it.

"Close the door," Kelly said urgently as soon as her mouth was free.

"The door?"

"There's a tiger loose out there. I think it killed my sister."

"Was she a captive too?"

"No. She's the one who put me here. Her and Josh Jacobs. My husband is in the house. A basement somewhere and they're torturing him! You have to get him out!"

"Wait, I know who you are!"

"Please! You have to save him before they kill him! There's at least four other captives in there somewhere!"

"Slow down and take a deep breath."

He cut her free and she jumped to her feet.

"There's no time. They'll kill them all if they think they can get away with it!"

The other officer said, "Holy crap! Look at this." He was staring at the monitor. He nudged his radio and said, "We have a 10-54 and need backup. I repeat, we have a possible fatality and a hostage situation and need immediate backup. Armed men are on the scene and preparing to engage!"

Kelly ran to peer over his shoulder. The monitor still displayed footage taken in the basement the night before.

She said, "There's at least fourteen guards and all are heavily armed."

The officer said, "Send us SWAT. And warn them there's a tiger on the loose."

Kelly lifted her hands to hide her satisfied smile; only remembering she was naked when the officer draped a blanket over her shoulders.

She wadded the material to hold against the bleeding gash on her stomach.

"How bad is it?" the officer asked as he reached to pull her hand down.

She slapped his reaching hand away. I'll live but my husband won't if they know you're going to go in for him. You will go in for him, won't you? Josh talked about another entrance, one not in the house. It's how he planned to sneak me inside.

"Why would he?"

"To make Howard Cirillo believe I was that wolf."

She pointed to the wolf on the screen.

Both officers returned to their car where they spoke at length on their radios.

Kelly examined the computer a minute then clicked the button that said *live feed*. Mark's hand was bandaged and the cages empty now but it looked mostly the same to her. She hoped they wouldn't realize they'd been looking at old footage before.

She grabbed the sweatshirt containing Marcus and rummaged in the drawers for a pair of sweatpants then headed to the bathroom.

An officer tapped on the door a few minutes later. "Miss, you really shouldn't shower until the doctor has examined you.

"I'll be out in a minute," Kelly said. "Good boy," she whispered to Marcus when he resumed his mouse shape and jumped back into the pocket when she pointed at it.

She took a deep breath and opened the door. Now, if Marcus would stay a mouse and the police got to Mark before the guards did, they had a real chance of getting out of this alive.

Chapter 36

A loud clank and a spate of gunfire pulled Mark back from the darkness.

The scent of smoke was thick in the air. A man yelling "Over here!" coincided with another spate of gunfire and someone on a bullhorn saying, "Police! We have the building surrounded!"

Mark tried and failed to get his feet under him.

"Kelly!"

The banging continued, ending suddenly in a wave of fresh air.

"Kelly!"

He tried again to stand, panting hard with the effort. They'd kill him before letting the police take him. That his wife hadn't barked was terrifying. If they'd moved her already...

His wolf was as frantic as he was but didn't press for release.

They won't kill her, he thought at his wolf. *She's too valuable. The police would send her to a zoo somewhere and they'd try to steal her back. He'd find her first. We'll find her!*

His wolf remained deeply unhappy. They both knew if Kelly wasn't answering then she wasn't here. Cirillo could've already moved her. They'd never be able to track all of these people.

"Fuck," Mark muttered as he pulled himself to the door of his cell, which was just a few feet away.

He could hear people running but wasn't sure if it was above him or in the cellar. The man on the bullhorn continued to yell directions. The scent of smoke grew alarmingly.

"Hand me the cutters," a man said.

Police, Mark thought in relief, letting himself lay and pant. Cirillo's crew wouldn't need cutters. They had the cage codes.

"Kelly!"

"We have a live one! Police! Call out!"

"In here! Behind the paneled wall!"

"I think it's coming from over here," another man said.

It took them a good ten minutes to get the wall open.

An officer crouched to peer through the door slot.

"It's Mark Miller and he needs medical," he said in aside then to Mark, "Do you know the code for the door?"

"Not this one. The one that leads to their lab is one-nine-seven-six-four-one."

The lab… the white rooms?"

"Yes. And hurry. They have at least four women captives down there."

"Jesus," one of the men behind the officer at the door said.

"Where is it?"

"There's a panel behind the desk in the library. It opens by pressing the bottom. The elevator uses the same code although maybe it takes one of their men to press it in. The place is pretty high tech and could've had biometric scans I didn't notice.

While he described the layout of the lab, men behind the officer discussed ways to get his door open.

He'd be free soon, he thought in relief. *This would make the news and Richard would come. They'd be able to track his wife.*

"Mark! Mark!" the officer said loudly and Mark realized he'd fallen asleep again. "Hang in there, man. Help is coming."

Muffled gunfire was met by renewed yelling on the bullhorn.

The whir of a helicopter drew closer.

"Feds have arrived," one of the men said.

"SWAT found the entrance," another said.

The officer at the door said, "Get this shit open!"

"They've got the fire under control."

A dull rumble shook the floor.

"Get back!" a new man yelled. "Paddy can cut that fucker off."

Mark hoped they'd hurry before Cirillo blew the entire place.

Another closer rumbled knocked a few of his ceiling panels loose and made the men outside his door exclaim.

"Gas," one said, right as Mark smelled it.

The fallen tiles revealed piping and wires. A fine white mist was flowing from a ceiling vent but even if he could reach the pipe he had no way to block it.

He debated warning them.

A line of dark orange marked where they were cutting the hinges from the metal door. He only needed another few minutes.

"Get out of here," someone said in a thick Irish accent. "I've got this."

The orange line continued to grow.

Mark pulled himself up, which made his head swim alarmingly.

"They're gassing this room."

"You'll be out in just a minute. I'm almost through."

His calm tone made Mark laugh. He was still laughing as darkness claimed him.

Mark opened his eyes to see a man he didn't know leaning over him with a small flashlight. His nose told him he'd been moved.

"He's coming around, I think," the man said.

"Mr. Miller, can you hear me?" another man asked.

Mark squinted, trying to force the whirling colors into a recognizable shape.

He called for his wolf.

"I'm officer Green and you're safe now."

Mark groaned as he pulled the wolf back. It fiercely wanted to manifest and he panted hard as he forced it back.

"My wife?" His words sounded hollow and breathless.

"Can you give him some water?" Green asked.

"I hate to move him. He could have internal injuries. He has an IV."

"I'm okay," Mark said as he tried to force himself upright. He wrinkled his nose at the filthy gown he wore. "Can I get some clothes or a blanket or something?"

The paramedic helped him sit up more and handed him a water bottle and draped a blanket over his shoulders. He unwound the soiled bandaged around Mark's left hand, making a tsking noise when he saw the mangled remains of Mark's fingers. Mark chugged the entire bottle while the paramedic poured a bottle of sterile water over the wounds, catching the resultant mess in a metal bowl. Mark was so thirsty that the filthy water drew his eyes. He squeezed them shut before he could lose control and snatch it to drink.

He said, "What the hell did they shoot me up with? I feel like shit."

"Chloroform, I think." Green withdrew a notepad from his pocket. "Can I get a statement."

"He's in no shape to do anything," the paramedic said as he gently wrapped Mark's hand in gauze.

"My wife?" Mark asked again.

"I'm not sure. They're still removing captives from the house."

A round of gunfire made them all tense.

"Wait here," Green said.

The paramedic closed the door behind him and reached for his cell phone. "Jerry, let's get out of here."

Mark said, "No, please, my wife could be here."

The paramedic bit his lip. "It isn't safe here."

"Jesus, fuck! There's a tiger loose!" Jerry exclaimed loudly enough Mark could hear him from the cab and over the cell.

"Please." Mark struggled to stand but the room wavered alarmingly.

The paramedic pulled him back. "We'll wait a few more minutes but, Jer, if you see any of these gun toting maniacs, get us out of here."

Jerry said, "We shouldn't have been called in until the fucking scene was clear. These idiots are going to get us all killed." He hung up but Mark could hear his continued complaints through the cab as could the paramedic by his wincing scowl.

"Well, let's get you cleaned up a bit." He began to dab Mark's face with a damp cloth.

Mark batted his hand away. "I'm fine."

"You're not. Your pulse is too fast and your obviously dehydrated. You're covered with scrapes and bruises and healing knife wounds although I saw no obvious serious injuries besides the hand. You've been drugged and are in shock and not thinking straight. Killing yourself won't help your wife. Let us take you to the ER where you can be checked out."

Mark laughed a bitter bark of laughter. "I assure you, the doctors here have checked me thoroughly."

The paramedic's expression darkened. "They experimented on you?"

Before Mark could answer, the door opened, and Green stuck his head inside. "They've found your wife."

Mark's breath caught hard in stunned amazement. Goosebumps pebbled his skin as he waited for Green to shoot him or freak out but his eyes were pitying as he said, "Dave, can you and Jer take her in too? She's right up the road there and we've secured the scene."

He gestured to three ambulances visible through the open door. Mark leaned forward to peer out. Four fire trucks were parked on the lawn, blocking the view of the house, but he could see all sorts of vehicles, most with lights on their roofs or in their windows, lining the entire drive two deep. Police cars from two different counties were parked in front of a big barn. Three black hummers and men in black combat gear with the word

SWAT emblazoned across it milled around the barn. Two more ambulances were on the way or just leaving, he could hear the sirens. Dead men lay in rows covered by white sheets while cuffed men and women were being herded to green vans and injured to ambulances.

A helicopter flew overhead as a man said something on a loudspeaker that distance made unintelligible.

"Ask Jerry," Dave said, and he pulled Mark back inside. "Lay down and rest a moment."

Green shut the door and a minute later the ambulance began to move.

The motion made Mark feel sick. He swallowed convulsively trying to hold back his nausea.

Dave leaned over him to press a stethoscope against his chest then took his blood pressure.

In the front seat Green was saying, "He's Mark Miller, you know the supposed werewolf. His wife was found tied up in one of the cabins. He had her tied naked to his fucking bed. She was beaten and I'm sure raped. She's coherent though and giving names. Some of the guards were scamming the sick fuck who runs all this. He was trafficking in human organs, stealing people right off the fucking street. The shit in there will give me nightmares."

Dave said, "You're doing better but your pressure is still high." Mark snorted and Dave winced. "So many fucking crazies in the world..."

Mark wasn't sure if Dave could hear the conversation in the cab with his weaker human hearing, but he supposed it didn't matter.

Dave's mouth was open to say more but the ambulance came to a stop. Mark sat as the back door opened.

His wife—in her human form—stood in the road.

He was too stunned and thankful to form words.

Kelly burst into tears when she saw him, collapsing at Green's feet. He and another officer pulled her up and handed her inside.

"Careful, she's pretty bruised up," Green said gruffly as Mark grabbed her in a hard embrace. She was human again and he was struck by her beauty. He'd forgotten how beautiful she was. Even dirty, bruised, and scared she took his breath away.

"I'm so sorry," he mumbled, and she cried harder.

"Our children…" the breath caught in his throat and he was crying too.

He buried his face in her matted hair and breathed deeply. She smelled of pain and Marcus under the blood. It tore a moan from him.

"Am I hurting you?" she asked in a gasping sob, lightening her hold.

He tightened his and kissed her bruised cheek.

Dave said, "Let me give you an IV—"

Kelly slapped Dave's reaching hands away. "Don't touch me!"

"You need—"

308

"I said no! No medical treatment! Nothing! No one is touching me. No one…" and she began to sob again.

Mark glared at Dave, motioning him away.

"Get them to the hospital," Green said gruffly.

He closed the door and slapped the side.

Dave picked up his cell. "Let's go, Jer."

"As soon as they move the fucking tiger corpse. It looks like it mauled a few of them."

Kelly growled softly against his neck.

Mark said, "They deserved it, the fuckers."

Chapter 37

Mark sat in the indicated chair, sliding it closer to Kelly's so he could put an arm around her. She hunched as though she were cold, hugging herself, keeping her hands in the pockets of the sweatshirt she still wore. It worried him how withdrawn from him she was.

Doctors and nurses who passed them gave them sympathetic glances or hurried their steps. Two police officers that Mark didn't know and Green waited with them. They'd been there over an hour already.

"I want to go home," Kelly said again.

Green said, "You need medical attention."

"Mark, they can't make us. Let's just go."

"He needs medical attention too," Green said.

Kelly lifted her face to glare but lowered it quickly, hunching against Mark's side.

He said, "It will just take a few minutes. I'll feel better if I know you're okay."

310

"I'm not okay but medicine isn't going to help."

Mark winced and bit his lip. Green cleared his throat. "Our counselors are very good and will be happy to help you."

"Shut up!" Kelly yelled, surprising Mark who jumped and then put both arms around her.

She began to cry again, and Mark stroked her hair murmuring endearments. She shuddered and jerked against his side and it worried him anew that she was having such a hard time controlling herself. He needed her out of here before she lost control of her wolf, but it would be suspicious as hell if he didn't get his damned hand tended.

"Can I borrow a phone?" he asked. "My family will be worried."

"Of course. You can use mine." Green handed over his cell phone.

Richard answered on the first ring.

"It's Mark. I borrowed a kind officer's phone to make this call.

"Kelly?"

"With me."

"Thank God."

"How's—"

"Everyone here is fine. Bryant's cabin was a total loss."

"My daughter…" Mark's breath hitched on a sob and Kelly moaned.

Richard said, "Come home, Mark."

"As soon as we can." He couldn't go. Not when Stacy had Marcus. He wanted to ask where Richard was but didn't dare with the police listening. He hoped his pack was here already searching and he was fiercely glad now that Marcus was pack and that Richard would be able to track him.

Richard said, "I sent the jet. We'll have you home in an hour."

"I can't take much more of this…" He'd been about to mention John's murder but remembered Kelly supposedly didn't know of her parent's death. He lowered the phone to say, "I'm so so sorry, sweetheart, they murdered your parents too."

Kelly hunched forward until her head rested on the table.

Mark picked the phone back up. "Can you arrange funerals?"

"Jesus, Mark, what happened?"

"Not now. I can't tell her like this."

"Yes, of course. What can I do?"

"I— nothing, I guess. I'll see you soon."

He handed the phone back to Green.

"You're certain about her parents?" Green asked.

"Yes. Stacy shot her father and her mother had a heart attack."

Kelly picked her head up and angrily rubbed her eyes. "I thought he was lying when he said they fed them to the tigers."

"Jesus," Green muttered as he turned away to make a call.

"I have a tentative ID on the remains you found." He walked away still speaking and Kelly laid her head back down. Mark stroked her hair. She made an odd coughing snort then coughed for a minute and asked for a water.

"I'll get it," one of the remaining officers said, "And I'll see what's holding them up. This is just ridiculous."

He closed the door behind himself and Mark shrugged his tense shoulders.

Someone knocked and a different police officer poked his head inside the room.

The officer still in the room said, "They haven't been seen yet, Bob."

Mark said, "We can give a statement. I want it over with."

The man entered, extending his hand, "Detective Robert Weaver and you already know Agent Prescott."

Mark ignored the offered hand. Bob cleared his throat, stepping aside to make room for Carvalho.

Carvalho said, "I'm sorry to see you again under these circumstances. I feel terrible about this. I really do. Howard Cirillo was completely under our radar though."

"Stacy wasn't. Steve wasn't. How many of those assholes got released?"

"We're still looking into how it happened."

Mark snorted derisively.

Carvalho said, "If you're up to giving a statement, it would be helpful in rounding up those who might still be at large."

"Stacy got away, *huh*."

Carvalho winced, and Bob cleared his throat again. "We have men searching for her. She won't get far."

Kelly said, "She tried to kill me. I was surprised she was working with Josh. I thought holding me was his idea, but she knew I was there and she would've killed me if that tiger hadn't shown up."

"Let's back up a bit. You're referring to Joshua Jacobs?"

"Yes. The entire thing was his idea. He knew they could sucker Howard into paying and that the price would go up the more they could convince him. So, they got a wolf and took me. They let Howard have my husband and Stacy promised Howard she could get me to become human with enough incentive. They planned to put me into the cage eventually, switch me and the wolf as needed to keep Howard convinced. Howard was paying Josh a fortune for security, never mind the finders fee and the bonuses. Josh and Stacy were working on a list of other possible people they could do the same too. They have more wolves somewhere, but I don't know where."

"*Ahh*," Mark said as if he were enlightened. "I'd wondered about Doctor Fisher. Doctor Smith seemed legitimate. He was a sadistic asshole but he conscientious about the tests he ran and I think he believed their bullshit, while Doctor Fisher lied about his exams. He never really ran many and the ones he did run were perfunctory as if he didn't care about the results. He must have been working with Josh. I wonder if they'd have killed Doctor Smith when it came time to prove werewolves existed."

"I hope they did kill him," Kelly snapped.

Prescott said, "We'd like you to look at our mugshots and put names to the faces if you can."

"Of course," Mark said.

Bob cleared his throat again, "I hate to bring up such a sensitive topic but we haven't found a sign of your daughter."

"You won't," Mark said harshly. "They murdered her."

Kelly squeezed his hand hard in both of hers. She pressed their clasped hands to her chest, gasping.

Prescott said, "I'm sorry but I have to ask…."

"She died in the fire. We were hiding out at a friend's cabin. They set it on fire. I have no idea if that was planning or accident, but they came in with guns blazing and shot us both up with some kind of tranquilizer. I could hear her screaming…"

"She didn't burn, Mark," Kelly whispered. Her wide horrified eyes were locked on his.

"I'm sorry but Steve told me she did, and I heard her screaming…" He couldn't speak past the lump in his throat. Kelly was grasping his hand so tightly that he'd have been bruised if he were human.

"She didn't!" She released him suddenly, hunching away. "Stop it right now," she said shrilly.

No one said anything for a moment.

Finally, Carvalho said, "This cabin was where?"

Mark gave them Bryant's address. A doctor entered while he was describing the medical procedures he'd undergone. The officers left the room and Mark repeated them for the doctor's benefit and let the man examine him. His hand was x-rayed stitched and bandaged and he was given a clean pair of scrubs and offered the use of a shower. Kelly glowered and paced the entire time and refused to be examined.

Mark said, "I won't ask again but it would put my mind at ease if the doctor can examine you."

She pursed her lips then shook her head. "Fine, you stay with me though." She stood and turned away to remove her jacket that she placed on the chair. The fresh scent of blood made the hair on Mark's neck rise.

Her back was a mass of discolored welts and splotches that he realized with horror were healing gunshot wounds.

"I'd like to get an x-ray," the doctor said, "You might have broken ribs. If you'll lay on the exam table—"

"No." She turned to glare, holding a hospital gown over her breasts. A jagged cut across her abdomen oozed blood.

"Were you sexually assaulted?" the doctor asked.

"That's none of your damned business!"

She reached for her sweatshirt.

"Let me treat this wound at least," the doctor said as he opened one of the cabinets. He began removing supplies. "You should have told us you were bleeding!"

Mark said, "Don't yell at her. She did say she'd been stabbed and no one here gave a shit. You were all too busy helping the men who did this to her."

The doctor's lips tightened. Kelly lifted her hand as she said, "It's nothing just a shallow cut."

The doctor leaned forward to examine it and then cleaned and bandaged it. When he was finished, he called for a nurse.

"Mrs. Miller's cut should have been seen to immediately. She'd be within her rights to sue us over this neglect. I see by their charts they were offered no medical care besides blood pressure and temperature checks." As he was speaking he was writing and he ripped off two sheets of paper from his pad that he handed to Mark. "Scripts for pain medication. Get your wife to a gynecologist at the earliest opportunity." He wrote furiously for another minute then tore off another script. "The morning after pill if you feel it's needed. Get her help."

He turned to the nurse. "Get them their discharge papers and I want the entire shift to be in my office at shift change."

"Yes sir," the nurse said to his retreating back.

"Can we go now," Kelly asked as she donned her sweatshirt, keeping her back to everyone and hunching again.

Mark said, "Yes. We're going in five minutes whether we're discharged or not."

The nurse hurried away. Mark stuck his head out the door to tell the police officers they were leaving whether they liked it or not.

Chapter 38

Kelly kept her back to the room and cradled Marcus. He'd been remarkably quiet and cooperative but she knew it couldn't last much longer.

Her breasts ached and she knew he must be hungry. She was starving and thirsty but had been afraid to ask for food. She wasn't sure how much it would heal her but was more worried about it enticing Marcus.

"I need a bathroom," she said and left the exam room without waiting for a reply. The hall bathroom was small but it had a lock and she gratefully locked the door and set Marcus down. He immediately resumed his wolf form and jumped around her whining softly.

She turned the water in the sink on and drank deeply then held him so he could drink too. She cuddled him a moment as a human and then stripped to take her wolf form and cuddled him as a wolf, licking him while he nursed.

He didn't nurse long. He was almost weaned and wanted real food. Her low warning growl quieted him, and he watched with wide eyes when she resumed her human form. Before she could really see it, his wolf form shimmered and a human child sat at her feet. She picked him up to hug him.

"You're a good boy, Marcus. Mommy needs you to be small and quiet for just a little while longer." He tugged on her hair and licked her cheek. She had no idea if he understood any of her words or not.

"Quiet as a mouse," she whispered as she set him on his feet. He grinned up at her and became his mouse self. As a mouse he was surprisingly light, much lighter than a normal mouse of his size. It worried her to hold him. He felt warmer than a mouse. The heat of him felt delicate, almost insubstantial. His heartbeat reminded her of the delicate flit of butterfly wings. She imagined he could be as easily crushed as a butterfly and knew he didn't like being in her pocket but he remained still when she gently placed him there.

"Just a little while longer, sweetheart. Quiet as a mouse."

She took a deep breath and walked back into the exam room. Mark was signing papers that he handed to her. Tears filled his eyes and he hurriedly looked away.

"We're fine," she said firmly as she scrawled her signature. He likely smelt the milk and maybe Marcus and he thought both their children were dead. His wolf would be frantic.

She'd hoped they could get a taxi and speak privately but a police car waited to drive them to the airport.

"We should stay here," Mark said.

"We're going home!"

"We're needed here," he said insistently.

She glared, grabbing him by the shirt and shaking him. "I know what I need, and I need to go home!"

He said nothing else although it was clear he longed to argue.

Six agents waited at the plane that Richard had sent, obviously planning to accompany them, and she groaned with frustration.

"We're going home, Mark. I have nothing more to say to them. I'm going to go lay down."

Mark said, "My wife is exhausted and we need some space." He followed her to the rearmost cabin.

She locked the door and sat on the narrow bed with relief.

He said, "Kelly, we can't go. Stacy has Marcus. Her trail is going to get cold."

"Marcus, come to Mommy." She reached into her pocket while Mark gaped at her in horror, likely afraid she'd lost her mind. She mentally urged Marcus to shift, not quite knowing how she pushed him into his wolf shape but knowing she was. She couldn't force him to switch shapes; she could only stop it, but Marcus cooperated.

Mark grunted in surprise and fell to his knees when Marcus stuck his head from her sweatshirt. He'd resumed his wolf form and scrabbled from her shirt to prance happily around Mark.

"Oh my god! How? I thought he was lost to us."

"Richard has our daughter."

"Are you sure."

"Yes, I spoke with him. Frank brought her to his pack and they gave her back."

Tears trickled from the corner of Mark's eyes. Marcus yipped and Kelly growled low in her throat.

Mark said, "They can't hear us. I can't believe you had him this entire time. How?"

"Marcus, show Daddy how you can be quiet as a mouse."

Mark gasped in astonishment, lifting a trembling hand to lightly touch the furry gray mouse that now stood on his hind legs where Marcus had been.

Kelly said, "He's starving. We both need food."

"Kelly—"

She shrugged angrily. "I don't know how. I don't know how much he understands. He needs me, Mark." She resumed her wolf shape and stepped out of the loose sweatpants she wore. She lay on the bed and a moment later Marcus jumped up to curl against her. He nursed for a moment before curling up beneath her chin and falling asleep.

Mark watched with tears in his eyes then kissed her forehead and went to find them food, she hoped.

Chapter 39

Mark had never seen so many reporters or news vans. Richard had sent a limousine to pick them up and it couldn't get through the press of people that filled the road in front of Richard's gate.

Agent Carvalho reached for his phone.

Mark said, "Don't bother. We're going home if we have to walk."

Carvalho said to the driver, "Honk the horn. Don't stop but go slow. He dialed and said, "We need more men here before this house is mobbed."

Mark strained to hear the reply.

"We already have backup on the way. Local police should be there momentarily. I've called the governor and asked him to prepare to call in the state militia."

"Have you received threats?"

"Not yet but the turnout for this is staggering."

"Keep me appraised."

Mark said, "Should we be concerned?"

"I think we should move your entire family to a safehouse until this gets straightened out."

"I'll speak to my uncle."

"Mark," Kelly said then heaved a heavy sigh. "I just want to sleep in our own bed and pretend this never happened."

He kissed her forehead and had to resist laying his hand across the small bulge that was Marcus.

His nerves felt taut from the strain. He was afraid his son would lose patience any moment and emerge from her pocket.

It seemed to take a year to reach the gates, which swung open when they approached.

Armed security pushed the crowd back so that the gates could close again.

Kelly practically ran from the car and passed Richard who held the door open.

Richard greeted Mark with a hard hug before shaking the agents hands.

"I'm afraid I have more bad news for you. I thought it best to wait and tell you in person," Richard said as he led the way to his office. "My father has passed away."

"Jesus, Richard," Mark said as the agents murmured condolences.

"He was old and while we were expecting it… this situation didn't help any. Not that I'm blaming you," he added hurriedly.

"I'm so sorry," Mark said. He sniffed deeply but only smelled older scents. None of his pack were present, not even Leah.

He didn't ask.

Richard said, "I'd wanted to bury him in the family plot, but I think it best if we release all the ashes."

Mark said, "Kelly is—traumatized. I don't think she can take another funeral. This is going to kill her. She loved that old man. *I* loved that old man."

Richard laughed sadly.

Mark said, "I'm exhausted. Can we do this later?"

"Of course." Richard stood to hug him again.

Mark gratefully returned the embrace. His wolf stopped pressing, comforted by Richard's presence. Richard patted his shoulder when he released him. "See to Kelly. I'll take care of everything else."

Mark headed directly to the conservatory.

Marcus greeted him with a happy yip and ran circles around his feet.

Audrey held his daughter and he closed his eyes to breathe in her scent and didn't realize he'd fallen until Marcus put his paws on his shoulder to lick his face.

Kelly whined and Marcus left him to return to her and an enormous, lightly roasted, haunch of meat.

Kelly licked Marcus while he ripped at the meat. He and his mother ate hungrily until their stomachs were bloated. Kelly transformed into her human self and held out her arms.

325

A little boy with brown curls and a mischievous smile reached to her and she cuddled him to her breast.

Mark had begun crying, not even realizing it until Audrey knelt beside him to rub his back.

You have a beautiful son," she said.

"Can I have her?" Kelly asked.

Mark crawled forward to place their daughter in her arms. He gathered his son and rocked him, examining his rosy cheeks and silky curls with a feeling of awe and anger.

"I'm so sorry," she whispered as she offered their daughter a breast. "I love you just as much but he needed me."

"You chose to stay away."

"Not at first. I didn't know who I was until you gave me that shot but Marcus needed me. I was afraid to come back. What if I lost my hold on him? He'd have died. He still might. I'm not sure how much he understands. He shifts his form so quickly that he could easily become something that gets him killed."

"You let me worry all this time..."

"What was I supposed to do? Look at him! He needs me!"

Audrey placed a blanket over Kelly's shoulders as she said, "He's a miracle and Kelly is right. He'll need all of us. What urges will he have to fight, Mark? Until he's old enough to understand the risks, we'll have to watch him like a hawk."

Kelly laughed a soft unhappy breath of laughter. "He can become a hawk or a fish. Should I have become a human woman and let our son drift away in a stream to be eaten by crows or become lost to us forever?"

"It would have taken minutes to tell me, Kelly!"

"And if in those minutes I lost the connection that let me stop him?"

"But you didn't!"

"I might have. It wasn't a risk I was willing to take!"

"Please, you're upsetting her," Audrey said as their daughter began to fuss.

Mark said, "If you had told me, all of this might have been avoided."

Kelly paled, jerking back as if he'd slapped her.

She said, "You're going to blame me for this?"

"No, I didn't mean that."

Audrey said, "You're both exhausted. Get some sleep and talk about this later."

Richard said, "No time for sleep."

Mark started in surprise. He hadn't heard or smelled him coming. Both he and his wolf were exhausted and not making good decisions. Audrey was right, yelling at Kelly now was a mistake.

Kelly rose slowly to her feet. "Do you blame me too?"

Richard said, "Of course not. None of us do, but we need to know what they know and what proof they have."

"I told Leah."

327

"But you don't know what's on the drone footage?"

"No but whatever it is convinced Howard, and Josh thought it was worth a lot of money."

Mark said, "Josh needs to be silenced permanently."

Kelly loosed a hard bark of laughter. "I killed that fucker."

Mark said, "The cover story is good but footage of us in the mountains will disprove it. And once word gets out, more people will be flying drones over these hills hoping to spot us."

"I'm aware and we're already taking precautions. The pack is safe."

Mark winced, "I told Howard that everyone at Howls is a werewolf."

Richard laughed. "Good. We're you able to hide the laptop?"

"What laptop?" Mark asked as Kelly said, "Yes. It's beneath the couch, up in the springs with a bunch of USB drives. But we aren't the only source of information they had. I have no idea what Frank told them."

Richard squatted beside Mark to examine Marcus.

Mark said, "Frank was denying everything too. I doubt they could get him to talk by torture but he might have volunteered information. I mean before he turned on them. They ate his wife…."

"Jesus." Richard made a mou of distaste.

"Oh my God!" Kelly said, pressing a trembling hands to her pale cheeks.

Audrey knelt beside her to support the baby.

"Take some slow deep breaths." She put her arm around Kelly, glaring at Mark.

Mark said, "Stacy didn't need us anymore. Her actions told us that. She was just there to hurt Kelly. I assume Frank or maybe even the entire Delmont pack is helping her."

"The pack isn't. Delmont declared Frank a fugitive and sent wolves out to look for him. He's also called in some favors as have I and we have a man on the inside who might be able to help us."

"What are we doing to help ourselves?"

"Leah is overseeing the computer search and Alan is putting together some drone footage that we can hopefully use in place of the original if we can find it, but we need some help with that. You and Kelly and your daughter need to be in some of the shots. He'll be calling in any minute to arrange it.

"Audrey, see if you can fix Kelly's hair and cover those bruises if shifting doesn't do it, and get her some clean clothes. Mark, shave and shower after you eat something. I can hear your stomach rumbling from here.

"And someone tell me how Marcus is here and in human form when I have wolves out looking for him there."

He leaned down to kiss Marcus's forehead. "JJ will be thrilled to meet you. I know I am."

Mark kissed his son's forehead too, overcome with gratitude.

He avoided Kelly's eyes. He didn't want her to see his anger.

"Let them sleep," Richard whispered.

Mark's children lay with their heads on Kelly's furry flank. All three slept deeply. Mark didn't like how exposed they were beneath the pines. The trees were almost touching the wall of Richard's house but it felt wide open to him. Kelly had flopped to the ground gratefully when filming had ended and he hadn't the heart to order her inside when his children slept so peacefully, but he hated that he could hear the crowd noises and see the lights of the news vans on the road in front of the house.

He said, "It's a risk staying. They could find something too incriminating to explain any minute."

"If we need to fight our way free, we will, but I don't think any footage will convince enough people, not with the way video can be manipulated. If we keep calm, we can get through this."

Richard squeezed his shoulder. "You have to let go of the anger and I don't mean Stacy. We'll find her and she'll get what's coming to her, but Kelly will sense your anger with her and she's really hurting now. She doesn't need your anger on top of it."

"I know but she could've fucking came back and said something."

"Could she? She had human senses but her wolf was in control. I think her wolf is more in control than she realizes. Kelly wouldn't have a ripped a man's throat out. Kelly would have avoided him but she didn't. She sought him out and attacked. Does that sound like she's in control?"

Mark said, "She shifted to her wolf form while unconscious. At least I think she was unconscious..."

Richard shook his head. "Your wife is something new, something different, or maybe she's just more intergrated than us or less integrated, but whatever it is, she has special needs as does your son. Let her take care of him as her instincts demand."

"I need her too."

"Motherhood changes them and we have to accept it. The kids will come first with her but that doesn't mean she loves you less."

"I want her to take care of them but..." Mark trailed off as he considered Richard's words. His anger fled and he was suddenly exhausted.

Richard said, "Go sleep. Audrey and I are watching. We've got the footage we need. No one is getting onto the property. You and Kelly can stay here as long as she needs too. If anything changes, I'll come get you."

Chapter 40

Two Days Later

Mark shook Derek's hand and took the seat he was offered. This visit to the police station remained him of the last one. Like on his last visit, he meant to take his family into the hills as soon as he left here.

Derek said, "I'm sorrier than I can say about your baby girl. Tell your wife she has my deepest condolences. If there's anything I can do, Mark...."

"Did Howard say if her murder was planned?"

Ted, the lawyer Richard had arranged, said, "He'll be charged with her murder whether it was planned or not."

Derek said, "He's seriously deluded. I think you can believe he never meant to hurt her. He'd meant to take her too."

"I suppose we can be grateful he never got his hands on her..."

Derek winced. "I saw the footage."

Ted interrupted to say, "No one should be seeing that footage. I'd like to know how it's getting leaked to the press. My clients have a right to privacy, never mind the tainting of the jury pool."

"Those fuckers should all hang!" Derek snapped.

Mark said, "Argue about that later. I have funerals to get to. What I want to know is how much danger have I put the employees at Howls in?"

Star was leaking the footage. The USB drives they'd stolen had records and video of the people who'd used Cirillo's services. Josh had kept backups of all of the security footage on his laptop. He'd hacked Howard's cell phone to get a copy of their very first talk, which Star had posted online.

Derek said, "The chief will be here in a minute, but I can't imagine anyone believes anything you said to him. It's clear you were under duress and would have said anything. I know both Bob Atwood and Glen Hillsdale from Howls are reserve firemen and I can personally vouch that I've seen them numerous times on the scene at night on full moons and every other fucking time of the day. It's just bullshit that people would believe they're werewolves."

"So, they're in danger then..."

Derek made a face, waggling his hand side-to-side, "Maybe some. I find it hard to believe an educated man like Howard Cirillo could be so gullible and he was, so I suppose there could be others out there."

"But have you heard any threats or anything that might make you think the danger—"

The door opened, interrupting them. Derek said, "Chief Mathews, Mark Miller and his attorney, Ted Truman.

"Mr. Miller." Mathews shook Mark's hand and took a seat facing him. Derek left, closing the door behind himself.

Mathews said, "I appreciate you taking the time to come in."

Mark said, "What are you doing to protect the employees of Howls?"

"There isn't much we can do, I'm afraid. But I don't think they're in too much danger. In fact, I wouldn't mind being on that werewolf list myself. I hear they're being offered ridiculous sums of money to be on a reality television show. It might be unpleasant for some of them, but Mr. Henderson is offering generous severance packages for those who wish to seek employment elsewhere. I doubt many will leave though or I should say I doubt many are leaving over fear of werewolf hunters. I think most just don't like the publicity and do like the payoff Richard is offering."

Mark said, "I wish I hadn't said it and it pisses me off that it got leaked but I thought if Howard just considered it logically that he'd see how impossible it was. But I had no right to put them all in danger like that."

"I like to think there can't be too many crazy people with Howard's resources out there."

Mark said, "We know Stacy is still out there."

Mathews nodded agreement. "And she's a very dangerous woman. But her face has been plastered all over the news. There's probably not a man or woman in America who wouldn't recognize her. We'll find her soon, hopefully before she kills again."

Ted said, "What are we doing to track down these leaks?"

Mathews shook his head, leaning back in his seat to cross his arms, "There isn't a lot local law enforcement can do. I've spoken to the FBI whose jurisdiction it is, and I'm in contact with the police where the Millers were held. The chief there is keeping me abreast of developments but hasn't had any luck finding the leak either. Obviously someone involved there got away. The news stations claim the footage is being sent anonymously and while we can get injunctions to stop them playing it, we can't stop it from showing up on the web. I think you can assume that eventually everything that was recorded will be shown. I think you should have your lawyer speak directly to the FBI about releasing the footage they've confiscated to be sure it's seen unedited and in context. If the web has the only versions, I'm sure the facts will be obscured and sensationalized.

"I've seen all of the retrieved footage and while I'm sure it will be uncomfortable to watch, I don't think it puts any of your friends in danger to other possible werewolf snatchers. In fact, I think if the clip of the, *um*, doctor interrogating you is seen that it will be crystal clear that you made that up, not that a sane person would believe for a moment you hadn't."

Mark said, "My wife and I are leaving and I'm not telling a soul where we're going."

"You'll be needed for the trials."

Mark shrugged. "Make a public plea and maybe we'll come back but I doubt it. I'm not making her relive it, not even to put those assholes behind bars. We saw how easy it was for them to get out and it just isn't worth it."

Mathews said, "Four good men died trying to keep Stacy Anderson behind bars."

"And Steve Hermlin just walked out." Mark shrugged. "Look, I'm not saying it's your fault, but the system isn't working. I came in to tell you face-to-face. You can try to arrest us, but I doubt you can get a warrant before we're long gone. We're willing to make video statements now or anything else you need but we can't stay here and not just because of the danger but because it reminds us every day of what we lost."

Mathews stood and offered his hand again. "I can't say as I blame you and I wish you luck wherever you end up."

EPILOUGUE

"Uncle Mark!"

JJ's happy greeting pulled Mark from a sound sleep. He sat as JJ flung himself into his arms.

Marcus woke and was instantly his wolf form.

"Cool! How'd he do that?" JJ asked enviously. He squatted in front of Marcus and ruffled his fur. "Wanna play catch or go swimming?"

"He's just a baby," Mark said as Marcus wriggled excitedly and licked JJ's face.

Leah laughed and squatted beside Mark. "JJ, run and get some toys. Let's see what Marcus likes to play."

"Come on," JJ said.

Mark opened his mouth to call Marcus back, but Leah shook her head. "Richard is in the hallway and will go with them. How are you feeling?" she asked, and Mark turned to see that Kelly had woken.

Kelly stared after JJ a moment but then transformed into her human self. The ease and quickness of her changes left Mark breathless. He thought she was doing it faster than ever and he'd thought her past transformations had been quick.

Kelly picked up their daughter and cuddled her.

"We're good. Any word?"

"Star and Alan are still busy infiltrating their servers. We've gotten some good leads. It's nothing you need to worry about though."

"The drone footage?"

"We found some footage but it's not very incriminating. I don't think it would be enough to convince anyone who doesn't want to believe. I don't think it could be the footage that convinced Howard but maybe I'm wrong."

"He still isn't talking?"

"He'll never talk again. He's dead."

"Good," Kelly said with vicious satisfaction.

Mark thought it was good too, but he examined her surprised by the harsh response.

Leah nodded at her as she said, "Wolves kill their enemies."

Kelly said, "Did we find Stacy?"

"Not yet but we will."

"Marcus bit her. I have no idea if he drew blood or not."

Leah frowned.

Mark said, "I hope it kills her."

Kelly said, "I'd rather kill her myself," and again Mark was surprised. She'd told them how she'd fought her sister and he knew any feeling she might've once had for Stacy was gone. He was certain she wouldn't back down when they found her. Kelly was colder now and he was both happy and sad over it.

Leah said, "She deserves everything she has coming." She took Mark's hand and kissed it before laying in on his daughter's back. "Kelly and Marcus are pack now and will be compelled to protect us. I think we all have a lot to learn about being werewolves."

Kelly said, "I was learning a lot from Marcus." She bit her lip as she took his hand. "I love you so much, you have to believe that, but he needs me and you distract me. You make it harder to be my wolf. I don't hear Marcus as clearly—not hear—understand. I don't understand him as well as a human woman and I'm worried he'll be hurt without my total attention."

Mark said, "I want him safe too. It isn't all on you. I can watch him too."

"I'm not sure he'll listen to you. I can force him to be his wolf self. I haven't tried to force him into any other shape, or maybe I did with the mouse. I'm not really sure, but I know I can make him remain a wolf. I see him begin to go— or sense it maybe. It isn't something I can describe but I know and can stop it. It terrifies me he'll become something weak and helpless and be killed before I can change him back."

Leah said, "Richard and I can do that too. I can control JJ and some of the weaker wolves. Mark could probably learn to do it with Marcus. I bet all of our stronger wolves could. We'll be very careful with him and we can get monitors and make sure he's contained in a safe area."

"Nowhere is safe if you can become an ant and get stepped on."

Mark gasped in dismay. "He can become an ant?" The hair on Mark's neck rose when he remembered how furiously Kelly had attacked him for killing that mouse. He might have eaten his son. Bile burned his throat and he was suddenly sympathetic to how compulsively she watched him.

Kelly continued, "Who knows. But what if he does it while I'm sleeping and I step on him when I wake?"

Mark said, "We'll show him how dangerous it is. We'll teach him. Let's encourage him to be a boy. You can show me what he needs, and I promise I'll be as supportive as possible."

He hugged her and she relaxed against him. He breathed deeply of her scent, overcome with how lucky he was to have his children at all. Stacy might have managed to take Marcus or Frank could have kept his daughter, but here they were, safe and sound.

"We're so lucky. I thank God every day for giving me this family."

"Amen to that," Leah said.

Richard returned with the boys and an assortment of balls.

Leah called JJ over. "Be very careful with Marcus. He can assume other forms and some are small and fragile. If he becomes a mouse, you could kill him if you weren't careful."

"A mouse? I want to be a mouse too!"

"Maybe someday, pal," Mark said. "But meanwhile you teach him how to be a boy."

Kelly kissed his cheek and for the first time in months he was completely relaxed. His pack mates would take care of his family. His pact mates would take care of Stacy

THE END

Upcoming Book in the *Moon Caught* Series set in
C. M. Conney's *Realms of Man*

Pack Magic

C.M. Conney, a *non de plume* for S.M. Savoy, lives and works on the family farm in New England alongside her husband and two grown children. She loves animals and owns more than she'd like to admit. Most days, when she isn't baking or planting, she spends her time writing or working on her artwork. An avid reader since childhood, she appreciates work in all genres and likes to mix it up a bit in her own work.

C.M Conney can be reached through her publisher at Acelyonbooks.com

Books by C. M. Conney

Books set in the **Realms of Man**
Suggested Reading Order:
Moon Caught
Heaven Scent
Qarahpyr
Seethe
Lord Blackwood

Military Romance

The Real Deal
Take the Shot
The Deep End

Rubenstein -Wong: *Ms. Denali*

Company L: *The Enemy at Home*

Books by S. M. Savoy

Valor, a Fantasy Series by S. M. Savoy

When lightning irradiates Team Valor, led by Charlie Hayes, five professional video game players find themselves able to use the magic of their game characters. But there's no time to plan, practice, or recover from the lightning that transformed them. ISIS has kidnapped a squad of Marines and is beheading one soldier every eight hours. And Charlie's brother, Rick, is one of those Marines.

Valor

A Warrior's Fury

A Sun Priests Magic

Beyond Valor

A Rogue's Passion

Hidden Nature

A Vow Unbroken

Books in Related Series: *Return of the Fae*

Medieval England is a nightmare for a modern woman. Luckily for Jen Frey, when she arrives there through a magic portal, she possesses magic of her own. But now she's trapped with no way back to her own time. She's determined to make a safe place she and her fellow time travelers can live, one where women are equal and using magic won't get you burned at the stake.

Return of the Fae

The Makers: A Science Fiction Series by S. M Savoy

A previously unknown gas rises from the ocean floor and sweeps the Earth, reducing every manufactured item that it touches to its base elements, leaving a devastated world in its wake. But there are some survivors. And among them are those who can capture and use this gas to reform the elements to their will— They call them the makers...

A NEW SERIES: *DUSTED*

Dusted by an alien pathogen, Mia Sutton can now transform into a rat. The government is searching for people like her and making them disappear—she has no intention of becoming their lab rat.